THREE DOGS, TWO MURDERS, AND A CAT

By Rodney Strong

Silvermoon Retirement Village series
Poker Chips and Poison
Hip Flask and Hanging
Knitting Needles and Knives
Antiques and Assault
Diamonds and Drowning
Rubies and Revenge

Ghostly Hitchhiker series
Murder in Paint
Murder in Mud
Murder in Doubt
Murder in Pink
Murder in Disguise

Other Cozy Mysteries
Murder Most Confusing
A Pocketful of Blackmail

Standalone books
Troy's Possibilities
The 2nd Chance of Joshua Messer
The Last Time You Say a Name
Thanks for Coming

Children's Books
(published as R.G Strong)
Karmartha – The Last Garden
Escape From School

RODNEY STRONG

THREE DOGS TWO MURDERS, AND A CAT

ISBN 978-1-0670264-4-8

Published by LoreQuinn Publishing

Editor: Anna Golden

Printing by: YourBooks Limited

A catalogue record for this book is available from the National Library of New Zealand.

I have been lucky over the years, to have known many, many wonderful women. Thankfully most of them haven't turned out to be murderers.

This book is dedicated to two of them.

To my wife Sarah, who's continued support can never be repaid, so I'll just bring you a cup of tea in bed every now and then.

And to the real Nicolette, who isn't an animal detective, but would make a kick-ass one if she wanted to.

ONE

'I don't do humans.'

Nicolette waited for the inevitable questions, *what do you mean you don't do humans, who hurt you, you shouldn't be afraid to let people in.* It was ridiculous because Nicolette wasn't afraid of anything – for herself.

'Fair enough,' the woman responded.

Nicolette couldn't conceal her surprise. Perhaps this old lady was different from everyone else who looked at her in confusion when she made that statement, before deciding there was something wrong with her. Like she was a broken watch. But Nicolette wasn't broken, she just told time differently.

Nicolette looked down at the tabby cat lying on the charcoal-coloured carpet. Now, *cats* she did, and dogs, and occasionally farm animals (although there wasn't much need for that in downtown Wellington city).

She caught the woman watching her and returned the stare, which was rewarded with a grin. Alice Atkinson certainly seemed different than most elderly ladies Nicolette met.

'I can't imagine there are many others in your line of work,' Alice said.

Nicolette tensed for a second, then forced herself to relax. 'I'm the only one that I'm aware of.'

'Good,' replied Alice. 'Being unique is important.'

'Wish it paid the bills more,' Nicolette muttered, bending to scratch the cat behind the ear, immediately earning her a faint purr. She gauged the tabby to be about eight years old, lean but with an air of domestication. She was way too relaxed to be feral.

'She's not mine,' Alice said from her position on the couch. 'Silvermoon has a no pet policy, but that doesn't stop half the residents feeding her.'

Nicolette straightened up to look out the window of the second-floor apartment. Residents of the Silvermoon Retirement Village were walking and chatting, enjoying the sun, while others sat in the middle of a small rose garden opposite the apartment building. Past the fence line there were glimpses of the Wellington harbour lying below the suburb of Wadestown. It was like something out of a promotional video. She wouldn't have been surprised to find that they were all paid actors.

Nicolette eased herself onto the floor and leaned against the wall. 'When did you first notice she wasn't well?'

Thin, small and wrinkled, Alice was easily the oldest person Nicolette had ever met, but she was no one's vision of a friendly grandmother.

Her eyes were steely as she replied, 'Four days ago. She was all floppy. Vanessa insisted she be taken to a vet.'

'Vanessa?' Nicolette asked.

'She's my... employee, I suppose you could say.'

'What was the vet's diagnosis?'

'That Maddy had been poisoned. They kept her for a few days because... well.'

'They weren't sure she'd survive,' Nicolette finished.

'But this morning they said she was doing better so Vanessa brought her home and now I'm playing nurse maid.'

The cat eyed Nicolette without lifting her head from the carpet. Her breathing was shallow but regular. Nicolette had completed a year of veterinary training before an incident involving a professor had forced her to leave. In a way it had been the best thing that might have happened to her. She was bright enough to be a vet, but her temper and lack of tact would have made her a public relations nightmare for any veterinary clinic.

'Why did you call me?'

'It was my friend Freda's suggestion. You did some work for her granddaughter and came highly recommended.'

Nicolette looked up at the tone in Alice's words. 'But *you* don't see any merit in me being here.'

Alice held her gaze. 'I *didn't*. A detective who specialises in animal cases seems highly improbable.'

Nicolette shrugged. She'd heard it before. 'You *didn't*?'

Alice nodded and leaned forward in her chair. 'That's right. Because *I do* do humans. In fact, there have been several times when my life depended on my ability to read people. And I have a good feeling about you Nicolette Briggs.'

'A good feeling,' Nicolette repeated.

'Alright then, more specifically, you've barely looked around since you entered. Your focus has been on Maddy. Your tone with me is brusque at best, but when you're talking to the cat your voice is soft, even if your words aren't. And when I said she'd been poisoned, you clenched your right hand, like you wanted to hit someone.'

Nicolette looked down and was surprised to find her hand was still curled in a fist. She forced her fingers to relax.

'Alright, my turn,' said Nicolette. 'You're tough, but some of that bluster is to hide that you care about this cat. You say she isn't yours, yet you agreed to look after her, despite telling me that half the residents feed her. Presumably, anyone could have done this, but here you are. That tells me that you're used to getting your own way. You probably paid the vet bill as well.'

'What if I told you I don't care for her at all. I just don't like seeing animals abused.'

'I would point out that we're on the second floor.'

Alice cocked her head to the side with a curious expression.

Nicolette pointed to the front door of the apartment. 'No cat flap.'

Comprehension dawned and Alice nodded slowly.

'And no way for her to get up here even if there was,' Nicolette explained. 'Unless this cat can work an elevator.'

'What if I said Maddy was an inside cat.'

'Then how did she get poisoned?'

Alice clapped her hands and sat back. 'Excellent reasoning,' she said. 'I've never been a cat person, but Maddy likes lying in the sun on my living room floor and I'm not opposed to her doing that.'

Nicolette got slowly to her feet, masking the old familiar pain in her left leg, and eased herself onto one of the chairs opposite the couch. 'What do you want me to do?' she asked.

'What I can't,' Alice replied. 'Like I said, if that were a woman lying poisoned on my carpet, I would know exactly what to do. I understand humans. Cats are more of a mystery.' Alice gave a frustrated wave of her hand.

Nicolette looked thoughtfully at Maddy. 'Even if I can find out who poisoned her, the animal cruelty laws in New Zealand are pathetic. The most the person would get is a slap on the wrist and a laughably small fine.' She heard the bitterness in her words and swore internally. She really needed this job, and here she was trying to persuade the client not to give it to her.

Alice fixed Nicolette with a cold stare. 'You leave the outcome to me.'

Nicolette smiled uncertainly, then realised Alice wasn't joking. And what's more, she believed the threat.

Alice relaxed and offered her own smile. 'Now, let's talk money.'

Nicolette looked around the apartment. It was on the top floor of the main building, one of only two on the whole floor. Nicolette couldn't be sure without snooping, but she believed it was a two-bedroom. The furniture was upmarket, mementos were scarce, but if her vague memories of college Art History were correct, the painting on the wall by the front door was worth thousands of dollars. Everything about the place said that Alice was well off. But she was also incredibly old. Nicolette couldn't take advantage.

'My usual rate is $350 per day plus expenses.'

Alice snorted. 'Try again and this time pretend I'm forty years younger.'

'$450 a day. Although if you were *fifty* years younger, I'd have said $550.'

'Never assume based on appearances. I'll pay you $700 per day plus expenses. Plus a bonus of $1,000 if you complete the job within three days.'

Nicolette's mouth went dry. She thought of the single figure balance of her bank account and the unpaid bills in her email inbox.

'Why three days?'

'Sometimes one needs a little incentive to hurry things along,' Alice replied.

Nicolette stood up and glared at Alice. 'I don't need an incentive to do my job.'

Alice shrugged and got to her feet. 'I assume you will want to talk to some of the other residents. I can arrange for them to...'

Nicolette held up her hand. 'I'm good from here. I'll update you at the end of every day.'

She walked to the door, still fuming from the insinuation that she wouldn't give it her everything without a financial carrot.

'You know,' she paused, turning back to Alice, her hand on the doorhandle. 'I—'

'No,' Alice said firmly.

'I just—.'

'I look forward to your first report this evening, but until then, we're done, don't you think?'

Nicolette clenched her jaw, shutting her mouth before she could argue her way out of a job.

It wouldn't be the first time.

TWO

Nicolette emerged from the elevator into the ground floor reception area. A woman behind the desk smiled and called out something that might have been "Have a nice day". She said it through a mouthful of food, so it wasn't clear.

'You too,' replied Nicolette, hoping she hadn't just said something offensive.

She had a piece of paper with the vet's name and number in her pocket, and a deadline, which was a better starting spot than most of her cases. She called and left a message for the vet to phone her back.

The sun had trekked across three quarters of the empty blue sky, and Nicolette paused on the top step for a moment to enjoy the warmth.

One of the first things native Wellingtonians will tell you is to never believe the weather until you feel it for yourself. Many visitors to the city might glance through a window and think sunshine equals warmth, only to find themselves shivering in one of the ever-present winds that came off the harbour. Today though, the wind barely qualified as a breeze and Nicolette sighed at the warmth on her bare arms.

To her left was the long driveway leading to the main gate, which stood open on a small suburban street. To her right was the rest of the Silvermoon Retirement Village – a large exercise building with an indoor pool, occupational therapy rooms, and gym. Her car was parked in the car park next to the village café. Nicolette knew that most of the accommodation was tucked away behind the building she stood before.

She closed her eyes and listened for the birds. All other noise faded away. Somewhere a tui whistled and coughed, and for a moment she felt grounded.

Something tapped her on the arm.

Her eyes flew open and, stepping swiftly to the side, she twisted her body and grabbed the hand, pulling it down towards her hip. Her other hand came up and caught the man on the chin.

'Ouch.'

Nicolette released her grip and stepped back, warily watching the man rubbing his face.

'That's a hell of a reflex.' He grinned and tentatively held out a hand. 'At the risk of getting a broken hand, I'm Joshua Belford.'

'Nicolette Briggs.' Nicolette shook his hand. 'Sorry about the jaw.' Though she knew she hadn't hurt him as much as she could have, pulling the power at the last second.

He made a show of wincing as he touched his jaw, then laughed. Joshua was Polynesian, wearing jeans, a pale blue polo shirt, and an easy smile. Nicolette thought he was younger than her by ten years at least, which put him somewhere around twenty-three.

'What do you want?' she asked.

'Alice asked me to show you around.'

Nicolette frowned. 'I told her I had it handled.'

'In my experience Alice doesn't like to be told anything.' He looked up at the second floor and she saw the outline of a woman peering down at them.

'Who is she?' asked Nicolette.

'I'm not sure I can answer that. The best I can say is she's the most remarkable person I've ever met. She's helped me out a couple of times so I'm repaying the favour... for the next twenty years or so. Anyway,' Joshua continued, 'Alice asked me to introduce you to some people that might be able to help.'

'Because I'm an outsider and they won't talk to me?'

'Gosh no,' Joshua said laughing. 'Actually, the opposite. Most of these folks will talk so long you'll never leave.'

When she didn't reply, he added, 'And I understand you're on the clock?'

She stonewalled him another moment. Finally, she sighed and nodded.

'Come on, then. I saw Freda and Les heading to Charlie's earlier. They'll still be there.'

Nicolette was relieved when Joshua didn't attempt friendly conversation on the short walk to Charlie's, which turned out to be the café. A few residents waved to him. He seemed to know everyone by name.

Joshua headed straight to a table in the back of the busy cafe. The couple seated there were both in their seventies. She was short and thin, and he was broad shouldered. Before them sat two plates holding half eaten muffins.

Nicolette's stomach reminded her it had been a long time since breakfast and that maybe she should consider eating lunch on a more regular basis.

'Hey guys.'

'Hello Joshua, who's your friend?' asked Freda. Her grey hair appeared freshly-styled and Nicolette wondered if there was a hair salon in the village somewhere as well.

'This is Nicolette Briggs, she–'

'Nicolette!' Freda's face lit up. 'My granddaughter Michelle has wonderful things to say about you.'

Nicolette remembered the case. Michelle Tait's dog Buster had been taken from her backyard. Despite having security camera footage showing it happen, the police had made it clear that finding Buster was not a priority for them. Nicolette had tracked down the thief and returned the terrier to his very grateful owner. The thief had unexpectedly made a full confession. Unexpected to everyone but Nicolette.

'Forgive my wife, her enthusiasm masks a lack of manners,' said Les. 'Please join us.'

'Don't you apologise for me,' Freda said, but there was no heat in her tone. She continued her enthusiastic address as Nicolette and Joshua took the two empty seats. 'Are you here to find out what happened to Maddy?'

'I'm going to try,' Nicolette replied with a nod. 'What can you tell me?' Then, remembering Joshua's assessment of the lack of brevity of the residents, she added, 'About Maddy getting sick?'

'It was Les who spotted it first, which is a miracle because Les never spots anything. I got a new haircut the other day and do you think he said a word?'

'How many different haircuts do you think you've had in fifty years of marriage?' Les said. 'There's only so many times I can muster enthusiasm for hair.'

'Well, I think—'

'Maddy?' Nicolette prompted.

Freda gave her husband a look that suggested their conversation was far from done.

'As I was saying, Les spotted Maddy looking a little lethargic. She normally comes to us first thing in the morning for a saucer of milk.'

'Cow's milk is bad for cats,' Nicolette said.

'Oh... well, she finished it every morning. Except last Thursday. She barely looked at it.'

'I thought the milk might have expired,' Les said. 'But I checked, and it was good for two more days.'

'I told you it was still good because I made a cup of tea that morning and it tasted fine,' Freda said.

'What happened after she refused the milk?' Nicolette said hurriedly, hoping to cut off a lengthy conversation about dairy products.

'I asked Freda to take a look at her. She's better with animals than I am.'

'Listen to you,' Freda said, nudging her husband with her shoulder. 'Talking like you aren't the first one at the door every morning looking for Maddy, and worrying if she's late.'

'I... Well, I... Only because I know you'll worry.'

Nicolette stifled her irritation. She was going use up her three days on this one conversation.

Les ate a piece of his muffin. He winced and picked something from between his teeth with his fingernail. 'Walnut,' he explained. For a horrible moment Nicolette thought he was going to show her, but thankfully he didn't.

'I thought she was a bit floppy and she didn't purr when I scratched her behind the ear.' He stared at his wife defiantly who smiled knowingly.

'Was Maddy often late to your place?'

'No. There was the occasional day we wouldn't see her until she strolled past around morning tea time, but most mornings you could set your clock by her being there at seven.'

'Is she an affectionate cat?' asked Nicolette .

That seemed to confuse the older couple.

'Aren't all cats affectionate?' asked Freda.

'Not at all. Some are aloof, others are...'

'Downright nasty,' Joshua suggested.

'I was going to say more challenging, but yes.'

Freda smiled briefly. 'Well yes, Maddy was definitely affectionate. She would always stay after she had her milk and show her appreciation. Silvermoon has a strict no pets policy, so it's been nice to have a cat again, even if it's just thirty minutes a day.'

Nicolette sat back in her chair, automatically placing the couple in the "good" file she kept in her head.

'Do you know where Maddy goes after her visits with you?'

It was Les who answered. 'It depends on the weather. If it's sunny, she'll sometimes lie on the warm concrete outside the Olympic Complex – that's what we call the exercise building. If it's wet, I've seen her head to the Smiths. They're three doors down from us on the right.'

Nicolette spent the next hour talking to residents. Most people didn't realise cats were creatures of habit. They had routines just like humans. After sixty minutes, she had a pretty good idea of Maddy's daily schedule. Adding this to what Alice had told her, it seemed that Maddy showed up in the village around seven in the morning and stayed until late afternoon.

No one seemed to know where she spent her evenings, although one resident, a tall distinguished man called Owen, recalled seeing Maddy jump to the top of the fence by the rose garden late one afternoon.

Joshua insisted on accompanying her even though Nicolette knew the way. The rose garden was opposite the main building, where they'd started. It didn't take a great detective to find it.

She did her best to ignore him as she examined the wooden fence. 'Kārearea brown,' she murmured.

Nicolette, at five-foot-seven, was able to touch the top of the fence with her hand if she stood on her toes and stretched up. There were no braces or support beams on this side, just smooth wood.

‘What’s on the other side?’ she asked Joshua.

‘Houses,’ he said. ‘They come out onto a street running parallel with the village.’

Nicolette hopped up and, gripping the top of the fence, she pulled herself up to see over.

‘That’s impressive.’

‘Couldn’t you do it?’ she asked, peering into the neighbour’s backyard.

‘Yeah, but...’

‘Oh, you mean impressive for a woman.’

‘I was going to say yeah but I do crossfit and most people can’t do a pull up.’

The Silvermoon Retirement Village, like most of Wellington, was on a hill, so the house over the fence was below them, providing a good view of the section. The grass was neatly cut and a small vegetable garden sat in the bottom corner. The house was pale blue wood with white window frames. She searched for a sign a cat might live there but couldn’t see a cat door.

Dropping lightly back to the ground, she shook her arms to relieve the ache.

‘Sorry,’ she said. ‘I shouldn’t have assumed.’

Joshua grinned. ‘I’m used to people making assumptions about me.’

‘Why’s that?’

‘People see a Tongan and automatically think I’m a rugby or league player.’

‘And you’re not?’

He shrugged. ‘I was always more interested in talking than tackling. I’m studying law at Vic.’

Nicolette realised she’d also assumed that he worked full-time at the village.

She gestured further along the fence. ‘Care to join me?’

She had to admit he managed it with considerably more ease than she did, but she reasoned this was her second time while his arms were fresh.

A ferocious barking erupted as a dog came around the side of the house. This lawn was unkept and patchy, a description that equally applied to the dog. It was a mid-sized brown and white short-haired animal. He reached the fence and leapt up. Joshua flinched, though it would have taken a super powered dog to reach them.

'Who's a good boy,' Nicolette said in a low voice.

Instantly the dog stopped barking and started softly wagging his tail. She could see his ribs, he was obviously underfed, although seemed energetic enough otherwise. She scanned the backyard for a water bowl but couldn't see one, despite the warm day.

Dropping to the ground, she waited for Joshua to land beside her before asking, 'do you hear the dog barking often?'

Joshua shook his head. 'Every now and then, but I think they've only been living there a short time.'

'What makes you say that?'

'I don't know for sure, but about three weeks back I was talking to Lance – he's one of the gardeners and he said one of the neighbours had moved out and he was going to do the meet and greet.'

'The what?'

'There's a policy here that everytime there's a new neighbour, management likes to visit and introduce themselves.'

Nicolette wondered why on earth management would feel that was necessary. Were the Silvermoon residents secret party animals? If so, they weren't the sort of animals she was used to dealing with.

Then it clicked.

'They like to check out the new neighbours to see if they're going to be a problem for the village.'

Joshua shrugged. 'No one has come out and said it like that, but that's the general feeling, yeah. If there's going to be a thrash metal band rehearsing in their backyard at midnight, then management would like to know ahead of time.'

'Is that usual for a retirement village?'

'I don't know. My experience is limited to here.'

Nicolette nodded slowly as she turned back to the fence.

'How long has Maddy been hanging around the village?'

'Maybe, about a year.'

'So it's not likely she lives at the house with the dog.'

She walked further along the fence line without saying anything else, leaving Joshua jogging to catch up. Beads of sweat slid down her back and pooled at the base of her spine. She pulled her faded yellow T-shirt away from her skin, a fruitless gesture given as soon as she released it the material stuck to her again. She was glad her long black hair was tied in a high ponytail so at least her neck wasn't overheating.

By the time she'd finished walking the fence line, sweat had formed a ridge across her brow. If she'd known she was going to be doing anything so physical she'd have dressed for it, but the last thing she'd expected at a retirement village was to be raising her heart rate.

Joshua looked annoyingly unbothered by the exercise.

The problem she had was that cats tended to often take circuitous routes home. Maddy might have jumped onto the fence right beside her house, or she might live several streets away.

There was only one thing for it, she was going to have to door knock.

'Thanks for your help,' she said.

'Are we done?' Joshua said, looking disappointed.

'I'm done at Silvermoon for now.'

'Oh, okay. Well, it was nice meeting you Nicolette.'

'Likewise. See you around.'

She headed back to her car. It was, like many other things in her life, a loaner. A small white Honda with the name of the garage plastered on the side in black letters. Her own car was currently undergoing testing to see if it was salvageable or terminal. She didn't hold out high hopes given its age, mileage, and the fact the seats permanently smelt like wet dog.

Some days she could say the same about herself.

THREE

Nicolette eased out of the carpark. She gave Freda a sketchy wave as she passed the café, then drove slowly down the long driveway.

When she turned on the air conditioning, tepid air ebbed out of the vents, teasing her bare arms with a promise of a chill, but by the time she reached the main gates, the air had done nothing to deliver on that promise. Nicolette put the window down instead which was a marginal improvement.

She turned right out of the cul-de-sac, then took the first right after that and drove until she judged she was about halfway along the Silvermoon property. From this position on the road below the village, she couldn't see for sure but it didn't matter if she was off by a few houses. She'd check as many as she could.

The houses here were mainly older, made from wood a long time before she was born. Wadestown was one of the oldest in Wellington which put it about 180 years old. She didn't know much else about it, but the houses in the street looked generally well maintained, with neat lawns behind wooden fences.

Traffic here was light, which was just as well since by parking at the curb she'd virtually turned the narrow road into a one-way street.

She picked a house at random and knocked on the front door. After a short pause, a harassed-looking woman carrying a crying baby answered.

'Yes?'

'Sorry to bother you,' Nicolette said with a smile. 'I'm looking for the owner of this cat.' She held up her phone to show the picture of Maddy she'd taken.

The woman barely glanced at it as she gently jiggled the baby up and down. In the background, music was playing. The woman was about Nicolette 's age, with dark smudges under her eyes and hair that looked like it had last seen shampoo several days ago.

'Sorry, what? Shush bubba.'

Bubba was obviously at the developmental age where she considered "shush" as a challenge. She flung her head back and howled at the ceiling like she'd been branded with a hot poker.

'Sorry, I don't want to buy anything.'

'No, I'm not selling anything. I...'

Nicolette glanced at the baby irritably, brought her finger to her lips and exhaled sharply with a hard T sound. The baby looked at her in astonishment, completely forgetting for the moment to cry.

'How did you do that?'

Nicolette shrugged. 'It works with dogs. I figured it was worth a shot.'

'Dogs?' the woman repeated.

'Anyway, have you seen this cat?'

This time she gave the picture a decent look. She nodded. 'Sure, it cuts through our backyard all the time. Usually while I'm getting this one her afternoon feed.'

'Do you know who *she* belongs to?'

'No idea, sorry, but I go for a walk every morning and I've seen her disappear over the fence that way sometimes.' The woman pointed back the way Nicolette had driven from.

Nicolette thanked her and headed back down the path to the gate while the baby sent fresh wails into the air.

No one was home at the next three houses.

The door of the fourth house was opened by an elderly gentleman who perhaps should have been living in the retirement village rather than next to it. His clothes, like his face, were worn and weather beaten.

'I've been watching you,' he declared firmly. 'My daughter is in the police and I have her on the line.' He held up his cell phone, unfortunately directing the screen towards Nicolette. She could clearly see there was no call in progress.

'Excellent, you sound like exactly the sort of man I'm after,' Nicolette said with a warm smile.

He eyed her suspiciously, gripping the edge of the door.

'An observant man like you must know what goes on in this street. I'm looking for whoever owns this cat.' She showed him the picture and he peered at it for a moment.

'I know where she lives, but why should I tell you?'

Nicolette felt the beginnings of a headache forming just behind her left eye. She fought the urge to walk away, or worse, say what she was thinking.

'You're obviously up to no good,' the man continued, waving his phone in her face. 'My daughter is on her way.'

'You must be so proud.'

He looked taken aback.

'It takes a certain sort of patience and bravery to serve as an officer.'

The man lowered his phone and smiled. 'We've always been proud of her, no matter what she does.'

Nicolette nodded like she knew what it was like to have supportive parents, rather than a mother who had once called her the biggest waste of potential in the history of the country. That had been a fun eighteenth birthday.

'If she's anything like you then I'm sure she's an exceptional officer.'

He visibly straightened up and squared his shoulders.

'The thing is,' Nicolette continued, 'something has happened to Maddy and I'm trying to track down her owner to let them know.'

'Maddy?'

'That's what the residents of the Silvermoon Retirement Village call her.'

The man snorted. 'That village. You'd never catch me there.'

Nicolette waited for him to expand on this opinion, but he shut his mouth and kept it closed.

'Do you have a cat?' asked Nicolette.

'No,' he begrudgingly replied. 'Never liked them. I'm a dog man.'

'Oh, what sort of dog do you have?' She peered past him.

'Good grief, I said I liked dogs better than cats, not that I owned one.'

The headache came on fully and she took a deep breath and let it out slowly. 'Look, I'm sorry to bother you, sir. Have a good day.'

She started down the front steps and he called out. 'Wait, don't you want to know where the cat lives?'

Nicolette gritted her teeth before turning back. 'Yes.'

The man smiled smugly and she understood that his desire to be seen as important outweighed his suspicion.

'Next door,' he said. 'I've seen that cat go through the cat door around back.'

Nicolette looked at the house next door, a virtual twin to this one except with green window trims rather than cream.

'What's happened to it? You said something had happened.'

Nicolette decided on a modified version of the truth. 'We think she ate something she wasn't supposed to. She's quite sick.'

'Oh dear. So, I'm not in danger?'

'Why would you ask that?' Nicolette said.

The man took a step back into his house, his expression bordering on fearful.

'No reason. Don't listen to me, I'm just a silly old man. I have to call my daughter,' he said, forgetting that she was supposed to have been on the phone already.

He closed the door firmly before Nicolette could ask any more questions. She hesitated but decided against knocking again.

No one answered when she rang the doorbell next door. It was one of those video doorbells where people could see you on their phone no matter where they were in the world. What was different about this one was the small black rectangular box attached to the wall above it.

She pressed the button again and waited, casually looking around. The small front yard was a week away from overgrown, but the paint on the window frames was fresh. There was nothing out of the ordinary about this place compared to the rest of the street, except she could see at least two security cameras in addition to the doorbell. They were nestled in opposite corners of the house, just under the roof line. What was even more interesting is that both appeared to be pointing away from the front yard, angled up and down the street respectively. Whoever lived here was more interested in the neighbours than their own protection. The cameras appeared new, their white surface not yet stained with grime.

She pressed the bell one more time, then reached into her back pocket and pulled out a business card. Just as she realised she'd left her pen in the car, an amplified male voice made her jump.

'Yes?'

She looked around, then realised it had come from the doorbell.

'Hi, my name is Nicolette Briggs.'

'Good for you. What do you want?'

She showed her phone to the camera. 'I'm looking for the owner of this cat. The neighbour said he's seen her go inside your place.'

There was a delay before he said, 'Yeah, she's mine. What's she done?'

'Nothing. I mean, she didn't do anything. There's a possibility she has been poisoned.'

Another long pause followed.

'Show me the picture again.'

She obliged.

'No, I made a mistake, that's not my cat.'

'Are you sure?'

'I think I know my own cat. I'm busy, you can leave.'

'Wait, maybe if I described her to you. The photo might not be clear through the camera. Hello?'

Nicolette rang the doorbell again, then banged on the wooden door with the palm of her hand. 'Hey!'

When it became apparent he wasn't coming back, Nicolette took two steps away from the door and scanned the front of the house. She made a show of shrugging and looking disappointed before heading out the gate. Mindful of the cameras, she knocked at the next two houses up the street, but no one was home at either.

She trudged back to her car, did a careful U-turn and drove back the way she'd come.

At the intersection she sat for a moment. Left would take her back towards the retirement village, right went down the hill to the city.

She had many questions. But the biggest one right now was why someone would lie about owning a cat.

She turned left.

FOUR

Nicolette parked in the same spot in the carpark and headed towards the fences beyond the rose garden. She pulled herself up and realised she was looking into the wrong backyard. Dropping to the ground she moved several metres to her left then tried again.

This was right. She recalled how the backyard had been slightly unkempt, the grass overdue for a cut and there were more weeds than flowers in the beds running along both edges. The back door was made with frosted glass and in the bottom pane someone had installed a cat door.

What she hadn't noticed earlier was there were two security cameras here as well, pointing in all directions, including towards the back fence.

Nicolette dropped to the ground and pressed her back against the fence, feeling the rough wood pressing into her shoulders.

She knew two things about the owner of this house: they'd lied about owning Maddy, and they were extremely paranoid. People who were worried about security might put cameras up, maybe one at the front and one in the back. Whoever lived in this house wasn't taking any chances with blind spots. It would make sneaking in problematic. If required.

Pulling out her phone, Nicolette typed the address into Google maps. She used her finger and thumb to zoom in. Swiping into street view, she was able to see the front of the house. It looked the same, except from what she could see there were no security cameras.

Nicolette checked the date the street view was taken. Six months ago.

Next, she accessed a Greater Wellington property database. It told her that the property had changed hands a month prior, when it was sold by a G Downing to the Magnusson Family Trust.

So, half a year ago there had been no security cameras at all. Then the property changed hands and suddenly it was sewn up tighter than a prison. It could be as simple as security conscious owners, but she need to be sure.

Alice had told her the cat had been seen around the village for much longer than a month, so if that was Maddy's house then she didn't belong to the person living there now.

The property database couldn't tell her where G Downing had moved to and wouldn't provide contact information. With a sigh, Nicolette realised she was going to have to call in a favour.

She stretched her legs out in front of her and dialled a number she'd saved and deleted from her phone many times.

'Nic,' the voice said cautiously.

'Hi Archie.'

'It's been a while.'

'Yeah, life, you know.'

'I'm familiar with it, yes,' Archie replied. 'How've you been?'

Nicolette leaned her head back and considered the question as she watched the trees overhead rustling in the slight breeze.

'I've been good.'

'Are you lying?'

'Never to you, Archie.'

Archie laughed and Nicolette joined in, because they both knew that she was lying about lying.

'I need a favour.'

‘Of course you do. Not until you ask.’

Nicolette screwed her eyes shut and counted to five.

‘How’s the family?’

‘Why don’t you come around and find out,’ replied Archie.

‘Archie.’

‘I know, but you don’t get anywhere without asking. What do you need?’

Nicolette released the breath she was holding and opened her eyes.

‘I’ve got a name and an old address. I need to know where they are now.’

‘You know I could get in trouble for this.’

‘Since when has that stopped you?’

‘Give me fifteen.’

Nicolette relayed the details, then hung up and laid the phone on her lap.

She watched a car creep up to the main building. Two people climbed out of the backseat. They could have been prospective residents. She hoped if they were they got a ground floor apartment. The few steps up to the foyer appeared to take some effort.

She tilted her head and saw Alice standing in the window of her apartment. Nicolette couldn’t tell if she was looking at her or not. After a moment the old woman moved back, out of sight.

Nicolette wondered why Alice had employed her. Finding the owner of a cat wasn’t that hard, she’d basically achieved it in thirty minutes. So why not do it herself?

She was still mulling over that question when her phone rang. Expecting Archie, she didn’t check the number before answering.

‘What have you got?’

‘Er, hello? I’m looking for Nicolette Briggs?’

Nicolette glanced at the screen, recognising the number she’d called earlier. ‘Are you from Wadestown Animal Centre?’

'Simon Boland. You're calling about the cat brought in a few days ago?'

'I was wondering if you'd been able to determine if Maddy was definitely poisoned.'

There was a small pause, then Simon continued cautiously, 'She was definitely exposed to something. We are still waiting for some blood results to come back, but it appears to be cyanide based.'

'Cyanide!'

'Yes, it's surprisingly common and found in a wide range of places in nature.'

'So it was accidental.'

'I can't say that.'

'Then it was it deliberate?'

'I definitely didn't say that.'

'Mr Boland, I'm not a journalist or police officer. Anything you can tell me would help prevent an old woman wasting her money.'

'Er, what?'

'This nice old lady is paying me to find out who poisoned this cat. If it turns out the cat just had some bad chicken then I'd rather not charge her.'

'I see.' There was another pause, then he proceeded in a more relaxed tone. 'I can tell you that cyanide doesn't usually come from eating bad chicken.'

'But?' Nicolette said when he hesitated.

'I would have expected to see blistering or redness around the mouth if the cat had eaten anything toxic.'

'How else could it have gotten into her system?'

'I don't have much experience with it myself, but I have read of cases where animals inhale cyanide-based gas.'

'Could that be accidental,' Nicolette said.

'Statistically unlikely.'

'Statistically unlikely?' she repeated.

Simon laughed. 'That's as close as I'm prepared to go, Ms Briggs. I can tell you that we haven't had any other animals present with the same symptoms, and neither have the other local practices, which means whatever this cat was exposed to was isolated.'

'Fair enough. Thanks.'

'You know, the vet network talks about you.'

Nicolette frowned.

He continued. 'Tell Ms Atkinson that we'll refund her money.'

Nicolette blinked. 'Why?'

'Like I said, you're well known around Wellington. Goodbye, Ms Briggs, and good luck.'

As soon as he hung up, Archie rang back.

'Frank and Gladys Downing owned the property for forty years. Gladys Downing now lives with her daughter in Ngaio. Texting you the address now.'

Her phone dinged and she checked the message.

'Thanks, Archie. I owe you one.'

'You can start repaying me by not calling me Archie anymore.'

'Okay. This one time. Thanks, Veronica.'

'I'll take it.'

Nicolette hung up.

Now she had a lead, but she didn't move immediately. Between the quiet and the warmth, she felt herself drifting back in time to her parent's backyard. All she was missing was a book in her hands and a dog resting his head on her lap.

Reluctantly, she climbed to her feet and walked back to her car. She put the address into the Maps app and once more drove along the driveway and out the front gate of the Silvermoon Retirement Village.

FIVE

Gladys Downing had moved from a turn-of-the-previous-century wooden house in Wadestown to a mid-century wooden house in Ngaio. As the crow flies, it was a distance of only a kilometre, but thanks to the winding indirect road it took Nicolette ten minutes to drive there.

The woman who answered the door was thirty years too young to be Gladys Downing, but when an older woman appeared behind her their family resemblance was clear. They were similarly dressed in slacks and light-coloured blouses. The younger of the two held a set of car keys and Nicolette realised she had caught them on their way out.

'Sorry to bother you,' Nicolette said. 'But I need to talk to you about your old house.'

Gladys Downing studied her carefully over a pair of thin rimmed glasses.

'I sold that a month ago.' Her expression was neutral and her words seemed carefully chosen.

'Yes ma'am, I know that.'

'I'm Angela Downing. What's this about? We're on our way out.'

Nicolette retrieved her phone and showed them the photo of Maddy. 'Do you know this cat?'

‘What’s she done now?’ Gladys said resignedly.

‘So, you recognise her?’

‘Of course. That’s Kanga, my cat.’

‘We haven’t seen her for a few days. Mum’s been worried.’

‘I have not,’ Gladys replied in a tone that said she had.

‘Is it usual for her to go missing?’

Gladys sighed and shrugged. ‘She’s always been a roamer, but since I moved here she’s taken to disappearing all day, and coming back to sleep before leaving the next morning. And she’s never hungry anymore. I wondered if she’d found another family.’

She sounded upset by the betrayal which made Nicolette feel bad confirming her suspicions.

‘That retirement village! I knew it. All those people with nothing to do but steal another person’s cat.’

‘Mum, I’m sure Kanga had a lot to do with that.’ Angela turned to Nicolette. ‘She’s always been a little con artist. One day, just after Mum moved in here, we discovered she’d been given three breakfasts because we all thought she hadn’t been fed. She was very convincing at pleading starvation.’

‘Cat’s will do that,’ Nicolette said. ‘If it’s any consolation, the people at Silvermoon do seem to care about her.’

Angela fixed her with a look identical to the one her mother had given Nicolette earlier. ‘I’m sure you’re not here simply to tell us where Mum’s cat’s been spending her days.’

‘No. Unfortunately not. It appears that Maddy – sorry, Kanga – has got into something she shouldn’t and it made her quite sick. The vet says she’ll make a full recovery though.’

Gladys’ hand flew to her mouth and she sagged against the door frame.

Hher daughter gripped her arm. ‘Mum, let’s get you a cup of tea.’

Gladys patted Angela’s hand and straightened up. ‘I’m fine. Where is she now?’

'I'll give you the name and number of the woman looking after her at the retirement village.' She waited for Angela to programme it into her phone, then said, 'Can I ask what you know about the people that bought your old house?'

'Why do you want to know about them?' Angela asked.

Nicolette scowled at the whole answering a question with a question thing. 'There's a cat door in the back door of your house. It's possible your cat has been returning there and that's where she may have been exposed to something. Have you met the new owners? Do you have a contact number for them? I tried knocking on the door, but no one was home.'

'That was all handled through my real estate agent. I've got her card somewhere.' Gladys rummaged in her handbag and came up empty handed. 'I think it's on my dresser. Darling, could you go and get it please?'

After Angela disappeared into the house, Gladys turned to Nicolette with a shrewd expression. 'I met the new owner once. The day before I moved out, he showed up on my front doorstep asking if he could measure the rooms to make sure his furniture would fit inside.'

'What was he like?'

Gladys screwed up her face. 'I didn't like him to be honest. Oh, he said all the right things, complimented me on how neat and tidy the place was and so on and so forth, but there was something I didn't like about this eyes. They were shifty.'

'Shifty,' Nicolette repeated.

Glady's cheeks turned pink. 'I know how it sounds, but that doesn't make it any less true. His eyes were blue and always moving, like he was trying to memorise every little detail.' She shivered. 'He looked me up and down and it was like he was seeing inside me. It was...'

'Shifty,' Nicolette finished.

'You're making fun of me.'

Nicolette shook her head. 'I've met people like that before.'

'Then you do know. He had a scar on his face as well, here.' She touched the side of her face by her eye. 'Anyway, he only stayed for a few minutes.' Gladys frowned.

Angela returned and handed her a business card, which Nicolette slipped it into her jeans pocket without looking at it.

'I'll tell you something else, he said he wanted to measure all the rooms, but he only got his tape measure out in one. The old storage room. It's right in the middle of the house. It doesn't have any windows so we used it as a walk-in linen cupboard. He seemed very interested in it.'

Nicolette thought she saw a fleeting look cross Angela's face. She couldn't be sure but it seemed like anger.

'Is there anything else?' Angela asked.

'Yes, we do have to go I'm afraid. We have a market to get to and—'

'Mum, we're going to be late.'

'Thanks for your time,' Nicolette said. 'I'll let Alice know that you'll be in touch.'

Back in her car, Nicolette sat tapping her fingers on the steering wheel while she stared out the window. Her leg ached and she resisted the urge to rub it, knowing that wouldn't achieve anything other than leave her feeling more irritated.

She called Alice and reported everything she'd discovered.

'You've been busy,' Alice said approvingly.

Despite herself, Nicolette felt a flicker of pride at the old lady's praise.

'So, I've found the owner, but if Maddy-Kanga picked up the poison somewhere on her journey between the new house and the old one, then it'll likely be impossible to figure out where and how.'

'But?' Alice said.

Nicolette blinked at the response. She had expected Alice to receive the information, thank her for her work and accept the invoice.

Nicolette watched a purple Toyota Corolla back out of the Downings' driveway and drive past her. She'd become more aware of cars since replacing hers was becoming more likely with each visit to the garage. She'd even considered hybrids but they were out of her price range. Like everything else.

Gladys gave a little wave but was gone before Nicolette could reciprocate.

She tapped her fingers again. 'But why did the new owner lie about owning Maddy?'

'You don't believe he was simply mistaken.'

'He only changed his story when I said she'd been poisoned.'

'Yes, in hindsight that wasn't particularly smart.'

Nicolette winced.

'But quite enlightening, wouldn't you say?'

'It sounds like you want me to continue investigating.'

'As you say, Maddy could have been poisoned at any point between her house and here, but if there's a chance that the person who did it lives over the fence from my friends then I want to know about it.'

Her friends but not herself? Nicolette's curiosity about the old woman deepened.

'Alright, I'll keep looking.'

'Good. Keep me apprised of any further developments. There may be ways I can assist.'

Nicolette hung up. She highly doubted there was anything Alice could do that she couldn't do herself.

She glanced at the clock on the dashboard and saw it was three minutes past three o'clock.

'Damn,' she groaned. 'She's going to kill me.'

SIX

Death wasn't awaiting Nicolette outside St Mary's College in Thorndon, but an artic wind in a school uniform was.

'You're late.'

Nicolette glanced at her watch. 'Five minutes.'

'Late's late.'

'It's only 3.15pm.'

'I could have been snatched off the street.'

Nicolette gave her daughter a sideways glance and stifled a sigh. 'Sorry, Chloe, work got in the way. I was coming from Ngaio.'

Chloe Briggs, living proof that Nicolette had had sex at least once in her life, was a conundrum. Four days shy of her fifteenth birthday, with the attitude of a forty-year-old, and the haircut of a twenty-two-year-old hippie, the only task Chloe enthusiastically embraced these days was holding her mother to impossible standards. One minute late earned a frown, two minutes a scowl, and any more than three minutes a long spiel about motherless children in third world countries that received more love than her. Despite the differences in hair styles, there was no mistaking the two were related. Chloe had the same brown eyes, same slight build, and same stubborn streak.

'What's the case?' Chloe shed her blazer before clicking her seatbelt into place and impatiently gesturing to the road.

Nicolette told her everything as they started towards home. In the rare moments they weren't trying to outwit, outdo, and out shout each other, her daughter was extremely smart and insightful. For an ungrateful child.

'So how are you going to get into the house?'

'Why would I try and get into the house?'

'Duh, the guy lied about owning the cat, so he obviously tried to kill her. You need to get inside to see why. And find out what he's doing in that room he was so interested in.'

'Breaking and entering is against the law.'

'Mum.'

'Alright, but if anyone asks, I told you it was illegal.'

'Yes, yes, you're an upstanding member of society. Now how are you going to do it?'

Nicolette had been thinking about that all the way to the college.

'He's got cameras at the front and back. Those types of security systems send video straight to your phone, which means he'll instantly know if I try to... make my own way in.'

'You know, the school netball team needs new equipment.'

Nicolette filtered that through her teenage translator then firmly shook her head. 'Absolutely not.'

'Why not?'

'Because we've just established that a poisoner might live there. I'm not sending you to knock on the front door.'

Chloe slumped in her seat and scowled at the windscreen.

'How was school?'

Her daughter waited an appropriate amount of time to convey she was annoyed but not so annoyed she wasn't going to answer. 'A waste of time. I already know everything I need to know.'

'Lucky you. I'm not anywhere close.'

That one earned her a tight brief smile.

They got onto the motorway and headed out of the city. Sometimes the hassle of living so far away from the college made Nicolette reconsider her decision to send her daughter to a private school. That and the attendance dues. But Nicolette had gone to St Mary's and despite what her mother might think, she had turned out alright, so Nicolette was determined to give Chloe every opportunity to do the same.

Peak traffic hadn't started yet so their trip was quick and mostly in silence. Chloe seemed to communicate with her phone more than her mother, which Nicolette had been assured by several websites would be a temporary state, lasting a mere three to twenty years.

The Honda strained a little going up the Ngauranga Gorge road but eventually made it. As Nicolette took the Johnsonville off-ramp, she wondered if they needed anything for dinner. Then she smiled to herself. The answer was always yes. Between a teenage daughter and three dogs, trips to the supermarket were almost a daily occurrence.

Ten minutes and ten kilos of dog food later, Nicolette pointed the car towards home.

It was hard to believe that their semi-rural property was so close to the city. She'd moved into the house with Chloe as a newborn and had nervously watched suburbia creep closer and closer to her small piece of countryside. New builds accompanied by flashy new cars threatened to turn her quiet part of the world into yet another generic suburb. However for now Ohariu Valley remained her sanctuary.

The weatherboard house was built in the 1950s and had two bedrooms and a tiny kitchen. Its main source of heat was a fireplace which managed to warm the entire house if they left all the internal doors open.

The house had belonged to Nicolette's uncle. Initially, Nicolette had moved in as a favour. He'd insisted she would be helping him out by living there while he travelled for a few months. It was almost a year of "just a few more weeks" before she realised she'd been tricked. He was happily living in Spain with no intention of coming back. By then she'd become used to the space and privacy and was more than happy (behind a façade of grumbling reluctance) to take up permanent residence with Chloe.

Uncle Jack had returned only once, when Chloe was three. He'd stood in the middle of the lounge, turned a full circle on the spot, grunted, and declared that it was no longer his house. She wasn't absolutely clear on the legal status, but as far as she was concerned the place was hers.

And Chloe's.

Nicolette pulled the car into the gravel driveway and three sets of eyes watched her from behind a wire fence.

Nero, Teddy, and Fig. They completed her home.

Chloe was out the door and jumping the gate before Nicolette could pull the key from the ignition. Nicolette watched her daughter be enveloped in a crude hug of tongues and paws and excited yelps.

The dogs loved Nicolette, but they adored Chloe. Never mind that it was Nicolette who had rescued each of the dogs, bought the food, and did the majority of the walking. Chloe mysteriously had homework every time a walk was due.

A soft beep drew her attention to the passenger side of the car. In her haste to greet the dogs, Chloe had left her school bag behind.

Nicolette's fingers itched to check her daughter's phone. She trusted Chloe marginally more than any other fourteen-year-old, but the last time she'd been caught checking messages on Chloe's phone it had taken several weeks of bribery and coercion before she'd been forgiven.

She got out of the car and leaned on the fence to watch.

Chloe pretended to faint. As she lay on the ground, Teddy the border collie stood over her anxiously barking.

'Quit it, you know Teddy's background.'

Chloe immediately opened her eyes and sat up, wrapping her arms around the dog and murmuring words of apology.

Meanwhile the other two were chasing each other around the overgrown lawn, pausing every now and then to check that their antics were being admired. Nero, a three year old mixed breed, was mostly white, with a black patch over his eye and another down his back. Fig, a four-year-old mixed breed, was the newest member of the family, still working out the noises and smells of her new home. The mid-sized grey dog with a white patch over her left eye hadn't had the easiest of starts to life, spending most of it tied up in someone's backyard, fed only enough to keep her alive. It had taken two weeks of patient reassurance to get her not to flinch every time someone tried to pat her.

Nicolette liked homecomings. They gave her hope.

Later, with three dogs sprawled on the floor around the kitchen table and Chloe in her room *allegedly* doing homework, Nicolette opened her laptop and looked up the Magnusson Family Trust.

There wasn't much to find.

The problem was that while family trusts in New Zealand were legal entities, they didn't have to be publicly registered.

She scrolled through and clicked on dead ends and false starts. She found a family trust in Leicester, England, and another in Connecticut, USA. Neither of which appeared likely to have bought a house in suburban Wellington.

Above her, the house groaned and popped as it settled for the night. Fig raised her head and Nicolette scratched behind her ears.

'Good girl,' Nicolette murmured.

Fig stared around her a moment more, then laid her grey head down, keeping one eye on Nicolette as she worked.

Nicolette googled the name Magnusson which brought up a range of results, from a tailor shop opened in 1866 in Wellington, to a type of woollen jersey.

Retrieving Gladys Downing's real estate agent's business card from her pocket, she dialled the number. It was answered immediately by an energetic voice.

'Ursula Franklin, Franklin Real Estate. How can I make your real estate dreams come true?'

Nicolette moved the phone several inches away from her ear.

'Ursula, hi,' she replied in an equally bubbly voice. 'I'm so sorry to bother you after dinner. My name is Amanda Downing. You sold my mother Gladys's house in Wadestown last month.'

She waited while the woman mentally found the right memory.

'Of course! Amanda, how are you? How's your mother doing?'

'She's absolutely fine, you're such a doll for asking. Except, well the thing is she's a little embarrassed, which is why I'm calling.'

'Oh no,' Ursula replied in a concerned tone. 'Is everything alright?'

'Nothing major I can assure you. It's just, in the haste to pack up everything for the move, it seems she completely forgot about a box of things in the roof space. Honestly, I told her not to bother about it. If she hasn't missed it until now... am I right?'

Ursula laughed and Nicolette continued. 'There was some of Dad's things in it and Mum has been feeling a little... what's the word?'

'Nostalgic?'

'That's it. So, look. I know this is probably against all sorts of rules but I was wondering if you could give me the new owner's number so I can call and negotiate getting the box back. Mum is quite upset about it.'

She held her breath as the silence stretched out.

'Apparently there are some letters in there that Dad wrote to her when they first started dating. And Dad could be quite descriptive when he wanted to be. Hence her embarrassment. If someone else found them she'd be mortified.'

There was always a fine line in constructing a lie. Too little and it never works. Too much and it never works. And how much was just enough depended on each situation.

'Of course. Usually I would never do this, but just wait a minute.'

While Nicolette waited, Nero got up, stretched, and walked to the French doors. Nicolette let him out, leaving the door ajar for him to come back in after he'd done his business.

'Right. The buyer was the Magnusson Family Trust and the person I dealt with was Peter. This is his number.' She rattled it off and Nicolette scribbled it down on her notepad.

'Thank you so much,' she said. 'Mum will be relieved.'

'Good luck, hon.'

As Nicolette hung up, she caught a glimpse of Chloe standing in the hall doorway.

'Why is it okay for you to lie but not me?'

'Because it's part of my job.'

Chloe crossed to the fridge and took out the plate of leftover lasagne Nicolette had planned to eat for lunch the next day.

'Besides, I've never told you not to lie.'

'I know, I know,' Chloe replied as she grabbed a fork and started eating like she hadn't already consumed two platefuls earlier. '*If you're going to lie, make sure the consequences are worth it if you get caught.*'

'Right. Have you done all your homework?'

Chloe sighed through a mouthful of pasta and turned back towards her room.

'And that, Fig, is called parenting,' Nicolette said.

The dog opened her eyes at hearing her name, then went back to sleep.

Later, Nicolette stood, stretched and turned off her laptop. Time for bed.

Beneath the kitchen table, Fig began whining in her sleep, her back legs twitching. Nicolette lay on the floor next to her, stroking her back and murmuring soothing words. She didn't know if dogs dreamed but if they did, then Fig's weren't pleasant.

'Is she okay?'

Nicolette looked up as Chloe came and lay down on the other side of Fig. She wore pyjamas and her hair was mussed enough to show she'd at least tried to get to sleep.

'She will be. She has us.'

Chloe laid her hand on Fig's chest. Under their combined attention the dog quietened down and after a moment let out a soft sigh.

'She's lucky you found her,' Chloe said.

She knew her mother only brought home damaged animals, but Nicolette never told her the situations she found them in.

'You should be in bed,' said Nicolette.

'I had to pee.'

'Love you, honey.'

'Love you, too. Don't tell anyone,' Chloe replied with a grin.

'Your secret is safe with me.'

SEVEN

The next morning started badly. The mechanic called to say her car was going to cost her an amount of money she didn't have. She grimaced and told them to go ahead with the repairs. There was no choice, she had to have her own transport.

The mechanic cheerfully told her it should be ready by the middle of the week and she was free to keep the courtesy car until then.

'Everything alright?' asked Chloe.

It wasn't until Nicolette had banged on her bedroom door twice that Chloe had grumpily reminded her it was a teacher only day, so she had no school. Then, instead of going back to sleep, her daughter had risen and was now polishing off the remains of the lasagne she hadn't gotten to the night before.

'Fine. Are you going to be alright if I go to work?'

Chloe gave her the half incredulous, half scornful look that she'd somehow perfected in the last two months. 'Yes. Duh. Or... can I maybe come with you?'

Nicolette returned this with her own look and Chloe shrugged and went back to her phone.

'Do the dishes before I get home, please. And take the two dogs for a walk.'

'Two?'

'Teddy's coming with me.'

'How come he gets to go and I don't?'

'He has the right number of legs. Walk the dogs.'

'Mum!'

Nicolette stopped one street away from the old Downing house. She didn't want the nosy neighbours recognising her car and she didn't want her car showing up on the security cameras again. She dialled the number the real estate agent had given her the night before.

A recording told her the number was no longer in service.

Interesting.

Climbing out of the car, Nicolette adjusted her cap, then opened the rear passenger side door to let Teddy out. He immediately sniffed the grass, then peed.

'Come on,' she gently tugged on his leash and he happily trotted beside her as she walked down the road towards the Downing house. In her experience, people paid less attention to a dog walker than they did to someone walking by themselves.

The sun was fighting a losing battle with the southerly wind sweeping up the hill and she was glad she was wearing her warm tracksuit top. Teddy didn't seem to mind the wind, even when a sudden gust flipped his ear inside out. Nicolette reached down and straightened it, earning herself a lick of thanks.

As she rounded the corner to the Downing House street she slowed her pace. Two marked police cars were parked outside, and a dark sedan she identified as a plain clothes car sat opposite. A uniformed officer stood guard at the gate.

As she approached a man in a suit exited through the front door of the house and come down the path. He conferred with the constable and turned back to the house. He stopped suddenly when he caught sight of her.

They stared for a long time, then he beckoned her over. Nicolette crossed the road, furiously thinking of an excuse for her to be walking Teddy so far from home.

When she stopped, the man bent down to pat Teddy, who wagged his tail happily.

'Hello, Nicolette.'

'Hello, Dom.'

Detective Senior Sergeant Dominic Lister was frustrating, smug, annoyingly intelligent, and, in a convoluted way, Nicolette's stepbrother. He was also taller than her, two years older and according to many women quite attractive.

'What's your connection to the resident of this house?' Dominic asked.

'None.'

He shook his head. 'You decided to drive twenty minutes from your place just to take Teddy for a walk in this street?'

'He likes hills?'

'Nic.'

'You know I hate that name.'

'And you know I hate when you lie to me.'

'Fine,' Nicolette replied with a sigh. 'It's possible the man living here tried to kill a cat.'

Dominic's eyes narrowed and he flicked the fingers on his left hand. She knew that meant he was trying to decide what to tell her.

'Kill how?'

'Poison. Why?'

'Nic, tell me you've never been inside this house.'

'I've never been inside this house.'

'Nicolette!'

'Dominic!'

They glared at each other until Nicolette suddenly realised something.

'He's dead, isn't he?'

'What makes you say that?' Dominic asked sharply.

Teddy whined and backed around behind Nicolette, who crouched down to reassure the dog.

'You're homicide,' Nicolette said, ruffling Teddy's ears, 'and you asked me if I'd been inside the house, which means you're hoping they won't find my prints or DNA in there. Who's a good boy?'

'What?'

She stood up. 'I wasn't talking to you.'

'Right. Sorry Teddy.'

Teddy yawned an acceptance of the apology.

'Obviously, I can't officially comment on an ongoing police investigation.'

'Obviously.'

She waited patiently and eventually a ghost of a smile crossed his face.

'Unofficially, you're half right. There is a dead body, but the victim is a woman. You know I'm going to have to question you.'

'Formally or unofficially?' One would mean a trip to the central police station, while the other could happen here.

Dominic beckoned for the constable at the gate to come over.

'Take some notes will you, Ethan. We are questioning Nicolette Briggs, age 34.'

'Thirty three.' For another month anyway. 'And Teddy, aged 4,' Nicolette added.

Dominic scowled. 'Nicolette has prior knowledge of this household and she will now tell us how and why she's here today.'

If it had just been him, she would have teased Dominic about his officious tone, but she drew the line at undermining him in front of his colleagues. She succinctly relayed everything that had happened since she'd first arrived at the Silvermoon Retirement Village the day before.

'Who's your client?' he asked. She'd left that bit out.

‘I’ll have to check with her before releasing her name.’

‘Nicolette, this is a murder investigation.’

‘Which has nothing to do with her. For one thing she didn’t even know which house the cat came from, and for another she’s about a hundred and fifty years old. Do you really think she vaulted the back fence, broke into the house, and murdered someone over a poisoned cat?’

The constable smothered a grin which Dominic missed.

‘The first two are unlikely,’ Dominic begrudgingly accepted. ‘But the last one? You of all people know what people are capable of when it comes to protecting their animals.’

Nicolette nodded. ‘Okay, so two points to me, one to you.’

‘It’s not a game, Nicolette.’

‘Look, my involvement began and ended with the cat. I don’t do humans.’

‘I hope your daughter knows that.’

‘Leave her out of it,’ Nicolette snapped.

She took a deep breath and tried to relax her shoulders. This was how her and Dominic’s relationship had always been. One third nice, two thirds niggle.

‘Okay, that’s all for now.’

He turned to leave.

Annoyed that she was being so casually dismissed, Nicolette said, ‘Whoever killed her obviously came from inside the house. It was unlikely to be an intruder. Not with all the security cameras around the place.’

Dominic turned back. ‘What security cameras?’

‘There.’ She pointed to the corner of the house, but the camera was gone. A quick glance confirmed the camera in the other corner was also missing.

‘Now there’s something,’ she muttered.

Pushing past the constable, she headed towards the side of the house.

'Nicolette, you can't go in there.'

'Relax, I'm not going inside.'

'But still.'

She heard his footsteps crunching across the gravel path and she quickened her pace.

'Nicolette!'

She rounded the corner at the back of the house and stopped.

'I will arrest you.'

'Don't be stupid,' she replied. She pointed up at the corner where the wall met the roof. 'Yesterday afternoon there was a security camera there. And one on the other side.' She looked at her brother who was frowning. 'And two more at the front of the house. So, where are those cameras now?'

'It doesn't look like anything is missing. I'd expect the paint to be a little faded.'

Nicolette shook her head. 'The cameras were less than a month old, not long enough to cause fading.'

Dominic pulled out his phone and took a picture of the empty spot, then he walked over to the other corner and did the same.

'How did you find out about the body?' asked Nicolette.

'I thought you didn't do humans?'

'But I do do puzzles.'

'You know I can't talk about that,' Dominic replied. He came over and gripped her by the arm. Teddy issued a low growl and he let go. 'You need to get off the property. I'll call you later.'

Once they were back on the footpath, Dominic gave her his serious look. The same one he'd given her when she was seventeen and packing her bag to run away from the chaos that was their home.

'We only found out about the body earlier this morning. You need to step away and let me do my job. Promise me you won't get involved, Nic.'

'I promise you I have no intention of getting involved.'

He grunted.

'I'll call you later.'

He turned away as a car pulled up and another detective she recognised got out. She hurried off before he could glance in her direction. Dominic was a giant pain in her butt, but he was family. The other guy was just the first part.

Teddy wasn't happy about cutting the walk short, but she persuaded him to get into the car with a treat from the bag she kept in the glovebox.

It was all gone by the time she put her seatbelt on, but he was happy to sit down on the back seat, especially when she lowered the window so he could stick his head out.

She pulled into the Silvermoon carpark and he looked at her incredulously when she raised the window most of the way, leaving a gap for fresh air. She made sure she parked in the shade. Normally she would take Teddy with her, but he was still skittish around too many people, and old people, like kids, were unpredictable in their reactions to dogs.

A young woman answered when she knocked on Alice's door.

'I'm Nicolette Briggs. Is Alice home?'

'No, I'm out dancing,' a voice called from inside.

The woman smiled and opened the door wider. 'I'm Vanessa. Ignore her, she's in a mood.'

Alice was sitting on the couch where she scowled at Vanessa.

'I don't get in moods. Sit down,' she commanded, with a wave towards a chair.

'I'll make some tea.'

'You'll have to forgive Vanessa, she thinks she's a 1950s housewife.'

'Oh, I'll do some cucumber sandwiches too then.'

Alice coughed. 'Only if you put a thick piece of ham in there. And hold the cucumber.'

'You know you can't eat ham,' replied Vanessa.

'Am I interrupting something?' Nicolette interjected.

Vanessa laughed. Nicolette put her at around twenty-two or three, casually dressed in jeans and a light green T-Shirt. Silvermoon staff wore a blue T-shirt as a uniform so it was clear the girl didn't work for the retirement village. There didn't appear to be a family resemblance between Vanessa and Alice, although they were both slim. Alice had said the relationship between the two was complicated.

'Not at all,' Alice said. 'Do you have something to report.'

Nicolette relayed everything that had happened over the last hour. She expected the two women to be shocked, but both took the news calmly. Once again Nicolette felt like she was missing something important.

'And what are your next steps?' asked Alice as Vanessa handed Nicolette a cup of tea.

'Sorry, I assumed milk and no sugar.'

'That's fine,' replied Nicolette. 'I'm not sure what you mean. There's nothing left for me to do. It's a murder investigation now.'

'Yes, but you said the victim was a woman, and you think the person who poisoned Maddy was a man.'

Nicolette looked from the younger to the older woman and back again. 'But it's likely the man was the killer, or at least involved. Either way it would mean interfering in a police investigation.'

'Which is a problem for you?' Alice asked.

Nicolette opened her mouth to answer, then closed it again. The truth was the grey element to her investigations usually brought her into the disapproving spotlight of many police officers.

But there had always been a reason for it, and she just couldn't see the motivation here. She looked over to the patch of sun where Maddy was cleaning herself. The cat looked like she was going to make a full recovery.

Yet there was something strange about this case that made her feel uneasy.

'What's troubling you?' Alice asked.

'I guess it's the security cameras. They were put up for a reason and, unless they were taken down before the woman was killed, it shows a certain level of...' She searched for the right word.

'Forethought,' Alice finished.

Nicolette looked at her thoughtfully. 'Yes. Let's assume for the minute that the man I spoke to yesterday is the killer. He does away with the victim, then climbs up a ladder, four times, and removes the security cameras.'

'Presumably because there's footage on there that is incriminating,' Alice said.

'But those cameras don't record to the device. Everything is stored in the cloud,' added Vanessa, with a grin.

Nicolette waited for Alice to ask what the cloud was. Instead she said, 'So why remove them?'

'Exactly.'

'That's a puzzle worth exploring, don't you think?'

'I'm sure the police will look into it. I know the detective in charge of the investigation and he's thorough.'

'So, you won't continue? Your three days aren't up yet.'

'I don't want to take your money.'

'It's my money to spend. And I'm sure you want the bonus?'

Nicolette very much wanted the bonus, especially in light of the news about her car.

'Why do you care so much?' she asked.

Alice took a sip of her tea. It was Vanessa that answered.

'Because she collects strays. Me, Joshua, Maddy. Once she decides you're worth it, you become part of Alice's inner circle. And when you're in that, she'll do anything to protect you, whether that means cracking open her purse or cracking a bone or two.'

Alice pursed her lips but didn't contradict her.

Nicolette smiled at the idea that the elderly woman was capable of breaking any bones other than her own.

'Maddy picked my apartment to spend time in. Granted she had a little help at first,' Alice glared at Vanessa, 'but I've grown accustomed to her presence. If someone deliberately hurt her then something must be done. You suspect the man at the house was the poisoner, but you haven't proved it. Until you do, the job is incomplete. You have two days left in your three-day deadline. Unless you are so well off you can afford to forfeit the pay and bonus, or worse, you lack the moral fortitude to complete the job...'

Nicolette knew she was being manipulated, but she still bristled at the insinuation.

'Fine. I'll keep going, but I won't interfere in a police investigation.' Not after last time, she added in her head.

'Excellent,' Alice said, looking satisfied. 'What's next?'

Nicolette hesitated. In her experience clients mostly just wanted the happy outcome, rather than to hear about the steps taken to get there.

'If you're worried about her delicate sensibilities, don't be,' Vanessa said. 'Alice doesn't have a sensitive side.'

Alice scowled, but Nicolette saw the twitch of her lips.

Nicolette rose from her seat and crossed to the window. From there she could see the top half of the house beyond the fence, where a police officer was balanced on a ladder, inspecting the corner where the security camera had been.

She turned to face the others.

'Does the name Magnusson Family Trust mean anything to you?'

They both shook their heads.

'The police will no doubt look into it and chances are it'll lead nowhere, but that seems to be the best place to start. And for the time being I've got one advantage they don't.'

'What's that?' asked Vanessa.

'An eyewitness.'

'Carry on,' Alice said. 'Unless you need anything, I won't expect another update until the end of the third day.'

'I'll walk you out.'

Vanessa didn't speak until they were in the elevator.

'She can be a bit crotchety, but underneath it all...'

'...she has a heart of gold?'

'Gosh no,' Vanessa laughed. 'More like a heart of diamond. Pretty to look at but just as likely to cut you if you get close.'

'I'm not sure that analogy works.'

'Probably not.' Vanessa shrugged. 'But what I said back there was true. She gets a little obsessive about things, especially mysteries like this. She won't let it go. There have been some deaths at Silvermoon over the last year. Not usual old-age sort of deaths, but the other sort.'

Nicolette glanced at her and Vanessa shrugged.

'Alice wants to know if this is something to be worried about,' Vanessa said. 'But she tends to stick to the village grounds these days, which is why she needs you.'

The elevator doors opened, and they stepped into the lobby.

'I won't take her money if I don't think I can do anything.'

'I understand that and, believe it or not, that's probably one of the reasons she wants you to keep going. She's a complicated woman, but she reads people, and she obviously thinks you're up to it.'

They paused outside on the top step.

'I've only met her twice. Why do I have this sense of not wanting to let her down?'

Vanessa grinned. 'That's the Alice effect. It's annoying, but you get used to it.'

'Who is she?'

'Like I said, that's complicated. And not my story to tell.'

EIGHT

Nicolette walked back to the car where Teddy greeted her like she'd been gone for hours. When she let him out, he had a sniff around and found a discrete tree to pee against.

While she waited, she called Gladys Downing. 'I was wondering if there was anything else you'd remembered about the man who came to your house.'

There was a long pause, during which Teddy looked at Nicolette anxiously to make sure she was still there before resuming his exploration of the car park.

'He wore a suit. I remember thinking it seemed strange to wear a suit to come and measure a room. I decided he must have come up on his lunch break, but...'

'Then you noticed something else?' Nicolette prompted.

Gladys let out a tiny laugh. 'It's silly. My husband worked in the city for thirty-six years, and he wore a suit every single one of those days. He never particularly liked it, but after all that time it became comfortable, like putting on your favourite pair of sweatpants in the weekend. Oh he looked so smart in his crisp white shirt and suspenders.'

Nicolette bit her lip to stop her impatience spilling out.

'Sorry, that was probably more than you wanted to hear. Anyway, I can recognise when someone is not comfortable in what they are wearing.'

Teddy checked on Nicolette again and she flicked her fingers. He happily trotted over and nuzzled her hand.

'So, you think the man wasn't used to wearing a suit?'

'I'm sure of it. Well, mostly sure. He kept pulling at his sleeves and adjusting his jacket. It could have been a new suit, I suppose. It's probably just a silly old woman's imagination.'

'Gladys, I doubt there's a single silly thing about you.'

A giggle came down the phoneline and Nicolette found herself smiling.

'What about his car?' she asked.

'What about it?'

'Do you remember anything about it? The colour or make.'

'Oh, I didn't get a good look at it, I'm afraid...'

Nicolette struck that off as a potential line of investigation.

'...but I think it was a black 2020 Subaru Outback. I didn't get the licence plate, but it started with KDP.'

Nicolette blinked.

'So not a good look then,' she said dryly, and opened the car door to let Teddy jump in.

'It was a game we used to play with the kids when we were on road trips. We'd read out the letters on the number plates and the girls would have to come up with as many words that contained those letters. Even though the kids are all grown, I still do it when I'm out. I suppose it reminds me of happier times.'

She sounded down and Nicolette shuffled her feet uncomfortably. Give her a sad cat or dog and she'd instantly know what to do, but people were a minefield of potential wrong things to say.

'Going back to the man, I know from our earlier discussion that he had shifty eyes, but can you describe him in more detail?'

'Well, he would have been about Angela's age, early thirties. He had short brown hair, as if it had been cut using the... what do you call them?'

'Clippers?'

'Yes, that's right. He was taller than me and I think he'd recently lost some weight.'

'Why do you say that?'

'He was too thin in my opinion. I like a little meat on my bones.'

Nicolette winced and quickly ended the call. She climbed into the car and Teddy poked his head between the seats to give her face a lick.

The man had obviously borrowed a suit to wear. The question was why? Was he trying to impress Gladys Downing or appear to be something that he wasn't? Much as she liked Gladys, Nicolette doubted it was the former. Which brought her right back to why?

Another question struck her and she dialled Dominic. It went to voicemail and she left a message. He called back as she was going out the Silvermoon gates.

'Nic, please don't tell me you're calling about the case.'

'I am, but I've got some info for you.'

'Alright, what?'

'First, a bit of quid pro quo.'

'Nic!'

'All I want to know is how you found out about the body?'

'Nic!'

'You're going to be asked this by the journalists anyway.'

He sighed. 'I guess you're right. One of the neighbours was out for a walk when they saw the front door wide open. She called the police and when the constables arrived, they discovered the body inside.'

'Right, in the lounge.'

'No, the bathroom. Damnit, Nicolette.'

Nicolette grinned smugly.

'You know you're annoying, right?'

'I've been told,' Nicolette replied.

'Yeah, the trouble is you take it as a compliment.'

He hung up, leaving Nicolette feeling mildly regretful. She realised she hadn't given him an update on what she found. Chances are she would need more information from Dominic at some stage and now he was less likely to give it. That, and the next family gathering would be an interesting affair. Not that she attended family gatherings.

Aside from tricking Dominic into revealing where the woman was found (interesting but not overly helpful for now), she was pretty sure she knew who had alerted the police.

A short time later, she parked down the street from the old Downing house. Teddy gave her a resigned expression as she cracked open the driver's window for him and climbed out of the car.

'I won't be long, I promise. Then we'll go to the park and throw the ball.'

His ears perked up at the word ball and he looked around hopefully.

Nicolette laughed. 'Soon.'

Keeping an eye on the flurry of activity happening at the crime scene, she crossed the street and knocked on the front door of one of the houses she'd visited previously.

The same woman from yesterday answered. Different clothes, but the same exhausted expression and wailing baby in the background.

'Yes?'

'Hi, I was just speaking with the police and thought I'd come and see if you were okay.'

'Oh, thank you.' She looked over her shoulder as the crying got louder. 'She's teething,' the woman said. 'I've tried everything but as you can hear, nothing works.'

‘Perhaps I can help,’ Nicolette said. She didn’t wait for a response, gently pushing past and following the sound of crying down the narrow hallway.

The baby was lying on her back, tiny fists waving in the air like a drunk boxer. Nicolette plucked her from the cot and began rocking her gently. The crying slowly subsided to hiccups and ragged breathing and finally silence.

‘How did you do that? She won’t do that for me,’ asked the mother from the doorway.

‘She can sense that you’re stressed, so it’s a vicious cycle of you getting upset because she’s upset and she’s getting upset because you’re upset.’

The woman’s lips trembled and Nicolette quickly said, ‘Can I make you a cup of tea?’

‘That sounds wonderful, but I’ll make it.’

‘I’m Nicolette by the way.’

‘Abbie, and this little one is Emma. Come on, the kitchen is this way.’

Abbie may have been a mess, but her house wasn’t. There was the usual clutter found in most homes, but the surfaces were clean and there was nothing to trip over as they walked to the kitchen.

Nicolette perched on a wooden stool at the counter, still jiggling Emma gently in her arms, and studied Abbie while she boiled the kettle and made the tea. She revised her earlier age estimate down to late twenties. Abbie’s hair was cut into a bob which, judging by the photos on the hallway wall, was a recent change. Probably out of practicality rather than fashion. Her T-shirt hung loose and her grey tracksuit pants were cinched tight around her waist.

Emma seemed fascinated by Nicolette ’s necklace, pulling it with both hands and trying to put it in her mouth. Nicolette casually extracted it from her little fingers each time.

Abbie opened the fridge door and Nicolette caught sight of a fridge magnet that read:

Shopping List:

Milk

Bread

My Sanity

'The police have already asked me a bunch of questions.'

Nicolette smiled at her. 'I know, but sometimes it pays to circle back to see if you've remembered anything more.'

'Honestly, there wasn't much to remember,' Abbie replied, sliding a mug of tea across the counter. 'Sorry, we're out of milk. Black okay?

Nicolette nodded, even though black tea was marginally above cold tea on the list of things she disliked.

'I saw the door was open when I passed on my walk, and it was still open when I was coming back. That's pretty weird around here. There's been a few break ins recently, but even before that people didn't leave their doors open.'

'So, you called the police?'

Abbie shook her head. 'Not at first. I called out from the gate, just in case someone was home. When I didn't get a reply, that's when I called the police.'

Abbie's eyes darted to the right as she said it. Nicolette waited patiently for her to continue.

'I couldn't stay, because Emma was hungry, but I told them my name and number and a detective came to see me. He told me there had been an unexplained death. What does that mean?'

'It means they don't think it was natural causes.'

Abbie's eyes went wide and she bit her bottom lip.

'You seem like a sensible woman, Abbie,' Nicolette said. 'Your house is organised and tidy, even if you're not.'

Abbie tugged at her T shirt and scratched at a dried food stain with her fingernail.

'I'm sure you're not the sort to just wait at the gate, are you?'

Abbie stopped working at the stain on her shirt and looked stricken. 'I didn't go inside.'

'Of course not. But maybe to the doorstep?'

Abbie tried to take a sip of her tea but her hands were shaking too much. 'You don't think the police will be angry, do you?'

'If you didn't go inside then you'll be fine. But why did you lie about it?'

'I panicked,' Abbie replied. 'The emergency services operator sounded annoyed when I called, like I was wasting their time with something silly about an open door. I wanted to get off the call as quick as I could, because I did feel silly. It was probably as simple as someone forgetting to lock the door and the wind blowing it open.'

'Except you weren't silly, Abbie. If it weren't for you, who knows how long that poor woman would have lain undiscovered.'

'Oh, I didn't think of that.'

Nicolette's arm began to ache so she switched sides and flexed her sore hand. She'd forgotten how heavy babies became after holding them for a while.

'While you were on the doorstep did you see anything?'

'Not the body,' Abbie replied quickly.

'No, but anything else, no matter how small.'

'It was just a hallway.'

'Any pictures on the walls?'

Abbie frowned. 'Come to think of it, no. The walls were bare.'

'What about smells?'

'Smells?' Abbie repeated in surprise.

'Yes. Sometimes we remember smells more than what we see. Close your eyes and take a deep breath and try to remember the doorway.'

Abbie looked at her uncertainly before closing her eyes. She took a big breath in, then opened her eyes again and shook her head.

'Sorry, I can't smell anything, other than baby vomit.' She glanced down at her T-shirt and shrugged.

'That's okay. I should get going though.'

She handed Emma to her mother and they walked to the front door.

'Hang on. I don't remember smelling anything, but there was a sound.'

'What sort of sound?' asked Nicolette.

'It was faint. But I'm sure there was music playing somewhere inside the house.'

'Do you remember the song?'

'No,' Abbie replied with a frown. 'It wasn't a song. I mean there was no singing. It was almost… classical or jazz maybe? I'm not very good with anything older than 90s pop.'

'I'm not much better. Could you tell where it was coming from in the house? Like was it loud or faint. Did you think it might have been coming from the back of the house or near the front?'

'It was definitely faint. I didn't hear it until I got right up by the door. I get the impression it was coming from somewhere in the back of the house, maybe. I know that's not helpful, but it was so low I almost missed it completely.'

'That's been helpful. I do have one more question. The dog next door?'

Abbie scowled. 'That man. He ignores the poor thing. I sometimes throw some food into the backyard, because I don't think he ever feeds her. And she barks all day because she's left alone. I called the SPCA and they came around but left the dog behind.'

'Never mind,' Nicolette said. 'The police are in the street now, perhaps they'll go knock on the door and do something.'

'Oh,' Abbie's face brightened. 'I hope so, she's such a sweetie. She always licks my hand when I feed her.'

'Good luck with Emma. And trust me when I say it will get easier.'

'I hope so.'

Abbie closed the front door and Nicolette walked down the steps. Faint music wasn't much of a clue, but all these little things could add up to something big. It made sense if the victim was found in the bathroom though. Nicolette often listened to music when she had a bath or shower. She should have warned Abbie that there was a doorbell camera so the police would know she lied about not approaching the house. But she figured there was a plausible explanation and she'd be fine.

She looked at the house next door and decided she could spare a few minutes to scope things out.

The door was flung open, and Nicolette took a step back at the sight of the man who filled the door frame. He was dishevelled and his breath stunk of alcohol. He squinted at her and scratched the hairs on his cheeks.

'What do you want?' He belched and she took a step back as the smell hit her like a physical wave of stale beer and pizza.

'Good morning. I'm working alongside the police. There has been an incident down the street.'

'I didn't see anything.'

From inside the house a dog barked.

'Shut it!' He yelled over his shoulder.

'Oh, a dog. I love dogs, do you mind if I see him.'

Nicolette slipped past him before he could reply and strode down the hallway. The house was cluttered and there was a damp odour.

'Oi, get out.'

She ignored the man, continuing through the house, into the kitchen and out the back door, jumping down the two steps to the grass.

Now that she was close up, Nicolette could see how thin the dog was. His ribs were clearly visible, and his coat was matted and dirty.

'You can't be here.'

'Yet I am,' she replied brightly. 'Who's a good boy?'

'What?'

The dog slunk up and sniffed her outstretched hand, giving her a tentative lick. Nicolette scratched behind the ear and he flopped onto his side, tongue hanging out happily.

'He looks a little thin. When was he last fed?'

The man rubbed his neck. 'Let me see, that was... none of your damn business. If you're with the police let's see your ID.'

Nicolette gave the dog one more pat, then stood up and smiled brightly at the man.

'I won't take up any more of your time. My colleagues will be down to formally interview you later.'

She sidestepped around him and retraced her way through the house, taking in as much as she could on the way through. She heard the man following and quickened her step, only relaxing once she was through the front door.

'Oi!'

'Thank you, sir,' she waved over her shoulder and made it to the pavement before risking a glance back. The man stood there in dazed confusion, then stepped back inside and slammed the door shut.

With a sigh of relief Nicolette headed back to her car.

When she got a few feet away she stopped dead. Teddy's face wasn't pressed to the window. She covered the remaining distance quickly, her eyes searching the back seat.

He wasn't in the car.

'Teddy?'

She looked up and down the street but there was no sign of her dog. Rounding the car, she saw that the passenger door wasn't shut properly.

'Teddy!'

Nicolette strained to listen for an answering bark, but none came.

It was then she saw something on the dashboard. It hadn't been there before. She opened the door and snagged the folded piece of paper.

The note was short and to the point.

If you want to see your dog, come to Izard Park.

Nicolette jumped into the driver's seat and did a U-turn. It took all her self-control not to speed past the police cars outside the old Downing house. Once she'd turned the corner, that control slipped and her foot pressed down on the accelerator.

It took five minutes and one near miss with a bus to get to Izard Park, during which time she'd formed and discarded many theories around the dognapping. Teddy wasn't the most trusting dog, thanks to his early life, so he wouldn't leave with just anyone. In fact, she should have heard him barking from inside the house. This led to a flood of guilt because she'd left him in the car and if she hadn't then he wouldn't have been taken. It was all her fault.

Slamming on the brakes, she glared at herself in the rearview mirror. 'Sort it out, Nicolette.'

She flung open the door and jumped out, racing across the footpath and onto the grass. Izard Park was a playground beside a grass field, surrounded on three sides by trees. It was a nice, secluded spot for a meeting. But the exits were limited and that was good for Nicolette and bad for whoever took her dog.

On first scan the park appeared empty, but then she saw a mother and her young child on the slide. Next to the playground, a man was sitting on a bench with Teddy happily lying at his feet.

Nicolette strode over, forcing herself to take deep breaths and relax her hands. She was going to listen to his excuse before deciding on a course of action.

The man and dog both stood up as she approached. Teddy barked happily and strained at the leash connecting him to the man.

'Ms Briggs, I'm happy to—'

Nicolette punched him.

NINE

'Remind me never to annoy you,' the man gasped from the ground, clutching his stomach.

'Too late. Give me my dog.'

He passed up the leash and Teddy slunk over to her side.

'Can I explain, or do you want to hit me again?' He rolled into a seated position, leaning against the bench.

Nicolette saw the mother of the toddler watching her in alarm.

'My ex,' Nicolette called to her. 'He stole my dog.'

The woman eyed him and said, 'I would have hit him harder. And lower.'

Nicolette turned back to study the man. He had short brown hair and blue eyes, a couple of days' worth of stubble on his chin, and a pale scar running from above his left eye up to his hair line. He wore jeans and a polo shirt and didn't seem very upset that he'd just been clobbered.

'Okay, well you got my attention. What was so important that you had to steal my dog?'

'Borrow,' he replied. 'He was never in any danger. In fact, he was perfectly happy, until you decided to drive my kidney into my spleen.'

Nicolette sat on the bench. Now that the adrenalin was wearing off, she felt a little shaky. Teddy nuzzled her hand and she rubbed the top of his head. 'Silly dog, going off with a stranger. What if something had happened to you?' she murmured.

'I took good care of him.' The man pulled himself up, onto the far end of the bench.

'Let's start with your name,' Nicolette said.

'Mark Chaney.'

'Your real name.'

'How do you know that's not my real name?'

Nicolette sighed. 'You didn't dognap Teddy and lure me to a park just so you could give me your real name.'

He nodded appreciatively. 'Let's leave it at Mark for now.'

She took out her phone and snapped his picture.

'What was that for?'

'In case you take off with Teddy again. Alright, *Mark*. As I said, you've got my attention. What do you want?'

'I want to start by saying, I didn't kill anybody.'

It suddenly clicked as to how she knew his voice.

'How about poisoning any cats?'

Mark winced. 'That either.'

'So explain why there's a dead body in your house.'

Mark shook his head. 'That's the thing though. I've never been inside that house.'

'You didn't show up at the front door wearing a suit?'

'How do you know about that?' He grinned ruefully. 'Alright, so I have been into the house, but only to set the equipment up.'

'What equipment?' Nicolette asked, though she thought she knew the answer.

'Security cameras.'

'Why don't you start from the beginning.'

'Fine. A month ago, I was hired to install a security system at the house.'

'Hired by who?'

'The Magnusson Family Trust. They had recently purchased the house and wanted top of the range cameras installed outside.'

'And inside?'

Mark looked away for a second. 'Just in one room.'

'The bedroom,' Nicolette guessed.

'No, the kitchen.'

'The kitchen? That's a bit strange isn't it?'

He shrugged. 'It wasn't my job to question why. But the kitchen has a back door in it so I figured they just wanted to cover that.'

Teddy stood up and whined. Nicolette glanced around. The mother and child were walking away leaving Nicolette and Mark alone. She stroked Teddy and eventually he relaxed.

'Were you in the house when I came to the door yesterday?'

'No, I was at my office. I got a phone alert there was someone there.'

'Why did you lie about owning the cat?'

'I saw the cat go inside a few times on the cameras. I figured it would be easier to just say it belonged there. But when you said it had been poisoned, I panicked.'

Nicolette wasn't always the best judge of character, but she believed him.

'And what about this morning?'

'I got a call to come and remove the security cameras. Just the outside ones. They said they were selling the house again and didn't need them anymore. They offered me a five-hundred-dollar bonus if I did it before nine.'

'You didn't find that suspicious?'

'Of course I did, but I wasn't going to turn down five hundred dollars. They were my cameras anyway, the Trust was just leasing them, so the sooner I got them back the sooner I could start charging someone else.'

'But they weren't returning the inside camera, or the doorbell?'

'No,' Mark replied with a frown. 'They said I'd get those back next week, they needed them a little longer.'

'And you didn't find *that* odd?'

'You'd be shocked by some of the things my clients want done.'

'Okay, so then this morning you went to the house and took down the outside cameras. Did you go inside?' asked Nicolette.

'No, I told you, apart from setting up the camera in the kitchen, I never went into the house.'

'Did you see or hear anything while you were there?'

He shook his head. 'Honestly, I was only there for thirty minutes. All the cameras were wireless, so it was just a case of climbing a ladder and unscrewing them.'

'Was the front door open when you arrived?'

'No, of course not. Why would it be?'

'What time did you leave the house?'

'Around 8.50am. I wasn't going to risk losing the bonus.'

'How did they know you were done?'

'I called them.'

'Okay,' Nicolette nodded thoughtfully. 'So now, back to the important question, why did you take my dog?'

Mark looked guilty as he wiggled his fingers at Teddy who happily sniffed them. 'I went back to the house because I forgot a screwdriver. I saw you talking to the cop and then one of the neighbours standing at their gate told me there'd been a murder. I was freaking out. Then I saw you go into the house down the road. I figured out who you were and I wanted to talk to you away from the police. When I saw you back there this morning I thought taking the dog was the only way to get you alone.'

'You're an IT guy and you've never heard of a cellphone?'

'I didn't know your number. But I knew your name because you introduced yourself at the house. I searched the web and found you.'

Nicolette frowned. She knew there was no way of avoiding things going online but her job required an element of anonymity.

Teddy whined again. He was staring at an empty spot across the park.

'Who is your contact at the Magnusson Family Trust?'

Mark pulled out his phone. 'Her name is Kalliana Magnusson. I only ever talked to her over the phone and we emailed a few times.' He showed Nicolette a phone number and she took a photo of the screen with her own phone.

'You never met her in person?'

'No,' Mark confirmed.

'Was she the one you called this morning to get your bonus?'

He nodded and she noticed his leg jiggling up and down. 'But it wasn't her that answered. It was some guy.'

'What did he say?'

'Nothing much, he said she was busy. I said the job was done and he promised to deposit the five hundred dollars into my account today.'

'Who mentioned the money first, you or him?'

Mark thought for a moment. 'He did. Come to think of it, he was probably the same guy who called me this morning about removing the cameras.'

'Did he tell you his name?'

'Just once, at the start of the first call. He said it quickly so I'm not sure.'

'What happened to the camera footage? Can you access that?'

He slumped back against the bench. 'No, I set up the footage to run directly to their server and provided them with their own login. The only camera I had access to was the doorbell one, so that I could monitor the camera for visitors.'

'Do you still have access?'

Mark swiped and pressed, then turned the screen towards her. A video time-stamped yesterday showed the porch and street directly outside the house. 'It's motion activated.'

'Can you show me this morning.'

He swiped the screen and the video jumped to 8:00am. Nothing happened for a while, then at 8:10am a car stopped outside the house and Mark got out. He took a collapsible ladder from the back seat and hurried up the path, disappearing from view around the side of the house. A few seconds later the video cut out.

That's weird,' Mark said. 'That shouldn't happen.'

'What's weird?'

'It might be nothing. Let me take a closer look at it at home and get back to you, but it looks like the killer blocked the camera somehow. Oh god, they were there.'

He looked horrified at the thought, but she'd known too many liars in her life to be totally convinced.

'Can you send it to me?'

'Sure.'

She gave him her work email address and a few seconds later he'd sent her a link to the footage.

Mark went back to the video and swiped forward with his finger. The screen stayed black until 9.13am when it suddenly flicked back to life. They watched as Abbie approached the door carrying Emma and called out. When there was no reply, she retreated down the path and pulled out her phone.

Ten minutes later a police patrol car pulled up and two officers entered the house.

'Go back,' Nicolette said.

He rewound the video to before it cut out and they watched it again. She didn't learn anything new the second viewing.

'Why didn't you go to the police with this?'

'Isn't it obvious? Because I thought they'd think I killed whoever was in... Oh I get the video thing now. You think I blacked it out to cover my tracks. I swear I didn't kill her. I don't even know who the dead woman is. Besides if I could black out the video why wouldn't I just do it from before I arrived?'

Nicolette thought for a moment. 'How long were you around the back of the house?'

Mark shrugged. 'I don't know, maybe ten minutes tops. Like I said it was just unscrewing a couple of cameras.'

'You need to talk to the police.'

Mark looked at his watch, then jumped up. He strode several feet away before turning back. 'Look, I know I need to, but I was hoping...'

'What?'

'That you could find out what happened first. That way I'd be in the clear already.'

'Is that why you took Teddy?'

'Yes. Like I said, I looked you up.'

'I don't do humans.'

'What does that mean?' Mark stepped towards her.

Teddy instantly rose to his feet with a deep growl and Mark stopped.

'I don't know how you got Teddy to come with you before, but I'm his family and he's very protective.'

'I wasn't...' He backed quickly away.

'Your best bet is to go to the police. I know the detective in charge of the investigation, I can call him. Tell them everything you just told me. If you're innocent, they'll confirm it.'

'You've obviously never watched true crime documentaries,' Mark muttered.

He took another look at this watch, while jiggling up and down on the spot.

'What's wrong?'

'I get restless when I'm nervous. I'm going to do a lap of the field while I think. I'll be right back.' He took off jogging before she could reply.

'He's a weird one,' she said to Teddy, who huffed and sat down.

'What do you know? You were the one who went off with him.'

Her phone beeped with a message from Chloe asking if she could go into town with some friends.

Nicolette fired back "Which friends?"

She looked for Mark on the far side of the field. It took her a moment to find him.

He was facing the bushes, as if examining the leaves. Suddenly he took two steps back then slowly toppled to the ground. For a moment she thought he'd lost his balance, but he stayed down.

Teddy whined and pulled at his leash.

Nicolette stood up, counting off the seconds in her head. When she got to ten and he still hadn't moved she knew something was wrong.

Racing across the grass, Teddy loping beside her with his tongue hanging out, she covered the distance in no time. Skidding to a halt, she dropped to her knees.

Mark lay on his side, facing away from her. When she rolled him over, his sightless eyes were staring at the sky. A knife stuck out of the centre of his chest.

She checked for a pulse just in case, but didn't expect to find one.

Mark was dead.

TEN

'That's when I saw the blood,' Nicolette said.

Dominic looked over to where Mark's body lay a few metres away.

'Hell, Nic, what have you got yourself involved in?'

'I wish I knew. It's just getting stranger by the second.'

'And you didn't notice anything, like someone stabbing the victim?'

Nicolette frowned at her brother. 'I know how it sounds but I'm hardly going to forget seeing that.' She looked at her feet. 'Teddy knew something was up.'

Dominic followed her gaze. 'I'll just ask him some questions then.'

'Don't be an idiot, Dom. Teddy kept whining, but there was nothing there when I looked.' She peered towards the bushes close to where the body lay. They were about her height and densely spaced. 'Maybe someone was waiting in there.'

Dominic grabbed her arm. 'Please tell me you're not about to contaminate my crime scene.'

'Of course not. Wouldn't dream of it.'

'Good, because based on what you told me, you were the last to see him alive, which automatically makes you a prime witness. And suspect.'

Nicolette checked her brother's face to see if he was joking, then sighed. 'I could never read your poker face.'

He leaned towards her slightly. 'I'm serious, Nic. As soon as the brass hear about my connection to you, I'm going to get pulled off this case, and the only other detective that is free to step in is Phelps.'

'Phelps! You mean he hasn't fallen on his own career yet?'

'Nic, be serious.'

'I'm standing next to the dead body of someone I was just talking to,' Nicolette shot back. 'I'm aware of how serious it is.'

'Then go home and think hard about everything he said to you, because the next time you talk about it could be at the Wellington Police Station.'

Nicolette tugged on the leash and Teddy shot to his feet. He was nervous around crowds and had been sitting hunched over and leaning into her leg.

'You can't possibly think Mark has anything to do with Kalliana Magnusson's murder.'

'We don't know...Wait, how did you...?'

'Mark said she didn't answer her phone. The body found was a woman and the house was owned by the Magnusson Family Trust. I can add.'

Dominic scowled. 'Damnit, Nic, just go home.'

She went, but not home. Nicolette knew enough to navigate her way around most computer problems, but she was no expert. Luckily, she knew someone who was, and this was going to have to be an in-person visit.

Teddy had settled himself into the back seat and looked hopeful when Nicolette opened the back door and clipped the leash onto his harness.

She paused to lock the car and tried to ease the tingly feeling in her stomach, before walking up the path to the front door of the townhouse. The front lawn was small and immaculate, and the driveway lined with colourful flowers. Nicolette felt like she was walking into a show home.

The door opened before she could knock. A tall, athletic woman with short black hair leaned against the door frame and looked her up and down. Even in paint-stained shorts and pale white singlet top, she looked fabulous, much to Nicolette's disgust. No one would have picked them to be sisters, which technically they were.

'Well, well, look what the dog dragged in.'

'Hi, Archie.'

'Twice in the same week, and it's not even my birthday.'

Nicolette shifted uncomfortably and Teddy skittered to the side to avoid being stepped on.

'Before you come in you might want to know that Mum is on her way over.'

'Bugger,' Nicolette said. 'I'll come back later.'

'Like hell you will.' Archie grabbed her arm and pulled her into the house. 'You've got an hour and it's been so long I didn't think you'd remember where I lived. I'm not waiting another two years for you to show up.'

'It hasn't been two years!' Nicolette protested as she was dragged down the hallway and into the open plan lounge and kitchen. The place looked like it had just been unwrapped. No clutter, no dishes on the kitchen bench, and a single framed picture on the wall above the dining table that could have been a stock photo, except Nicolette recognised the young girl.

'Why do you have a picture of Chloe on your wall?'

Archie let her go and walked into the kitchen.

'Why not? She is my niece.'

Nicolette winced at the unspoken jibe.

'When was this taken? She looks about five.'

'She was. I had her for the afternoon. Shockingly. So, I got a friend of mine to take a few photos. That one is my favourite.'

Chloe was sitting on the grass, her hair going in all directions. She refused to let it be brushed back then, well before she became an image conscious teenager. She was laughing at something off camera.

'Teddy can wander round. Still drink those awful smoothies?'

Nicolette unclipped the leash and Teddy immediately began exploring the space with his nose. She went and sat on a kitchen stool. 'They're not awful smoothies. They're nutritious.'

Archie pulled a container from her freezer and placed it on the bench. 'They're filled with things that shouldn't be in a liquid form, like kale and spinach.'

Nicolette watched her reach into a cupboard and bring out a smoothie maker.

'What are you doing?'

'Making you a smoothie. You see when someone comes to your house it's considered polite to offer them refreshments.'

'Tea would be fine.'

'This, my dear Nic, is not a tea situation.'

Archie opened the container and scooped out a frozen lump of what looked like berries. She placed it in the smoothie maker, then added apple juice and Greek yoghurt.

'You just happened to have this lying around?' asked Nicolette.

Archie switched on the machine then mimed to her ear that she couldn't hear. After twenty seconds she switched the machine off and poured the smoothie into two glasses.

'You're joining me?'

'How do you think I maintain this fine physical specimen.'

'Vodka and cigarettes?'

Archie pretended to scowl, then laughed. 'I've given up one of those, I'll let you guess which.'

'It's obviously the cigarettes. The place doesn't smell, your fingers aren't stained yellow, and there's not an ashtray in sight.'

'Well, aren't you the detective. Come on.'

They carried their drinks through the sliding door onto the tiny patio and sat on a long swing chair, while Teddy sniffed his way around the tiny backyard. The property was ringed by a six-foot fence, so they were alone.

'At the risk of ruining a pleasant moment, why are you here?' asked Archie.

'The case I called you about yesterday. It's taken a turn for the worse.'

'And you want a fake passport so you can flee the country. Of course, I'll get it from my safe after we're done.'

'You have fake papers for me sitting in your safe?'

'My dear girl, this was always coming.'

'Well, I'm not going anywhere, but there is a dead body I'd like your help with,' Nicolette said.

'Certainly. I think there's a shovel in the garage.'

'Archie, after the last time I came to you for help with a dead body, you think I'd ask again?'

'In my defence, you were the one who killed the fish, I was just trying to help.'

They shared a smile, then Archie's expression turned serious as Nicolette told her everything.

'My darling step-brother obviously doesn't know you very well.'

'I agree he's being optimistic.'

Teddy finished his exploration and flopped down in the shade, keeping his eyes on Nicolette.

'So why not just leave it alone? It's a double homicide, if we assume that both murders are connected.'

'They have to be.'

Archie nodded. 'Yes, I can see that. But the police are involved and, assuming Dominic can connect the dots, there will be plenty of resources devoted to solving the case. Why not just sit back and let them handle it? I'm sure your client will understand.'

Nicolette frowned. She'd been debating that on her way over. The sensible thing would be to do what Archie suggested. And the last thing she needed or wanted was the police looking in her direction if she got in the way. But...

'I can't help feeling that I'm the reason Mark is dead. Think about it. How did the killer find him if not by following me to the park?'

'Oh, I don't know, by following him?'

'Right, but then why not kill him before I got there.'

Archie sipped her drink, leaving a thin dark pink moustache on her upper lip. She licked it away before answering. 'You said it yourself, there was the mother and her child when you first got there. They couldn't kill him with witnesses.'

'I was a witness.'

'But you didn't see anything. Mark was fifty metres away.'

'And why didn't I see anything?' Nicolette said in frustration. 'There are trees and bushes over there, sure, but I should have seen or heard something.'

'Okay, I understand now.'

'What?'

'You're not going to leave it alone because you'd rather drive yourself crazy with what-ifs and wonderings.'

'Is it wrong to want answers?' Nicolette shot back.

Archie just stared at her and Nicolette stood up in irritation.

'Stow the drama, Nic. It's not wrong, and much as I love you showing up on my doorstep, I know you're here because you want something, so just tell me, what can I do for you?'

Nicolette sat back down and looked guiltily at Archie. 'I do need your expertise.'

'It'll cost you.'

Nicolette mentally braced herself and gave a tiny nod.

'You and Chloe have to come around for dinner.'

'With just you?'

'And Dominic and Jemma.'

'But not Mum.'

'You can tell her she's not invited.'

To anyone else the price wouldn't have seemed excessive. But Nicolette had to think it over carefully. She didn't like being manipulated, but Archie was the best person she'd ever met where it came to computers.

'Fine,' she sighed.

'My people will call your people with the details. What do you need?' asked Archie with a triumphant expression.

She showed Archie the footage from Mark.

'Can you retrieve what's been deleted?'

Archie ran the video a few times. 'I don't know if it has been deleted.' She jumped to her feet and went back into the house. Nicolette followed her and found Archie sitting at the table. She'd plugged Nicolette's phone into her laptop and was viewing the video on the bigger screen.

She nudged the chair next to her with her toe and Nicolette sat.

'Usually if something is deleted, the video jumps or the time stamp will show missing time. This runs chronologically, it's just the image goes black for a period of time.'

'Any idea why?'

She looked amused which made Nicolette think she'd missed something obvious.

'Sometimes people look for high tech answers to something low or no tech. Watch.'

She clicked the video back to the beginning and slowed it right down. The image crept forward, then went black.

'Wait, show me that again.'

This time she saw it clearly and wondered how she'd missed it.

'The time keeps moving.'

'Exactly. I can't restore deleted footage because there is none. The image just goes blank, then after a period of time it comes back on again,' Archie said. 'I don't know how. Where was the doorbell mounted?'

Nicolette closed her eyes and tried to picture the entrance way. She opened her eyes again. 'On the wall to the right of the door.'

'These cameras generally have a wide range of vision, if you're in front of them. Notice you can't see the front door in any of the footage.'

Nicolette nodded slowly. 'So someone inside the house caused the image to black out. That makes sense. The killer knew Mark was coming and when. They waited until he went around the back, disabled the picture, then uncovered it once he'd gone.'

'But why?'

'That's easy. Mark's the IT expert. The police would think he disabled the camera, killed whoever was in the house, then reenabled the camera as he left. That's assuming they got to see the footage.'

Archie shivered. 'So he was working outside while a murderer waited inside the house to kill a woman.'

'Or she was already dead. But there's a major problem with this theory.'

Archie nodded. 'I went back, but the file only runs from 5pm the previous day. No one else approaches the house. Except, this.'

Archie went back to the beginning and they watched as a courier approached the front door with a small package. He rang the doorbell, and a short time later retreated down the path empty handed. 'Nothing else until the morning. She ran the footage of Mark appearing at the gate carrying a ladder. He disappeared from view around the side of the house.

'Which means either he lied and was the murderer all along, or the murderer had been in the house all night.'

Archie unplugged the phone and handed it back to Nicolette. 'Like I said before, you should let the police handle this. I know your work puts you in contact with some unsavoury people, but this is way worse than usual, Nic.'

Nicolette turned to watch Teddy lying peacefully in the sun.

'Did I ever tell you how I got him?'

'You know you haven't.'

'He belonged to Peter, a nice old man. He got Teddy after his wife died because he thought a young dog would keep him active. He died only a year later. Peter had told his daughter he was leaving Teddy to her, but instead his estranged son took him. He refused to hand Teddy back unless she signed over her share of the house to him. He sent her videos of him kicking Teddy and leaving him tied up in the pouring rain. Peter's daughter hired me to get him back. When I brought him to her, she said she never wanted him, she just didn't want her brother to win. She told me to dispose of him.' She looked at Archie. 'Those were her exact words, *dispose of him.*'

'Geez, Nic. That poor dog. What did you do? About the woman, because obviously...' She waved to Teddy.

'I charged her double and took Teddy home with me.'

'Why not take him to the SPCA?'

Nicolette whistled and Teddy's head shot up. He jumped to his feet and raced in to nuzzle her hand.

'I need a guarantee. I couldn't guarantee that whoever adopted him would treat him properly. But I could guarantee that I would.'

Archie watched for a moment, then said, 'And you're saying you can't guarantee that the police will do right by Mark. Like he's become one of your rescues.'

It was more than that, deeper than that, but it was close as she was prepared to admit.

'Something like that.'

Archie put a hand on her shoulder. 'You're one weird chick, Nic.'

'Yeah, well. A pot and a kettle.'

'I'm not weird, I'm eccentric. What are you going to do now?'

She'd been thinking about that. 'Find out everything I can about Kalliana Magnusson.'

'Now that I can do. Give me a couple of hours and I'll tell you her favourite type of perfume.'

Nicolette's phone buzzed. A message from Chloe.

'I've got to go. Apparently, my daughter has lost her debit card and is stuck without food in the middle of the city.'

'Sure. Ten bucks says she's found an outfit she wants and doesn't have enough money,' Archie replied with a smile.

'I am not going to take that bet.'

Archie showed her to the door, crouched to ruffle Teddy's ears, then stood and gave Nicolette a fast, strong hug.

'Thanks for helping, Veronica,' Nicolette whispered into her ear.

Archie let her go and stepped back. 'Don't start using my actual name now, Nicolette Charlotte Abigail Briggs.'

Nicolette laughed. 'Those aren't my middle names.'

'I'll text you what I find, and the date of our dinner. Bring Chloe and a good attitude.'

'One of those I can do.'

She was still smiling when she got into the car and started into the city. Archie always made her feel better. The smile slipped as she considered calling and visiting more often. Like everything else in her life, it was complicated, and unlike everything else in her life, when it came to family she was a coward. She'd always choose absence over dealing with hard feelings.

ELEVEN

Chloe was waiting on the corner of Lambton Quay and Panama Street when Nicolette and Teddy walked up.

'Where are your friends?'

'Hey, Mum.'

Nicolette studied her daughter. 'What's wrong?'

'I lost my card. Didn't you read my message?'

'Where did you lose your card? And where are your friends?'

'They're shopping.' Chloe vaguely waved towards some shops. 'I said I would catch up to them.'

Nicolette exchanged a look with Teddy. 'What do we think?'

Teddy sneezed and sat down.

'Yeah, me too. Teddy and I think you're lying.'

Chloe pressed her mouth closed and glared at her mother.

'Before you announce your innocence, you should know I checked your transactions after I parked the car. There was one a few minutes ago at Tandi's.'

Chloe's anger flared and she turned it in the direction of the store in question, across the road and down a bit.

'Let's pretend for a second that I'm not the smartest person in the world and you tell me everything while we go over to the store and get your card back from whoever stole it.'

Chloe clenched and unclenched her fists, causing Teddy to hide behind Nicolette's legs. She instantly dropped to her knees and apologised to the dog.

'Ashley, Yaswanti and I were hanging out. Then this other girl from school showed up. Kirsten. No one likes her but she's....'

'Not the sort of person you can tell that too.'

Chloe shook her head and stood up.

'She said she loved my bag and asked to see it, so I handed it over. When I got it back, it was undone, but I didn't think anything of it. You know this bag.' She held up the battered leather shoulder bag she'd had for seven years. 'It's always coming undone.'

'Which is why I've told you not to use it.'

'It's my favourite bag.'

'You have ten others in your closet.'

They crossed the street and as they approached Tandi's, a group of girls came out. Nicolette recognised Ashley and Yaswanti, which meant the third girl was Kirsten. She was a solid, light skinned girl who looked a little older than the others, and she was carrying a bag.

'Hi, girls,' Nicolette said brightly. 'Fancy seeing you here.'

'Hey Ms Briggs.'

'I was just out training Teddy when I saw Chloe.'

'He's so cute,' Yaswanti said.

She went to pat him and Nicolette stopped her.

'Sorry, he can't accept pats while he's working.'

Teddy managed to look surprised, disappointed and relieved. He was still getting comfortable in crowds, but loved pats, so there was always an internal struggle when he met new people.

'What sort of training?' asked Ashley.

'Great question,' Nicolette replied with so much enthusiasm she could actually feel her teeth hurting. 'He's going to be part of a new task force for the police focussing on pickpockets. Dogs, as I'm sure you know, have an amazing sense of smell. For example,

Teddy would get a sample from the victim, like one of you, or Chloe. Then he could track down something that person has touched.'

As she spoke, she saw out of the corner of her eye that Kirsten put her hand to her jeans pocket.

'Do you girls want to see a demonstration? Chloe can you give me your bag?'

She watched Kirsten begin to panic as she pushed Chloe's bag under Teddy's nose. He sniffed it and looked at her expectantly.

'Now I just need to give him the command and—'

'Hey, Chloe, I meant to tell you that I found your card on the ground.' Kirsten held it out and Chloe took it. 'I was going to give it back to you when you caught up to us.'

'You didn't tell me it was missing,' Nicolette said to her daughter.

'I didn't know. I swear, Mum.'

'Oh well, thank you for picking it up.' She turned to Chloe. 'We should do a quick check on your banking app to see if anyone used it. Especially if you don't know exactly when you lost it. Who knows who might have picked it up and stole something with it.'

Now there was full blown panic on Kirsten's face. Nicolette decided to wrap things up.

'On second thoughts, what are the odds that someone would have picked the card up, bought something, then dropped the card in the street for your friend to find?'

Chloe looked at her Mum.

'And if they did do that, we can always report it to the police later. Not that they'd do much about it given how under resourced they are. After all that's why I'm training Teddy.'

Chloe nodded like she was thinking carefully. 'Yeah, you're right. It's all good, I've got it back now.'

'You're right. Okay. Well, you girls have a good day. I better get on with training Teddy.'

She waved goodbye and by the time she got back to the car, Chloe had messaged "Thanks".

While she waited for Archie to come through with information on Kalliana Magnusson, Nicolette decided to stop at home and check on the other dogs.

Teddy was greeted like a long-lost friend, and only after they'd satisfied themselves with sniffing him from nose to tail did they turn their excitement on Nicolette.

As they raced around the grass, she felt some of the tension in her shoulders loosen. It was impossible to watch them play without remembering how they'd been when she'd first brought them home. Each one had experienced the very worst side of humanity and had taken a long time to be convinced that there were good people in the world too. She'd never intended to keep all of them, imagining herself as their short-term therapist, but now they were part of the family. Deep down she had known that was always going to be the case.

The family were now simultaneously squatting on different parts of the lawn. She sighed and fetched a paper towel from the kitchen, relocating the fresh deposits into the outside rubbish bin.

Back in the kitchen, her phone beeped with a message from Archie telling her to check her emails. She had sent a link to a folder in the cloud. Inside were a couple of screen shots, a document of bullet points, and a photo. Nicolette clicked on the photo first. Kalliana Magnusson was young and attractive and wore clothes straight from a fashion magazine.

She turned her attention to the document. Across the top Archie had written, 'I can only find info two years back. Fake ID? Need more time.'

Scanning the page, she saw Archie was right. Prior to 2022 there was nothing on Kalliana Magnusson. Since then there was a wide range of social media accounts, including some that Nicolette had never heard of. She did a quick google and found they were dating apps. Quite specific ones by the look of them. Nicolette hadn't been on a date for longer than she'd admit to anyone, and there'd never been an app involved.

She pulled up the social media accounts and flipped through photos of Kalliana smiling happily for the camera in a variety of places. After scrolling through them for a few minutes, Nicolette noticed a pattern. She went back and looked through them again.

They were all selfies, but they only showed Kalliana. There wasn't a single other person in any of the shots.

'Either she's the world's biggest narcissist... or the accounts are fake,' Nicolette said to the empty kitchen. 'Although these days it's the same thing.'

She went back to reading Archie's summary document.

'According to FB, KM works for the Magnusson Family Trust as a director. Prior she worked for a government agency. Nothing on education, family, etc. All photos from around Wellington.'

Nicolette went back and checked the selfies again. Sure enough, all the photos featured buildings or landscapes around Wellington city.

That told her one of two things, assuming it was a fake profile. One, that whoever created the accounts didn't have the computer skills to do a better job. (Archie could have put her into the crowd at a Queen concert from 1980). The second thing it told her was that Kalliana Magnusson – if that was her name – had been in Wellington, at least when the photos were taken. And in that case, she could be tracked down.

The latest post on Instagram was from a week ago – Kalliana on the waterfront, eating an ice cream. The caption read, "it's berry ice being in the sun".

'And now I know something else about them. Their sense of humour is from the 1950s,' Nicolette announced to Fig who had nudged through the French door and lay on the other side of the kitchen watching her.

There were only two places to get frozen yoghurt on the waterfront. Nicolette had done extensive personal research on this.

Scooping up the car keys, she ignored the hopeful looks from the dogs and drove back into the city. Luckily the garage hadn't seemed worried about recording the mileage on the loaner.

Parking was harder to find now that the local council had decided that everyone should ride a bike or catch a train, but eventually she managed to find one only a few blocks from where she wanted to go.

It was post-lunchtime but sunny, so there were still plenty of people walking and sitting and scooting along the wharf. Like a lot of other places around the city it was either being rebuilt, partially condemned, or waiting for one or the other. Nicolette stopped at the first frozen yoghurt place, by the large fountain/statue that never seemed to be going. She bought a cone and showed a picture of Kalliana to the person working behind the counter, without any luck.

She took a few bites as she watched a double scull rowing boat glide from the small lagoon, under the foot bridge and into the calm harbour. She'd given it a go once, before deciding rowing was firmly on the list of things she wasn't good at.

She finished the cone as she ambled around the corner towards the second shop. In the sixty-metre journey she had to take rapid action to avoid two scooters, three groups of runners, and a group of mothers pushing strollers and gossiping without watching where they were going. Ahead and to the right the rescue helicopter took off. She tracked its flight for a while, until she almost tripped over a dog leash, earning her an apology from the owner and a lick from the corgi.

The second frozen yoghurt place was a little hole-in-the-wall with a cheerful woman who greeted her like a long-lost friend. For a panicked moment, Nicolette thought she must come here too often. Then she realised the woman was just being friendly.

'Oh yeah, I remember her,' the woman said.

'Are you sure? You must see hundreds of people a week.'

'Yeah, but she threw away her cone without eating any of it.'

'She did?'

The woman nodded. 'She asked for a perfect cone – actually made me redo it a couple of times because she said it wasn't round enough. I wanted to tell her it wasn't going to stay round once she ate it, but the customer is always right, or so they constantly tell me. Anyway, it was pretty quiet when she came in, so I remade her "perfect cone" until she was happy with it. Then I watched her walk over to the edge of the wharf, take a couple of photos, and toss the cone straight into the bin.'

'What a waste,' Nicolette said, eyeing the enticing tubs of frozen yoghurt behind the glass display case and wondering if she could justify a second one while the first was still sliding down towards her stomach.

The woman grinned. 'You don't get into the yoghurt business without expecting a certain amount to end up on the ground, but I have to admit that one hurt.'

Nicolette stepped to the side to let a woman and her daughter order, chocolate for the daughter and black doris plum for the mum.

'Was anyone with her?' she asked.

The woman behind the counter handed over the cones and took payment before answering. 'Not when she was ordering the cone, but after she dumped it, I saw her talking to a guy.'

'What'd he look like?'

That got a shrug. 'White skin, brown hair, sorry, I wasn't paying that much attention.'

Nicolette pulled out her phone and scrolled to the photo she'd taken of Mark. 'Was it this guy?'

The woman squinted at the screen then nodded. 'That looks like him. What's this about?'

'He's my husband and she's the woman he's having an affair with. I'm trying to get proof for my lawyer.'

'Damn. My ex cheated on me and it didn't end well for him... or my sister. I hope you get what you need. Here.' She scooped a big helping of chocolate frozen yoghurt into a cup and handed it over. 'On the house.'

Nicolette's guilty feeling went away after the first spoonful.

'I tell you one thing though, if he's cheating on you, then he's cheating on her too. After she left, another woman came up, and by the way he greeted her they definitely weren't related, if you get my drift.'

'Can you remember what she looked like?'

'Blonde, full of herself. Wore workout clothes that probably never saw the inside of a gym. You know the type.'

Nicolette nodded thoughtfully, while eating more yoghurt. It was very rich and very good.

'I'd love to nail him for multiple affairs. I don't suppose you can tell me anything else about her?'

'Sorry, no. I served a customer and when I looked back they were gone.'

Nicolette thanked her and walked to the spot where Kalliana had taken the photo. She sat on the edge of the wharf and enjoyed the sunshine while she finished the rest of her yoghurt. After dumping the container in the rubbish bin nearby, she checked her phone, going through Kalliana's social media accounts again. She found a photo that looked right. She zoomed in, studying the people behind Kalliana. At the edge of the photo was a blonde woman riding an e-scooter.

She went back to the yoghurt shop and showed the image to the woman.

'Yeah, that's the other reason I remembered her. She came up on one of those e-scooters. I don't know if she left the same way.'

'Do you know what time of the day it was?'

'Around half-eleven, I think. I don't open until eleven on weekdays and it doesn't typically pick up until closer to twelve.'

'What brand scooter was she riding?'

'The purple company named after a bird.'

'Albatross.'

'Yeah, that's the one.'

Nicolette thanked her again then headed back towards her car. She knew that e-scooters all had GPS so the companies could collect and recharge them. The company would know where the scooter was on that date and time, and who had hired it.

Inside her car she googled the customer support number for Albatross E-Scooters. When a cheerful woman came onto the phone, she launched into her story.

'Last Wednesday I was walking my dog on the waterfront when I was knocked over by a woman riding one of your scooters. She didn't even bother to stop and check I was okay.'

'I'm so sorry to hear that. Liability rests with our hirers and not the company.'

'I completely understand, but because she didn't stop, I didn't get her contact details, and well my dog got spooked and ran onto the rocks and cut her paw open. She was hurt pretty bad and I'm looking at a huge vet bill that I can't afford. I'd like to contact the woman and give her the chance to apologise, and... maybe help out financially. It happened last Tuesday at 11am on Queens Wharf.' She was pleased at the level of self-righteousness she managed to put into her voice.

'I hear you. My dog ate something she shouldn't and it cost me hundreds of dollars. I can't give out a customer's name though, we have privacy policies. I could contact the customer for you. If she agrees with your version of events, then I can put the two of you in touch.'

'I understand,' Nicolette replied sadly. 'I was hoping to get this sorted quickly but you're right, there are procedures. I'm sure the school will understand.'

'The school?'

'My daughter is due to go on a once in a lifetime school trip to study wildlife in Antarctica. Her final payment is due tomorrow but with the vet bills... If she doesn't pay in full, the school will give her spot to the next person on the list. But that's not your problem, it's mine. I'm sure they'll understand.'

She held her breath and counted cars driving past.

'I'm sorry, I wish I could help but senior management would fire me if I gave out that sort of information. Perhaps you could file a police report?'

Nicolette thanked the woman and hung up. Privacy laws were all well and good, but they made her job a lot harder.

A few seconds later her phone dinged with a new message.

She read it and smiled. The woman had been swayed by her story after all. She'd sent through a name and phone number.

'Skylar Goodman. Now we're getting somewhere,' she said to the empty car. 'Dogs and kids – chuck them into a story and you can get pretty much anything.'

She resisted the temptation to immediately call the number. She needed to do some research first, especially on Mark Chaney.

It was mid-afternoon and she'd barely eaten anything, other than two frozen yoghurt, which were sitting uneasily in her stomach. She messaged Chloe to see if she wanted a lift home and got an instant "yes please".

None of her friends were old enough to drive yet and, while she was happy taking the train, Nicolette knew her daughter hated the two kilometre walk from the station to home. And given some of the tight corners and non-existent footpaths in places, Nicolette wasn't always happy to let Chloe walk.

Chloe was quiet when she got into the car, and Nicolette let her work through whatever was going on in her head.

As they were starting up Ngauranga Gorge, she finally spoke.

'Mum, why did you let Kirsten get away with the top? You knew she stole my card, and you knew she had used it. Why didn't you say anything?'

Nicolette had been waiting for this question.

'I don't know Kirsten. I don't know her background or her family situation. She could be desperate, or poor.'

'Or just trash.'

'No one is trash, Chloe. Some people make poor choices, and some are terrible people, but no one is trash. The point is I could have said something to her, and we might have got her to return whatever she bought, but we might not. The only thing we know for absolute sure is that I would have backed her into a corner and embarrassed her in front of her peers. When you embarrass someone like that, you're not just attacking them about one thing, you're attacking their whole character, and when you do that, you're not leaving them any room to change. Do you understand?'

'Sort of. You're saying by not confronting her, you were giving her a chance to not do it again.'

'Something like that.'

'But you're also letting her think she got away with it, so she might do it again.'

'That's a risk,' Nicolette replied.

'What if she does? Will you give her another chance?'

'No, people only get one shot, at least with me.'

Chloe didn't speak again until they were almost home.

'Does that one shot rule apply to me as well?'

Nicolette glanced over to her daughter who was staring straight ahead.

'You should never need to know the answer to that question. You're a good kid. A pain in the butt sometimes, but a good kid.'

Chloe grinned. 'And you're not too bad a mum. For an old lady.'

Nicolette choked. 'Who are you calling an old lady?'

'Have you looked in the mirror lately?'

'You're grounded for a week.'

'I can see some grey hairs coming through.'

'Two weeks.'

'And there are so many wrinkles on your face it's like someone is adding a new one every day.'

'Six months. And that someone is you,' Nicolette said.

'Are you saying I'm making you old?' asked Chloe.

'Let's just say the three dogs at home give me less worry than you.'

'Mum!'

They were still laughing as the car turned into the driveway. Nicolette stopped laughing when she saw the car parked there. A man leaned against it, waiting.

'Uncle Dom!'

Chloe jumped out of the car and ran up to give her uncle a hug. He kissed her on the forehead, then released her and looked at her mother.

'Are you still on the clock?'

He nodded and Nicolette told her daughter to go inside.

'Are you staying for a while?' asked Chloe.

'I need to talk to your mum first, then I'll come in for a coffee,' Dominic replied.

Nicolette waited for Chloe to go into the house before turning to her brother. 'How much trouble am I in?'

'Why do you think you're in trouble?'

She leaned against the car next to him. 'Because this is only the third time you've been here and the first two times it was to give me a lecture about a case. So... how much trouble am I in?'

She'd known him for almost twenty years. Ever since her mother had breezed into the kitchen one day and announced she was getting married again and he had a son slightly older than her and wasn't that amazing. Dominic was one of the most serious people she knew. Even his leisure activities were based around some form of competition, from his teenage years playing Dungeons and Dragons, to taking up squash at nineteen and running out of opponents because his friends quickly learned his "social" games were anything but. She also knew there were degrees to his seriousness. Right now, his expression was a three out of five.

'I'm here semi-officially. When they decide that you're a potential suspect, they won't let me be involved with that side of the investigation.'

'*When*?'

'We tracked down the woman with her kid, the one using the playground. She told us that you assaulted the victim.'

'Assaulted! It was a light tap.'

'He fell to the ground.'

'He'd stolen my dog. I got him back, so why on earth would I kill the man.'

Dominic looked around, his eyes coming to rest on the dog in question.

'You've got a reputation around Central as someone who is passionate about the welfare of animals.'

'Yes. But there's a difference between passion and murder.'

He gave her an amused expression. 'Not from my experience. Half the incidences I attend are a result of a wronged lover.'

'I didn't kill him.'

'*I* didn't say you did. But from an investigative standpoint, you always look at the last person to see the victim alive, and that's you. Someone who recently assaulted him – yes, *assaulted*,' he repeated as she was about to object. 'They will come and ask you questions, and it's most likely going to be Tyler.'

'Tyler! How does he still have a job?'

'Because he's good at what he does, Nic.'

'He's an ass.'

'I didn't say he wasn't.'

'You know, for someone who isn't saying a lot, you're saying a lot.'

He cracked a rare grin and rubbed his neck. She recognised it as a sign he was under pressure.

'Where have you been since you left the crime scene?' It sounded like a casual question, but he was never really off duty.

She told him about Chloe's stolen debit card and left it at that.

'You should have confronted her,' Dominic said. Then he sighed. 'But I know why you didn't.'

'Because I'm right.'

'I definitely didn't say that.'

'You didn't have to. You'd better come in and have a coffee or Chloe will never forgive you. She's fourteen, so she knows how to hold a grudge.'

In the kitchen Chloe had already boiled the kettle and filled the plunger with ground coffee. Three cups sat waiting on the counter.

'Uncle Dom, we're studying law at school. Have you ever testified in court?'

'Sure, a few times.'

Chloe's eyes lit up. 'Did someone object? Did a lawyer try and trick you? Were you ever told off by the judge?'

Dominic raised a hand in surrender. 'Whoa, first off it's nothing like what you see on TV. It's mostly boring, a lot of waiting around for your turn, a few questions, then you get to go.'

'Stink.'

'But rewarding.'

'Yeah, yeah.'

'Seriously, Chloe. It might not be all objections and trying to trick you into revealing damning evidence, but sitting in that chair and knowing that what I'm saying is helping convince a jury to get a criminal off the streets... It's important. The word guilty never sounds sweeter than at the end of a trial I've testified in.'

Chloe seemed happier at his response and poured their drinks.

'Is Mum in trouble?'

'Why would you ask that?'

'Because the only time you come here is when she is.'

'Are you two a double act or something?' Dominic frowned at Nicolette. 'That's something you need to talk to your mum about.'

'She won't talk about it.'

'*She* is standing right here.'

'I'm not blind.'

'No, but you might not be drinking coffee in a second either.'

'I've got homework,' Chloe replied, picking up her cup and disappearing down the hallway.

'She's getting tall,' commented Dominic.

'Yeah, well she doesn't get that from me,' Nicolette muttered. 'I saw Archie today,' she added.

'How is she?'

She gestured for him to follow her. She opened the French doors and stepped onto the small deck. When she sat down, all three dogs came to sniff the intruder. Fig gave Nicolette a sideways glance, then, deciding there was nothing to worry about, loped off after the others.

'I'm sure she was shocked by the visit,' Dominic said.

'You two make it sound like I never get in touch.'

'It doesn't take a detective to figure out you're not big on family. Or the reason why.'

Nicolette blew on her drink then took a sip. 'Now, Dom, let's not spoil a nice visit with heavy topics.'

‘I just informed you that you might be a murder suspect. You don’t think it’s already heavy?’

She shook her head. ‘That’ll never stick, even with Tyler investigating. He’d be wasting everyone’s time.’

‘Maybe. Probably. But he hates you, so don’t expect it to be pleasant.’

‘Hate’s a strong word.’

‘But accurate. Probably because you do a world class job of antagonising him every time the two of you meet. Honestly, it reminds me of the time you liked that boy at school, what was his name?’

‘Ew, I do not like Tyler Phelps. I did like Todd Mackay though, he was cute. Until I saw him throw a rock at a bird.’

‘Then you punched him in the stomach. I’m seeing a theme there.’

She smiled at the memory.

‘How’s Jamie?’ she asked.

‘She left me. A year ago.’

‘Oh. I’m sorry, Dom.’ She reached out and squeezed his arm. ‘She was nice.’

‘She said I was *emotionally distant*. I think *robot* was used several times.’

‘I never liked her.’

He offered a second rare smile and she waited for him to make a comment about staying in touch with family more. Instead Dominic sipped his drink in silence.

‘How was Kalliana Magnusson killed?’

He shook his head and smiled. ‘You know I can’t talk about an active investigation or comment on the identity of the victim. Besides, I’m not a pathologist.’

‘It doesn’t take an expert to point at a body and say, *she was shot five times*.’

'No, it doesn't. And if it were that apparent even a simple man like me would be able to figure it out.'

Nicolette scratched her head, idly thinking that she had forgotten to have a shower that morning.

'Archie conned me into a family dinner.'

Dominic looked at her in amazement. 'How on earth did she do that?'

'She's a tough negotiator.'

His eyes narrowed as he frowned. 'You're not still investigating this case, are you?'

'Which case?' she replied innocently.

'The Kal... the murder in the house.'

'Wouldn't dream of it. I just needed some IT help.'

He stared at her for a moment longer and she stared back benignly. She was thankful that Chloe chose that time to stick her head out of a window.

'Uncle Dom, can you stay for dinner?'

'Sorry, Chloe.' He drained his cup and stood up. 'I've got to get back to work. We're still on for the pre-season Phoenix game at the stadium next weekend though, right?'

'Totally.'

'What game? Why don't I know about this?'

'I told you.' Chloe withdrew her head before her mother could call her a liar.

'She didn't,' Nicolette said.

'Are you sure?'

'What's that supposed to mean?'

Dominic stood up and headed inside. 'You were never the best listener, Nic.'

'I'm a fantastic listener,' she replied, following him into the kitchen.

He made a noncommittal sound.

She scowled, which deepened when they walked out to the driveway just as an unmarked police car pulled up. Hate was too strong a word to describe her feelings towards the man who climbed out, but it was close.

Tyler Phelps was in his forties, with cropped light brown hair and a clean-shaven face. He was annoyingly good at his job, and just plain annoying at everything else.

'Detective Lister, what a surprise to see you here.'

'Just catching up with my sister.'

'Stepsister.'

'Same thing,' Dom replied.

'I just like things to be accurate,' said Phelps. 'You weren't discussing the case, I hope.'

'My *brother* knows how to do his job. It's very frustrating.'

Phelps looked at them both with narrowed eyes.

'I'm just leaving. Tyler, let's meet back at the station at 5pm and compare notes.'

That earned Dominic a curt nod.

Nicolette almost swore she got a wink as he got back into his car.

'Shall we do this inside?' Phelps gestured towards the house.

She led him in through the front door and they sat at the kitchen table, where Tyler withdrew a notebook from his suit pocket.

'Please go over the events that happened at the park this morning.'

She told him everything right up to when the police had arrived at the scene.

'And you'd never seen him before?'

'Never.'

'We have a witness who says you were aggravated when you arrived. That you assaulted the victim.'

'It was a light tap to the stomach.'

Tyle wrote that down. 'You told the witness he was your ex?'

She shrugged. 'It seemed the easiest way to divert attention.'

'Uh huh.' Phelps wrote something else down, then used the tip of his pen to scratch his head. 'So you punched him, once, then sat down and had a calm rational conversation with the victim.'

She didn't like the way he kept referring to Mark as the victim, like he was a statistic. True she didn't really know the man, but that didn't matter.

'Yes.'

'Uncle Dom, I thought you... Oh, who are you?' Chloe came the rest of the way into the room more cautiously.

'Detective Senior Sergeant Tyler Phelps. You must be Chloe.'

Chloe shot a worried look at her mother.

'I was just coming to get a snack. It can wait.' She walked back out, pausing in the doorway to gesture at the visitor with an enquiring look.

Nicolette gave a tiny head shake and her daughter disappeared from view.

'You were saying... you were angry with the victim?' Phelps continued as if the interruption hadn't occurred.

'No, I said I *had* been angry with him, but once I was sure Teddy was okay, I calmed down.'

Phelps looked at her with judging eyes and she had to stifle an urge to add assaulting a police officer to the list of her accomplishments for the day.

''Mmm, and you maintain you've never met the victim before today.'

'I don't have to maintain something if it's the truth.'

'Mmm.'

'How can I have met him before? I don't even know his name.'

Phelps leaned forward, an eager expression on his face. 'You said he told you his name.'

‘He told me *a* name. But he was cagey about it. How am I supposed to know if Mark Chaney is his real name?’

‘Any reason to believe it wasn’t his real name?’

‘He didn’t show me any ID, if that’s what you mean. And he seemed reluctant to give it.’

‘Reluctant to give his name to a woman who just attacked him unprovoked. How surprising.’

‘He stole my dog.’

‘Hardly a reason to punch someone. Oh, but that’s what you do, isn’t it?’

‘Some people don’t need much of a reason to be punched,’ she replied through gritted teeth.

His mouth twisted in a version of a smile. She knew he was getting to her, and he was enjoying it. She closed her eyes, took a deep breath. Opening her eyes, they were drawn to a short line of blue ink on his forehead from where he’d scratched his head with the pen. She felt her tension slip away.

‘Perhaps if I knew his real name, I could tell you if I’ve come across him in the past,’ she said. ‘Would that be helpful?’

Phelps pressed his lips together, then checked his notebook. ‘We still have yet to confirm the victim’s identity. He had no wallet on him.’

‘What about his car?’

‘There were no car keys on him either. We believe he may have caught an Uber or been dropped off by a friend.’

Nicolette laughed. ‘So, he impulsively took my dog then ordered an Uber?’

Phelps’ cheeks turned dark red as he slammed his notebook closed and shoved it into his pocket. ‘We are still canvassing the neighbourhood for witnesses. I don’t know what your involvement is with this, but you’ve meddled in official police investigations in the past so it wouldn’t surprise me to find you’re up to your neck in a double homicide.’ He stood up so quickly his chair scraped across the wood floor and knocked into the window with a bang. 'And if I find out your stepbrother has been feeding you information, I'll end his career.'

Nicolette shot to her feet. 'You're just jealous because he's a better detective, and person, than you'll ever be.'

A loud bark made Phelps jump.

Nicolette turned to see all three dogs standing at the door. Nero was shifting nervously and Fig barked again. Teddy looked part terrified, part angry, his ears up and teeth bared.

Phelps stepped away from the door. Then, without a word, stormed from the room.

She listened until she heard his car start and tires whip up gravel, before opening the door and reassuring the dogs.

Only then did she swear.

TWELVE

Despite Chloe's protests that it was another teacher only day, Nicolette bundled her daughter off to school the following day. Then she sat down with a cup of coffee, with the dogs in various stages of recline, from curled to sprawled around her, and started tracking down Skyler Goodman.

This proved an easy task. She was all over social media. In twenty minutes, Nicolette had built up a good picture of who Skylar Goodman was. It might not have been as deep or thorough a job as Archie could have done, but it was a start. She sat back and reviewed what she'd written down.

Skylar Goodman was originally from the United States of America, she moved to New Zealand a year ago – for love, if the public photos were to be believed, although Nicolette was sceptical. The woman was well educated, liked to put inspirational quotes about independence and strength on her Instagram feed, and was constantly working out. Although Nicolette noticed she didn't look sweaty or red faced in any of the photos.

If Nicolette even looked at a treadmill she broke into a cold sweat. Especially these days. She pulled the left leg of her sweatpants up and ran a finger along the scar that ran from just below her knee, down to the top of her ankle. Some days it looked angry, like it was reminding her she was the sole reason for its existence. Today the skin was pale and smooth and the ache that sometimes came was gone. She covered the scar back up, pushing the memory back into the vault from where it had come. No matter how hard she tried to forget, every detail of those five minutes was etched permanently in her brain.

She refocussed on her laptop screen. In all the many photos of Skylar with other people, the one person not present was Mark. Yet, according to frozen yoghurt lady, they appeared familiar.

She decided it was time to call Skylar.

Unfortunately, it went straight to voicemail. As she was urged to leave a message, Nicolette scrolled back through the photos. She left her name and number and a vague suggestion she needed to speak with Skylar about something important. Putting her phone down, she realised one of the gym related photos had a reflection in the large mirror behind Skylar. Zooming in closer she saw it was a sign. It took her brain a few moments to read the reversed letters but eventually she was able to determine it said "S&S Gym". A quick google search showed it to be a small boutique gym located in the middle of Wellington city.

Much to their disgust, she left the dogs behind again. Even her promising to bring home treats was not enough to relieve the soulful stares shot in her direction.

She wound down the window and turned up the radio as she drove, happily singing out of tune to songs that she knew half the words to. Thankfully Chloe and her great singing voice weren't in the car with her, always quick to judge and correct her when she got the words wrong, which was often.

If she had to say why she was in such a good mood, the explanation was that she liked puzzles. Specifically solving them. It was, in some small way, the reason she'd become a private detective. Then, as there was nothing puzzling in why people cheated on their spouses and that was a large part of the job, she'd quickly switched her focus to animals – lost, stolen, or hurt, people would happily pay to find out. Although she didn't always take their money. She didn't think someone should fail to get their four-legged companion back simply because they couldn't pay. Which explained her anaemic bank balance.

The S&S Gym was located on the third floor of an old office building two blocks from the waterfront. The rest of the building tenants appeared to be small businesses. The elevator opened onto a small reception area backed by a wall of glass. The clunk of weights hitting weights and the whirring of treadmills suggested fitness was being actively pursued nearby.

'Good morning. How's it going?' asked the young man behind the desk.

She returned his smile and stepped forward. 'Great thanks. Well, not really. Between you and I, my doctor tells me I have the heart of a forty-year-old.'

'Oh dear,' the man replied, his smile widening. 'And you want to shave those few years off? Well, you've come to the right place, we can get rid of those pesky extra kilos.'

Nicolette blinked, swallowed a vicious retort, and wondered whether she should have spent more time getting ready before leaving home.

'Does insulting potential customers usually work as a sales technique?' she asked politely.

'Oh, er, that is...'

'Everything alright here?'

Nicolette turned to see a big man filling the door frame of a side door.

'Oh, Steve, yes fine, just a little misunderstanding.'

Nicolette looked from the man to the sign above the door and back again. 'Are you the first or second?' When he looked confused, she added, 'S'.

He laughed, the infectious sort that had her smiling along.

'The first. Although, if you asked my partner Simon, he'd say the same. And you are?'

'Paula Jacobson.'

They shook hands and Steve gestured to the door. 'Unless you've wandered in by accident, would you like a tour of our facilities?'

'Yes please.'

He led her through the door and into one big space stretching from north to south. There were only a handful of people working out at this time of the morning.

'The changing rooms are to the left, where we have a spa and sauna as well. We don't do classes, space mainly being the issue, but we do have something most gyms don't.' He gestured to the corner of the room where a punching bag swung gently. Several sets of boxing gloves were stacked in a cabinet next to it.

'We find, especially being in the middle of the city, that a lot of people like to let off steam during the week. It's therapeutic.'

Nicolette nodded, then launched into her prepared story. 'It was actually a friend of mine that recommended the place. Skylar Goodman?'

Steve's eyes lit up and he nodded vigorously. 'Skylar, of course. She should be here shortly. She comes every morning around this time. Lovely lady.'

'Mmm,' Nicolette replied noncommittedly.

She listened as Steve showed her around, answering any questions she was asked about fitness goals.

By the time they had completed the tour and were back at reception, Skylar still hadn't shown. Nicolette didn't particularly want to sign up for a gym membership, but she was running out of questions to ask. Steve had already glanced at his watch a couple of times.

She was about to ask about bringing her own towel for the sauna when a ding announced the arrival of the elevator. The doors slid smoothly open and Skylar Goodman breezed out, clothed in workout gear, with a bag slung over her shoulder. She was late twenties with the sort of build that Nicolette might have had once in her life, pre-Chloe. Skylar wore a lot of make up for someone about to work out and clutched her phone in one hand.

The smiles of both Steve and the receptionist tripled in wattage, and Skylar returned them with her own.

'There she is, my favourite client,' Steve said in a voice that danced on the edge of creepy.

'Morning, everyone.'

'I was just telling your friend you'd be along,' Steve gestured.

Skylar's smile dimmed as she struggled to place Nicolette.

'I'm more a friend of a friend,' Nicolette said.

'Oh, right.'

The phone behind the desk rang and the receptionist picked it up.

Meanwhile, Steve promised to catch up with Skylar later, nodded when Nicolette said she'd have to think about joining, and then disappeared through the door again.

'Who's our mutual friend?' asked Skylar.

'Mark,' Nicolette said casually.

Skylar's looked puzzled. 'I know lots of Mark's,' she said.

'Tall, athletic, brown hair.'

Skylar laughed. 'You just described half the male population.'

'You met him on the wharf last week while he was talking to this woman.' She showed Skylar a picture of Kalliana.'

'Who are you?'

'A private investigator. I left a message on your voicemail for you to call me.'

'Damn it, I knew he was married.' All the colour flooded back into her cheeks as she clenched her fists.

'You can hit the bag later, first I need some info. How did you know Mark?'

'That's not the name he gave me. He said he was Grant Reed.'

'How did you meet?'

'I'm an influencer – do you know what that means?'

'Yeah, I'm thirty-three, not sixty. It means people give you free stuff for little to no return.'

'No, it means I provide great exposure to a range of companies.'

Nicolette decided to let that one slide. 'What does that have to do with meeting Grant Reed?'

'I was having major laptop issues. If I can't edit and post, it severely impacts on my livelihood. He works in IT and I hired him to fix it for me. We got to talking, which led to drinks and a couple of dates. I swear, if I knew he was married—'

'I don't know if he was married or not,' Nicolette said. 'Do you have his contact details?'

'Sure.' She dug into her back and pulled out a purse. After rummaging through it she handed over a business card for Reed Electronics.

'When was the last time you talked to him?'

'Just yesterday. We were supposed to have breakfast this morning, but he called to say he had an urgent job. We're going to meet up for a drink tonight. What's this about?'

'How about last week on the wharf? He was talking to another woman when you met him. Did he introduce her?'

'No. He said she was another client. I said hello to her and then Grant and I went for a walk.'

'Can you recall anything that she said?'

Skylar looked confused. 'Like what?'

Nicolette shrugged. 'Anything at all.'

Skylar wrinkled her nose as she thought, then her face cleared. 'Not to me, but she got a phone call as we were leaving and she was not happy about it. She basically yelled at the guy to stop calling.'

'Did she say a name?'

She started to shake her head, then stopped. 'It was weird. I don't know if it was a name or nickname or something, but she said, *Blue, I told you to leave me alone*.'

'Blue?'

'Yeah, I know, but I'm sure that's what she said. Look, if you don't work for a jealous wife, why are you investigating Grant?'

'It's part of a wider investigation.' She grabbed a pen and gym timetable from the desk and wrote down a phone number. 'I suggest you give this number a call. Detective Senior Sergeant Dominic Lister will want to speak with you.'

Skylar took the offered paper tentatively, like it was about to burst into flames. 'Do I...? Is it completely necessary for me to talk to the police?'

'Not at all. You could wait until they track you down, but in my opinion that would look way worse for you.'

'Is... Is Grant okay?'

Nicolette pressed the elevator button and the door slid open.

'You see, now that would have been my *first* question,' she said.

The doors closed on a confused Skylar.

Walking back to the car, Nicolette examined Grant's business card. There wasn't a physical address, just an email and mobile phone number, plus a website. She reflected on her conversation with Skylar. She probably could have handled it better, but people like that annoyed her. It took a certain type of ego to assume that other people would be interested enough in your opinion they would buy things just because you raved about it. It reminded her of the popular girls at school. She had not been one of them.

She didn't see the man until he grabbed her arm.

'Ms Briggs. Let's have a chat.'

She tugged her arm away, but he gripped tighter.

'Now, or I'll go to that fancy school and talk to your daughter instead.'

THIRTEEN

The first thought that went through her brain was to do what the man said. Unfortunately, her brain wasn't fast enough to stop her hand. She reached across and twisted one of his fingers. The man grunted and his grip on her arm loosened a little. So Nicolette lifted her foot and brought it down sharply on the side of his shin.

He yelped and let go.

She stepped towards him, eyes blazing and fist raised.

'Wait, wait!' He hopped back and raised his hands in surrender. 'I'm sorry, it was a stupid thing to say.'

She slowly lowered her arm, but kept her fist clenched.

Her assailant was young, tall, and slightly overweight, with glasses and a tattoo poking out from the bottom of his T-shirt sleeve.

'Damon, what the hell were you thinking?'

Damon slowly limped over to lean against her car. He rubbed his ankle. 'I thought it would be funny. I didn't know you were going to go all ninja on me.'

'Having known me for three years, you thought it would be funny to sneak up on me and threaten Chloe?'

'Hey, I would never threaten Chloe.'

'And that's the only reason you're not rolling on the ground with testicular trauma.'

He winced, then grinned. 'I've been following you for the last few minutes. At the start, I just wanted to see how long I could before you noticed. Then I thought it would be funny to grab your arm as a joke.'

'Piece of advice for you, Damon, never grab a woman. For one thing, it's assault. For another, they might not always be as gentle as me.'

'You almost broke my finger and ankle!'

'Almost.'

'Alright, fair point. What are you working on?'

'Know anything about two suspicious deaths in Wadestown yesterday?'

The grin slipped from Damon's face. He looked at her shrewdly. 'Are you mixed up in that?'

Nicolette leaned on the car beside him and considered how much to say. Recent prank aside, Damon was resourceful, intelligent and connected. He was also a journalist so there was always doubt about how off the record things were.

'On the periphery. What have you heard?'

Damon rubbed the stubble on his chin. He'd been trying for a beard for as long as she'd known him and it never grew to more than ragged wisps.

'I'm not working on it but, from what I've heard, the police are being tight-lipped about everything. They haven't even confirmed that the two homicides are related. Are they?'

'Two deaths in the same morning in the same suburb? Pretty likely, don't you think?'

Damon sighed. 'You know I love playing the question game with you, Nicolette, but how about some answers as well?'

She smiled innocently. 'I don't know what you're talking about.'

He grunted. 'Alright, the police haven't named the victims yet, but...' He looked questioningly at her and Nicolette nodded. 'Well, the rumour around the office is that they're struggling to identify one of the bodies.'

'Which one?'

He shook his head. 'Your turn.'

She showed him the business card and he took a picture of it with his phone. 'I need you to sit on this for a couple of hours first,' she said.

'Done. So, you are caught up in this. I knew it. But you don't do people. How did you get involved?'

She shrugged. It was better than trying to come up with an explanation that didn't involve admitting how broke she was.

'I hear your brother is one of the detective's. Have you talked to him?'

'A couple of times.'

Damon grinned. 'I would have loved to see that. Who ended up on the floor?'

She smacked his arm with her hand.

'Seriously though, two murders and no suspects. Be careful. If you are caught up in this, there's a dangerous person out there. Stay alive, will you?'

'Always the plan. How do you know they don't have any suspects?' asked Nicolette.

'*We are pursuing several lines of enquiry* is code for *we have no idea what the hell is going on*. It says a lot, don't you think?'

'In what way?'

'Most of the homicides we get around here are spousal or done by someone known to the victim. Usually the police are quick to reassure the public that there is no ongoing threat. In this case they don't seem to know what's happened.'

'Same here,' Nicolette muttered.

'Listen, I've got to go. Let me know when I can talk about this,' Damon said, waggling his phone.

She had just done her seatbelt up when her phone signalled a message. Her presence had been requested at the Silvermoon Retirement Village.

On the drive over, she called Dominic to warn him about the press finding out Mark's real identity and let him know what else she'd learned.

'You should tell Phelps.'

'You can do that,' she said, before hanging up.

There was a quiet police presence outside the old Downing house when Nicolette drove past, but she knew they'd be there for days going over every inch of the property.

She was let into Alice's apartment by Vanessa. The old woman was standing at the window looking through a pair of binoculars.

'The damn fence is too high,' Alice complained. 'I can't see clearly into the back yard.'

Nicolette stepped up next to her.

The fence surrounding the retirement village did a great job of maintaining the privacy of residents, and the people next door. Even at their elevated level, there was still a large chunk of the property's back section that was obscured.

'I hear yesterday was eventful.'

'How did you—?'

Alice lowered the binoculars and turned from the window. 'Hearing things second hand is not the same as first. Tell me.'

As Nicolette talked, Alice's eyes sparkled as if reliving past adventures.

When she finished talking, Alice picked up an envelope from the coffee table and handed it to her.

'What's this?'

'Full payment for your services, including bonus.'

Nicolette felt her mouth go dry. 'You're firing me?'

Alice fixed her with a stare and slowly shook her head. 'If I was firing you, you'd be getting nothing. I hired you to investigate whoever poisoned the cat, not to put your life at risk.'

'I don't think my life is at risk.'

'You were there when that man – What did you call him, Mark?'

'Yes, or possibly Grant Reed.'

'Whatever his name was. You were there when he died. Who's to say the murderer won't try and tie up loose ends?'

'You have to forgive Alice, she's prone to dramatics,' Vanessa said.

'I am not being dramatic,' Alice snapped. 'Nicolette, the fact is the nature of the job has changed and I'm not prepared to risk the wellbeing of you or your daughter.'

Nicolette switched her gaze from Alice to the envelope and back again. Part of her wanted to slip it into her pocket, say goodbye and get out as quickly as she could before the old lady changed her mind.

'I didn't complete the job though,' she said. 'I shouldn't get paid the full amount.'

Alice looked at Vanessa. 'Someone turning down money. I thought your generation never did that.'

'My *generation* isn't fuelled by materialistic things like money.'

'So I can stop paying you?'

'My generation also isn't stupid. I'll take the money,' Vanessa replied.

'I can't take money I didn't earn,' said Nicolette.

'You've more than earned it,' Alice replied. 'The nature of the investigation changed considerably, and you kept going. That deserves some compensation, don't you think? After all, if your mechanic finds something else wrong with your car you wouldn't expect him to fix it for free, would you? Just take the money, say thank you, and drink a cup of tea with me. Unless you'd prefer something stronger.'

'Tea is fine... thank you.'

While Vanessa made the tea, Alice asked uncomfortable questions.

'Do you often encounter danger in your line of work?'

'Some. It depends on the case. '

'Is that how you injured your leg?'

Nicolette's hand automatically went to her leg. 'Dog bite. She was out of her mind scared because of the way she'd been abused. She had wire wrapped around her leg. It had cut so deep I could see the bone. I thought I could calm her enough to get it off, but she was too far gone. She was crazy with pain and fear, and she latched onto my leg. Tore things that shouldn't be torn.'

'What happened to the dog?'

Nicolette rubbed her scar and focused on the bookcase behind Alice.

'What about the owner?'

Nicolette continued to stare. She noted the lack of personal items on the bookcase. Most people kept trinkets or knickknacks next to their books, reminders of travels or life in general, but Alice's had neither.

'I'm sorry,' Alice said. 'I never had much time for animals, I suppose because I never lived in one place long enough to get one. And now it doesn't seem fair to take in a life when it might become homeless anytime. Old age is a ticking timebomb.'

'Don't listen to her,' Vanessa called from the kitchen. 'She's going to be around to see my grandchildren.'

Alice snorted and Nicolette felt herself relax a little. She was still trying to get a handle on her employer... ex-employer now. At least Alice had the sense to know a pet was a long-term investment.

'How is Maddy?' she asked.

'She seems fine. Certainly, well enough to eat multiple cans of tuna every day.'

'Have you been in touch with her owner?'

Alice nodded. 'We've come to an arrangement.'

'What does that mean?'

'It means,' Vanessa said, placing mugs of tea in front of them, 'that Alice got her own way, again.'

'You're keeping her,' Nicolette guessed.

'I'm allowing her to keep visiting me, and Gladys Downing has no expectation that she will make her way home any time soon. Honestly it didn't take much, she didn't even realise the cat was missing for two days. It sounds like Maddy was more Mr Downing's cat.'

Nicolette got up and went to where the cat in question lay on the floor. The tabby started purring and nuzzled her head against Nicolette's hand. 'She seems happier.'

'What's next for you, dear? Do you have another job lined up?'

Nicolette thought of her email inbox, filled with offers for discount lingerie, the opportunity to launder Nigerian millions, and pet food discounts, but no jobs.

'I've got one or two things bubbling away.'

If Alice saw through her lie, she didn't comment. Instead they talked for a short while before Nicolette excused herself.

'If you ever need anything, you know where to find me,' were Alice's parting words.

It was only as she stepped out of the building that Nicolette realised that was what *she* usually said to clients at the end of a job. She had this niggling feeling she hadn't seen the last of the strange nonagenarian – a word Nicolette had looked up after she'd first met Alice, and which seemed too small to contain Alice's personality.

Before she reached her car, her phone rang. The number looked familiar but wasn't saved in her phone. She thought about letting it go to voicemail, but since she was recently unemployed and it might be a prospective client, she answered it instead.

'Ah, Ms Briggs. It's Simon Boland, from Wadestown Animal Centre?'

'Yes, Simon, how can I help you.'

'Actually it's me that can help you. Are you able to swing past the clinic? It would be easier to do this in person.'

Nicolette glanced back towards Alice's apartment and chewed on her bottom lip.

'Are you still there?'

'Sure,' she replied. 'I can be there in five minutes.'

'Great, see you then.'

He clicked off.

What could be the harm in hearing what he had to say, she thought.

It just proved she should never listen to her thoughts.

FOURTEEN

The Wadestown Animal Centre was located on the edge of the main shopping centre. From the front, it looked like someone had slapped a sign on an old house. The reception area was small and crowded with dogs and caged animals.

Nicolette said who she was there to see, and the receptionist made a quick call. A minute later a tall man stuck his head through the door behind the counter and beckoned to her.

She followed him down a narrow hallway to a consultation room at the back of the clinic.

He closed the door and turned, and she got a proper look at him. Simon Boland towered over her. He looked late thirties and had ragged brown hair. She looked into his blue eyes and saw he was appraising her the same way.

'You're shorter than I imagined,' he said.

Nicolette scowled and he immediately stumbled out an apology. 'I just meant, with your reputation I expected someone seven foot tall, breathing fire.'

'I can't do anything about the first part, but say anything else stupid and you'll get to see the second.'

He laughed and she grinned back.

'Fair enough. Let's start again. I'm Simon, of course, and you're Nicolette. It is a pleasure to meet you.' He held out a hand which she shook. 'After we talked, I arranged for some more tests, using the blood samples we had taken. I was concerned this might not be an isolated incident and the idea that there might be a nutcase out there deliberately poisoning cat was... Anyway, the results came back this morning. Maddy was exposed to tea tree oil.'

'Tea tree oil,' Nicolette repeated.

'And a touch of eucalyptus. They're both common ingredients in essential oils.'

'They're poisonous to cats?'

'Absolutely. And they fit the symptoms – wobbliness, drooling, respiratory distress. But there was something else there as well. I asked them to double check the results. There were definitely traces of cyanide.'

'Surely that's not common in essential oils.'

'Not at all,' Simon replied grimly.

'So, now you think she licked some essential oils? Because based on our previous conversation it sounded like there were no indications of that.'

'No. It's more likely she inhaled it. Quite a strong amount of it in my opinion.'

'Could it kill a person?'

Simon frowned as he shook his head. 'It's difficult to know. I'm not an expert, but given the difference in body weight, if it made the cat sick then it would be unlikely to kill a person. It could make them sick though. Possibly very sick, depending on how much they were exposed to.'

Nicolette leaned against the table and tried to imagine someone using essential oils as a murder weapon. No, actually it wouldn't have had to kill Kalliana. She was found in the bathroom, which is where most oil infusers go. Nicolette could imagine Kalliana lighting the infuser, then slipping into the bath. All it had to do was knock her out long enough that she'd drown. Nicolette would have to run that theory past Dominic. Assuming he would listen long enough.

'Could the cyanide have gotten into the oils by accident?'

'Cyanide does occur naturally in some foods, including the pits and seeds of some common fruits. Theoretically, apricot pits contain cyanogenic glycosides, but I think most people would notice an apricot pit floating in their oil diffuser.'

'So someone could have been poisoned by accident?'

Simon shrugged. 'I can't say one way or the other. You're better off talking to a doctor. I don't do humans, only animals.'

She thought he might be mocking her, but his face suggested not.

'Okay. You know, you could have told me all this over the phone.'

Simon grinned sheepishly. 'True, but I wasn't lying last time we spoke. You have a reputation amongst vets. I was curious to see if the reality lived up to the legend.'

'It usually doesn't in my experience.'

'No, nor in mine, but as someone who spends his days trying to make sick animals better, and seeing the fallout when I can't, I appreciate everything that you do.'

Nicolette dropped her eyes from his. Compliments were up there with humans that she didn't do well.

'Thanks,' she muttered. 'I better get going.'

'Sure, I've got a hypochondriac hamster waiting on me.' He laughed at her expression. 'To be fair, it's his human that thinks he has everything wrong under the sun, including a few things it's biologically impossible for a male hamster to suffer from.'

'Sounds complicated.'

Simon opened the door and gestured for her to lead the way into the hall. 'Being a vet is learning to manage the owners as much as the animals. If I think of anything else, I'll let you know.'

He gave her hand a firm, brief shake and by the time she was at the front door he was shepherding an old man carrying a cage through to the back.

Simon's information had been interesting, but she was no longer being paid to investigate, and everything she was learning would be found out by the police. Perhaps not as quickly, or thoroughly, but eventually. She had faith in Dominic, much less so in Tyler Phelps.

Archie called as she was driving home.

'Family dinner tonight, six-thirty at my place.'

'Tonight!'

'Don't be late.'

'What's the rush?'

'I'm not giving you the chance to think of an excuse to weasel out of it.'

'I think I'm busy tonight.'

'No, you're not. I already checked with Chloe, you're completely free. Tonight, six-thirty. Bring wine.' Archie hung up.

Nicolette didn't know what stung more – the fact that Archie was right, she had been thinking of an excuse to get out of family dinner, or that her own daughter had sold her out.

'Mum, it's not going to be that bad.'

Nicolette stared at her daughter and wondered how she could have raised such a naively optimistic child.

'You poor thing. It is going to be *that bad* and *worse*. For me. They love you.'

Chloe looked her mother in the eye and opened her car door. 'Of course they love me. I'm adorable.'

'If they love you that much, they can keep you,' Nicolette called.

Her daughter slammed the door shut. 'I'd miss the dogs too much.'

Nicolette joined her on the pavement. 'What about me?'

‘What about you?’ Chloe grinned at her sour expression.

‘And to think I birthed you.’

Chloe’s face twisted in mock disgust, and it was Nicolette’s turn to grin.

At the front door her finger hovered over the bell. She knew she was over thinking things. It was only a family dinner, and she’d survived many in the past. What was one more?

Chloe nudged her finger out of the way and pressed the bell. As they waited for the door to be opened, Chloe squeezed her hand. Her daughter knew some of why she was reluctant to spend time with her family, but not all. She wasn’t sure she understood it fully herself.

The door was flung open and a hand pulled her into the house.

‘What the hell, Archie?’

‘I couldn’t risk your flight mode kicking in,’ replied Archie as she closed the door behind them. ‘Hey Chlo.’

‘Hey Aunt V.’

‘Chlo? Aunt V? Who are you people?’

‘It’s called family, Nic, you should try it more than once every couple of years.’

Archie had dressed up for the occasion in black slacks and a colourfully patterned top. Nicolette immediately wished she’d put on her good pair of jeans.

Chloe had gone down the hall and into the lounge where a chorus of voices greeted her enthusiastically.

Archie looped her arm around Nicolette’s, obviously feeling her tension.

‘I’m sorry Nic,’ she murmured as they walked slowly towards the noise.

‘You should be, you know I dislike these things.’

‘No, I mean I’m really sorry.’

Before Nicolette could ask why, they entered the lounge. If she’d been tense before, she was now a block of granite.

'Mum invited him,' Archie whispered. 'Play nice.' Despite the smile on her face, her words were tinged with anxiety.

'Nicolette, there you are.'

'Here I am. Hello everyone.'

The greeter was sitting in the middle of the couch, from where she could dispense advice and disapproval in equal measure, sometimes in the same sentence.

Olivia Briggs was a year shy of sixty, looked five years younger, dressed ten years younger, and when it suited her, acted twenty years older. She was manipulative, sneaky, intelligent, and when it came to her daughter, perpetually disappointed.

'Hello, Mum.'

'You only call me that because you know it makes me feel old.'

'Actually, I call you that because you are my mother.'

'Drink!' Archie said. 'Let me get you a refill, Olivia.'

Olivia held up her empty glass. 'I was thinking no one would offer. Thank you, dear, just a half.'

A half of the large wine glass she handed over was roughly equal to a full standard glass. By the dull stain on her lips and the sheen to her eyes, Oliver had arrived early and started drinking immediately.

Dominic rose from the arm of the chair where he'd been perched and gave her a hug. 'We need to talk before you go,' he said in a low voice.

There were three other people in the room, not including Chloe or Nicolette. The first two were relatives – Jemma, her youngest sibling and the one Nicolette had spent the least amount of time with, since she'd arrived after Nicolette had left home, winked and tipped her glass in greeting. Her husband Nick was a relaxed man and possibly the only one she could have a decent conversation with, although his name had caused a few issues at family gatherings owing to its close proximity to her own. The last person in the room was literally the last person she had any interest in talking to, ranking somewhere next to Tyler Phelps on her least favourite people scale.

He stood up and took the three steps across the room to stand awkwardly in front of her.

'Hello, Nicolette.'

'I thought you were still in prison.'

'Er, really?'

'Maybe that was just wishful thinking. What are you doing here?'

'I was invited.'

'Nicolette, stop with the dramatics and give your brother a hug.'

'He's not my brother. Not anymore.'

Olivia made a frustrated gesture with her hand. 'Just because his father and I aren't married anymore, doesn't mean he's not family.'

'That's precisely what it means.'

Lewis smiled at Olivia. 'It's alright, I expected a cold reception. After all, we didn't part on cordial terms, did we, Nic?'

She clenched her fists and glared at the man who, after a five-year absence, could still get under her skin with a single sentence. He was two years older than her, taller, wider, smarter (at least in his mind), and definitely more arrogant. He'd always been stocky but had a leanness about him which along with his trimmed beard made him look more untrustworthy

'Nicolette, could you give me a hand in the kitchen?' Archie asked.

Grateful, yet slightly disappointed she didn't have the chance to verbally accost Lewis, she followed Archie into the kitchen. Due to the open plan nature of the house, they were only a few feet away from the others.

'What the actual hell, Veronica?!'

Archie squatted down to open the oven. She looked up at Nicolette and shrugged helplessly. 'I didn't know he was coming.

Olivia invited him. He showed up at the door five minutes before you.'

'How's it going in there?' Olivia called out.

'Dinner is almost done,' Archie replied, softly adding, 'Quick, grab a cloth and put this on the bench.'

Nicolette did as requested, inhaling the wonderful aroma as she did. Archie was a fantastic cook, taking food well beyond the lack of enthusiasm Nicolette applied to all her dishes.

Archie's specialty was lasagne, compiled using a secret recipe she'd vowed on more than one occasion to never reveal even under threat of torture.

'If people knew how to make it themselves, they'd never come and visit,' she always said.

Nicolette assumed Archie was joking, but as she glanced over to the crowded lounge she wondered if there was some truth to it.

'Has he said anything?' she asked under her breath.

'No, but from his reaction when Chloe walked in ahead of you, I don't think he knew you were coming.'

'If Mum knew, then he knew.'

'I can make an excuse for you.'

Nicolette squeezed her arm in gratitude. 'I owe you and I always pay my debts. Just don't put me next to him at the table.'

'Oh, don't worry. We don't want any knife slipping accidents,' Archie replied with a grin.

'It was one time.'

Dinner, the meal itself, was wonderful and Nicolette ate too much. Dinner, the conversation, not so much. True to her word, Archie had placed her and Lewis at opposite ends of the table and Nicolette managed to reach the end of the meal without interacting with him.

Her mother spent most of her time talking to Chloc, somchow eliciting more information from the teenager in half an hour than

Nicolette could in a week. They would be talking about that on the way home.

It was much easier engaging Dominic and Archie in small talk. They talked a bit about his broken relationship, her current contracting gig, and she told them about the newest addition to her family, Fig the dog.

Before dessert, Dominic announced he was stepping outside to have a smoke. He briefly looked at Nicolette who took the hint and said she needed some fresh air.

'You know those two things are diametrically opposed,' Lewis said.

'Shut up, Lewis,' she said irritably.

She cut off Olivia's protest by closing the sliding door.

'That went well,' Dominic said as he pulled out a vape pen. 'You managed an entire meal at the same table without killing each other.'

'I have cramp in my hand from clutching my knife too tightly,' she replied.

When he grinned, she reluctantly joined him.

'What's happening with the case?'

He breathed in deeply and let the smoke escape into the air. It smelt vaguely of strawberries. With the light spilling from inside, and the full moon sitting above them in a cloudless sky, the small backyard was dull grey rather than pitch black. As her eyes adjusted, she saw the branches in the bordering trees waving softly in the warm breeze.

'Why don't you tell me what you know,' he replied. 'I suspect it's as much if not more than what I've found.'

'I doubt that. You're a good detective.'

He shrugged, then looked over his shoulder. 'Just between us, so are you. But I'll deny ever saying that.'

'So will I.'

‘Right, so now we’ve got that out of the way, have you found out anything?’

She hesitated, wondering if she should admit how far she’d gone.

‘I think I’ve found out how Kalliana Magnusson died.’

He froze with the vape pen halfway to his mouth. ‘How?’

‘How did she die or how did I find out?’

‘Both. Either.’

‘Cyanide in her essential oiler diffuser.’

His expression told her he knew this already. And she’d hit the nail on the head.

‘Officially, she drowned in the bath. But she had high levels of cyanide in her system. Cyanide gas is extremely dangerous. While the pathologist hasn’t officially ruled on cause of death, I’m leaning towards that. We’re testing the contents of the bathroom, but the diffuser makes sense. How did you figure it out?’

‘Cat.’ She explained the conversation with the vet.

‘Strange that the cat survived, but the victim didn’t.’

‘I’ve been thinking about that. I wonder if the cat was a guinea pig.’

‘How?’ Dominic said. ‘Oh, you mean they tried the method out on the cat first to see if it would work.’

Nicolette nodded. ‘A lower dose, but yeah. That was stupid because animals and humans have different physiology so there was no guarantee that even if it worked on Maddy it would work on Kalliana.’

‘Maddy being the cat?’

‘Obviously. Did you find one in the bathroom?’

‘A cat?’

‘Keep up, Dommy, an oil diffuser.’

‘I know I’m in trouble when you call me Dommy,’ he said with a mock wince. ‘Yes, there was one in the bathroom.’

She saw concern cross his face.

‘You need to be careful here, Nic. Tyler Phelps would love to pin something on you for one of the murders. He’s never going to forgive you for the Garfield murder.’

‘I wasn’t the one that screwed it up.’

‘No, but you humiliated him in court. My point is if you know more than you should he’s going to try to use that against you.’

‘I’m not worried about Tyler Phelps. Besides, if I can help you solve the case first then it’ll benefit your career, right?’

‘I suppose. Wait, are you the reason I got a call from Skylar Goodman today?’

‘You’re welcome.’

‘Nicolette, if you’re keeping information about this case from me...’

‘Have you seen the doorbell video?’

‘We’re still trying to get access to it. The Trust handed over the password to the account for the other cameras but that one wasn’t on it.’

‘Grant told me that it was because they wanted him to answer the door if they weren’t at home. Here, take a look at this.’

Dominic was furious when she showed him the footage.

‘You should have given this to me straight away.’

His anger was undermined by the smell of strawberries on his breath, and she struggled not to smile.

‘I know, but in my defence, I expected you to have it already.’

‘Nic—’

‘What about the picture cutting out? Archie says it looks like something was covering the camera.’

Even in the dim light she could see his face turning redder. ‘You showed this to Archie?’

‘Of course, now I’ve been thinking about it. There was a black box attached to the wall above the camera. Maybe that had something to do with it.’

He took several deep breaths with the vape and when he finally replied his voice was calm. She wasn't fooled. Calm could be at either end of the anger scale for him and if she could see his face more clearly she no doubt would see the lines around his eyes indicating he was not happy.

'There was a device above the camera, it looked homemade, but we tested it. Essentially it was like a rat trap on a timer. When the timer ran out, the trap snapped down, blocking the camera. We haven't figured out what it was for, but this makes sense. It was installed to cover the camera. But why did it go off after Grant arrived?'

Nicolette didn't know the answer, but she had a theory. She just didn't know if he would want to hear it.

Dominic sighed. 'Spit it out Nic.'

'What if he meant to cover the camera so no one saw him arrive or leave, but something went wrong, and the device didn't operate straight away.'

He took two more puffs, then put his vape away. 'Perhaps. We'll never know for sure since the owner of the house, and Grant Reed are both dead. But if that's the case, then he just moved up to the top of the suspect list.'

Nicolette shook her head. 'That doesn't make sense. Why not just destroy the footage? And why go to all the bother of stealing Teddy, just to show me the video.'

'He must have known the police would find it eventually, maybe he was hoping you'd believe his innocence and help persuade the police.'

'It just doesn't seem right,' Nicolette replied with a frown.

'Nicolette, it's bad enough you've hidden important evidence from the police, now you want me to dismiss a perfectly good theory because it doesn't feel right.'

'Oh look, I think it's time for dessert.'

He grabbed her arm as she tried to step past. 'Stay out of the investigation.'

'Of course.'

His bitter laughter followed her inside. As she walked into the lounge she immediately saw someone was missing. She assumed a bathroom trip but as Archie handed her a bowl of Apple Crumble she said, 'Lewis had to leave, so you can relax.'

Nicolette couldn't help feeling relieved as she enthusiastically took a big spoonful of dessert.

She almost managed to get through the rest of the evening without being cornered by her mother, but just when she thought she was free and clear, she found Olivia waiting for her outside the bathroom door.

'Hello, dear, I thought we should have a chat before you sneak away.'

'I wasn't planning on sneaking away.'

Olivia gave her a perceptive look. 'You've been planning how to leave since you got here, Nicolette.'

'That's not true. Technically I'd already planned how to escape before I arrived.'

Olivia sighed as she leaned against the opposite wall.

'It pains me when you use words like escape to describe a simple dinner with family.'

'It would have been much simpler if you hadn't invited Lewis.'

'He's your brother.'

'He's your ex-husband's ex-wife's son.'

'He's family. And he very much wanted to talk to you.'

'Why?'

Olivia sighed with exaggerated frustration. 'Perhaps he wanted to say sorry. If you'd given him a chance he might have told you himself. You should consider taking that chip off your shoulder and giving him a minute or two of your time. After all, he is family.'

‘He’s one step above the pizza delivery guy. And we never got on, which you knew before inviting him. Plus, you know what he did five years ago. That was Chloe’s money. She almost didn’t get to go to St Mary’s because of that.’

‘He made a mistake, for which he has paid his price to society.’

‘But not to me,’ Nicolette snapped.

Olivia’s eyes narrowed briefly and Nicolette recognised there was about to be an abrupt change in conversational direction.

‘I don’t see enough of my granddaughter.’

‘You’ll need to talk to her about that.’

‘You’re her mother.’

Nicolette was too experienced to fall for the disappointment accompanying the words.

‘Chloe is smart enough to make good choices.’

Olivia pounced. ‘Are you saying staying away from me is a bad choice?’

In a proverbial case of being saved by the bell, Nicolette’s phone rang. Her relief turned to concern when she saw who it was.

‘Hey, Brooke, what’s up?’

‘Sorry to bother you, hon,’ her neighbour said. ‘It’s your dogs. They’re making such a racket.’

There was a sliding sound and suddenly she could hear them. She recognised at least two of the three were barking at the top of their lungs.

The sliding sound muted her dogs and Brooke was back. ‘It’s unusual behaviour for them. I sent Barry over with his torch to check on them, but he said he couldn’t see anything. Did you want us to use our key?’

Brooke and Barry were the best neighbours Nicolette could have asked for. Retired, they were always available at short notice to feed the dogs, and on occasion to feed Chloe, if Nicolette was stuck somewhere on a case.

'No, it's okay, I'm not far away. I'll come home now. Be there as soon as I can.'

'Are you sure?'

Nicolette pushed past her mother and walked quickly to the lounge. She beckoned for Chloe, then changed her mind and waved to Archie instead.

'No, it's fine really. I'm glad you called. Fig is still getting settled and I don't know how she'll react if something's upset her. Better if I come home and check on her. Thanks, Brooke.'

She hung up and grabbed her jacket from the back of the sofa.

'What is it, Mum?'

'Nothing, I just have to run home for a bit, but you can stay here with Arc... with *Aunt V* until I get back.'

'Why?'

Nicolette smiled reassuringly. 'It's nothing, honey.'

Chloe stubbornly followed her to the front door. 'You only call me honey when you're trying to reassure me. Is it the dogs?'

'What makes you say that?'

'Everyone else you care about it is here.'

Nicolette kissed her daughter's forehead. 'Don't read too much into things. I'll be back in an hour.'

'Come on,' Dominic said, pushing past Chloe and struggling into his jacket. 'I'll drive.'

'I don't need a ride. I have a car,' Nicolette replied.

'Mine's better,' he called from the front door.

'Why does he get to go, and I don't?'

Nicolette swung her head from her brother to daughter and back, rapidly feeling control slipping from her fingertips.

'Mum, why—'

'Enough!'

Chloe recoiled, her mouth dropping open in surprise.

'Come back in, Chloe,' Archie said. 'I'll break out the chocolate.' She took Chloe gently by the arm and lead her towards the lounge.

Nicolette paused for a moment, torn between rushing inside to apologise, and the urgency of the problem at home. She decided she could apologise later. The unknown situation with the dogs concerned her more than Chloe's hurt feelings. Because Brooke was right, the dogs never barked like that.

FIFTEEN

Dominic had the car warming up when Nicolette slid into the passenger seat.

'You're going to pay for that later,' he said.

'She'll get over it.'

'If I know my niece, not for a long time.'

'Just go.'

He eased away from the curb. 'Want to tell me what's going on?'

'I don't know. My neighbour called to say the dogs were going berserk. I could hear them from her place.'

'I'm guessing that's not normal.'

'No, but Fig is new, so maybe she got spooked and set the other two off.'

'But you don't believe that.'

'I don't know,' she repeated. What she did know was her hand was clamped to her right leg to prevent it jiggling up and down.

'You didn't have to come,' she said.

'No, but I took an oath.'

'I didn't know the police had an oath.'

'Not when I became a cop. When I became a big brother.'

In the dim light she saw the grin on his face. A nervous laugh escaped her mouth, and her hand relaxed its death grip.

As they got closer to home, Dominic asked, 'On a scale of one to ten, how certain are you we're about to walk into something?'

She didn't reply. She didn't want to admit she might be overreacting. When it came to her dogs – and her family – she knew she didn't always think rationally.

'What I'm essentially asking is should I be calling for the Armed Offenders Squad or has one of the dog's lost their favourite chew toy?'

'I can say I don't know again if it'll make you feel better.'

'I'm not asking what you know, I'm asking what you feel.'

She shifted her shoulders sideways so she could look at him clearly. 'I thought cops worked with logic rather than instinct.'

'Good cops work with whatever they need to solve a case.'

She watched him watching the road and forced her mind away from home. Dom had always been the logical one in the family, preferring facts to conjecture. Growing up, there wasn't a problem he couldn't solve by applying logic to it. On more than one occasion she'd teased him about being like a pointy-eared Vulcan, but it was said with affection, and because she knew it irritated him.

'Thank you for coming with me,' she said.

'Any time.'

'I'm sorry about you and Jamie. I liked her.'

'And I loved her. But there you go.'

'No AOS, but approach with caution.'

He risked a glance towards her before focussing back on the road.

'They don't bark. Not like that.'

'Ever?'

'Never. I think it's the insecurity of having been abandoned. They don't want to make a fuss in case they get dumped again.'

'That's not a nice way to live.'

'It's better than the alternative,' she muttered.

'Alright,' was all he said.

When they were fifty metres from her driveway, Dominic slowed right down and turned off the headlights. Nicolette widened her eyes to help them adjust to the darkness outside the car. Streetlights were few along the road to her house. They turned into the driveway and she waited for the sensor security light to click on. When it didn't, her anxiety ramped up. The tires crunched on the gravel and it was only as the car stopped that she realised she could only hear the tires because there was no barking coming from the house.

She was out of the car and halfway to the front door before Dominic's feet touched the ground.

'Nic! Wait.'

She ignored him, pulling her front door keys out of her pocket. In the dim light she saw that the door was already open a crack.

Dominic came up and placed his hand on her shoulder.

'I go first. Stay close though in case the dogs are aggressive,' he whispered.

Without waiting for a reply, he nudged the door open with his foot. A flare of light split the darkness in the hallway. Nicolette flinched, then realised Dominic was carrying a torch. He swung the light into every room they passed before continuing towards the kitchen.

The house felt cold and still. With every step, Nicolette's sense of dread increased.

'This is taking too long.' She pushed past him. 'Fig, Teddy, Nero?'

'Nic!'

She shook off his hand and stepped into the kitchen. Between the torch and the moon there was enough light to see that the room was empty.

She called for the dogs again.

A soft whimper came from behind the kitchen counter. She raced across the room.

Without the torch light to help it looked like one big blob of dog on the floor.

Then the overhead lights flicked on and she blinked rapidly to adjust her eyes.

The blob sharpened into two dogs curled up tightly in a ball. Teddy whined.

Nicolette dropped to her knees.

'It's okay boy.' She stretched her hand out and let him sniff it, before she gently stroked his head. He whined again, his ears flat against his head.

'Nero?'

Nero slowly raised his head and looked at her with soft, pain-filled eyes.

She couldn't see any blood. As she gently coaxed Nero to stand, he looked past her shoulder and cowered away. She turned to see Dominic standing in the doorway.

Understanding immediately, he stepped out of sight.

'Fig isn't here.'

'I'll check.'

This time Nero got to his feet, swaying slightly. He kept his left paw off the ground and yelped when she lightly touched it.

'What happened here, Teddy?'

Teddy whined once more, and that was all she needed. Between the front door being open and Nero injured, it was clear someone had broken in. Nero had been hurt in the process. But where was Fig?

Her heart and mind were torn between the injured dog in front of her and the dog that was missing. Quickly she dragged her mind to practical matters.

First, Nero needed an x-ray and probably some painkillers.

She pulled her phone from her jeans pocket and dialled the after-hours vet. She had most of the local veterinary clinic numbers saved in her phone.

Struggling to keep the rising panic under control, she gave a brief explanation and the calm voice on the other end told her they would be waiting.

'Nic?'

She jumped and almost dropped the phone. When she looked around, she saw Dominic had stayed in the hallway, out of Nero's sight. In that split second, she appreciated her brother more than any other time in her life.

'It's okay, baby, I'll be right back,' she murmured to Nero.

She stopped at the edge of the counter so the dog could still see her while she talked.

'The French doors were ajar. I've called it in. A patrol car will be here shortly.'

'Call them off.'

'What?'

She started to snap, then took a deep breath and smiled at her dogs as she said, 'They've been traumatised enough. I have to take Nero to the vet and I'm not leaving Teddy here with strangers in the house. He won't cope.'

As if he'd expected her to say something like that, Dominic agreed to call them back.

'Fig isn't in the backyard,' he said once he'd hung up. 'Is there any place she might go if she was scared?'

'Yes, to me. And I wasn't here,' Nicolette said bitterly. 'I was at a stupid family dinner.'

'Have you ever left the dogs alone during the day?'

'Yes, of course I have.'

'Then start using that brain of yours for something other than beating yourself up.'

She rounded on him, furious at his calm tone and sensible words.

'Go and call Fig,' he said before she could launch into a tirade. 'She doesn't know my voice, but if she's within hearing, she'll come to you.'

She stood frozen, hands clenched, her blood flipping between ice cold and red hot. He made sense but she didn't need sense. Someone broke into her house, assaulted one of her dogs, maybe took another. She needed a target and Dominic was right there.

'Bartholomew,' Dominic said.

She blinked in surprise. Then her anger slipped away.

'Bartholomew,' she repeated.

'Be angry once it's done.'

Nicolette nodded, then turned to the dogs. 'I'll be right back, guys. Stay here.'

She crossed to the French doors and stepped onto the deck. 'Fig!'

Nothing.

She called again, louder this time.

Again nothing.

Just as she was about to walk across the lawn to the fence line, there was a single urgent bark.

'Fig,' she called once more.

A small figure streaked across the grass and threw itself at her. She stooped and oompahed as twelve kilograms of lean dog cannoned into her stomach.

She grabbed Fig as the wriggling dog licked her face.

'Good girl, good girl,' Nicolette said over and over as she carried Fig inside the house.

'Nic,' Dominic said when he saw them. 'Look at her mouth.'

Nicolette put Fig onto the ground and knelt down. Fig leant against her as she examined the dog's mouth. There was something sticking out of it and Nicolette carefully pulled it free. It was a shred of torn black material. She showed it to Dominic.

'Looks like she bit the intruder,' he commented.

'Clever girl,' Nicolette said as she ruffled her ears. Fig's tail wagged so hard her whole back quarters moved.

'Do you want me to stay with the other two while you take Nero to the vet?'

'No, they can all come.'

'Nic, be practical, the vet won't want three dogs in the room.'

'I can't leave them alone.'

'Then I'll get the patrol car to come while you're all gone.'

She shook her head. 'I know the statistics. Even if they come the chances of finding the person who did it are slim.'

'Nic, we do what we can with—'

She squeezed his arm. 'It wasn't a dig, Dom. Just a fact. Besides I'm the only one who can tell if anything is missing.'

'Okay, but having three dogs at the vet is going to be chaotic. I'll stay,' he repeated.

She hesitated. He was right, she'd need to focus on Nero and the other two would be a distraction.

'Okay,' she said reluctantly. 'Teddy likes scratches behind the left ear, not the right, and Fig will watch how you treat Teddy before deciding whether to trust you or not. Call me if you find anything when you're snooping around the house.'

'Will do.'

She stood up. 'You're not even going to deny it?'

He shrugged as she held out her hand and he gave her the car keys.

'If it makes you feel better, I have no interest in what you have hidden under your pillow.'

She smiled briefly. 'It's your niece you have to worry about. I pity the person who tells her they've searched her room. I have to leave her clean clothes at the door.'

Dominic held up his hand. 'I solemnly swear not to invade her fourteen-year-old space.'

Nicolette picked up Nero and swore.

'What?'

'My fourteen-year-old is going to be fifteen in three days. I forgot. I haven't even got her a present yet.'

She started towards the door, then paused again. 'And I have to pick up my car tomorrow morning.'

'Maybe you should worry about all that tomorrow,' Dominic said.

'I'm a woman, I can worry about multiple things at one time.'

As she laid Nero on the back seat of Dominic's car, she knew she'd been thinking about day-to-day things to distract herself. Only it wasn't working.

She drove as quickly and safely as she could to the after-hours vet clinic at the bottom of Ngauranga Gorge. They knew her well there, as her work often involved bringing in injured animals in the middle of the night. The parking lot only had one other car and she was relieved to find the waiting room empty when she came through the front door. The receptionist took her straight into an examination room where Nicolette gently lay Nero on the table. He whined and licked her hand before looking anxiously around the small space.

She opened her mouth to reassure him, but the door opened before she could.

'Well, this is unexpected.'

Nicolette stared at the tall vet crowding the door frame.

'You work here too?'

'Not as a rule,' Simon said, his eyes firmly on Nero. 'They're short at the moment, so I'm helping out. What happened?'

'I don't know for sure, but I think he's been kicked.'

Simon looked at her sharply. 'You don't know?'

'Someone broke into my home while I was out. I came home to find one dog missing, one traumatised and one injured.'

He turned his attention back to Nero, gently probing at his leg and making soothing sounds every time the dog flinched.

‘Did you find the missing one?’

‘Yes, thankfully. My brother stayed home with the other two while I’m here.’

Simon examined Nero in silence, then straightened up, drumming the table thoughtfully with his fingers. ‘I’ll need to do an x-ray, but I don’t think there’s a break.’

Nicolette felt a tiny knot ease at the base of her neck.

‘I’d like to keep him here overnight, just to—.’

‘No.’

He blinked in surprise.

‘Nero was mistreated by his previous owner. It’s taken me months to get him to trust me and I’m not letting him think I’ve abandoned him. Unless there’s an essential medical reason to keep him here, I’m taking him home.’

Simon gave her an approving look. ‘I’ll give him something for the pain tonight, then you’ll need to bring him to my clinic tomorrow for a follow up.’

‘Thanks.’

‘I’ll be right back.’

She stroked Nero’s head and he rolled onto his side so she could scratch his stomach.

‘There’s nothing too major wrong with you, is there?’ she said with a smile.

Her phone pinged. Chloe wanted to know what was going on. And wanted to be picked up. Immediately. There was an emoji filled message which Nicolette didn’t fully understand, but the lack of smiling faces and dancing emojis told her it wasn’t meant to convey happiness.

Nicolette sent back a message promising she’d be there soon.

That’s not fast enough.

Slipping her phone away, she thought about the intruder. Was it safe for Chloe to be in the house? Maybe Archie could take her for the night.

As she struggled with that dilemma, Simon returned with a syringe which he injected into Nero.

'It might make him tired but it's just a mild painkiller. It doesn't seem like he's in a lot of pain.'

'He's been through worse,' Nicolette said.

Simon nodded. 'I looked him up while I was out the back. This is *the* Nero. Rumour has it you walked into a house filled with gang members and took him.'

'Don't believe everything you hear,' she replied. 'There were only three people in the house, and it was more a negotiation than anything.'

'You negotiated with three gang members to turn over their dog?' Simon repeated.

'You can negotiate with anyone if you have the right bargaining tools.'

'What did you have to bargain with?'

'I have to pick my daughter up.'

Taking the hint, Simon quickly x-rayed the leg, confirming there was no break. At the door Nicolette turned and said, 'thank you, Simon I appreciate your help. I'll see you tomorrow.'

By the time she loaded Nero into the car, Chloe had messaged five more times, with increasing levels of urgency.

Nicolette managed to get green lights on the few traffic lights, and there weren't many cars on the road, so she made it to Archie's house after only six more messages from Chloe. She parked and had barely turned off the engine when the passenger door was flung open and Chloe threw herself inside.

'You know there's laws against child abandonment.'

'Watch your tone. Frightened dog in the back.'

Chloe swung round in her seat and peered into the backseat. 'Nero, baby, why are you here?'

'Careful, he has a sore leg.'

'What happened!'

‘Let me go in and say goodbye to Archie first, then I’ll explain.’

She left Chloe telling Nero what an amazing dog he was and walked to the front door where Archie was waiting.

‘My niece can be melodramatic.’

‘Yes, she can.’

Archie smiled, then glanced over her shoulder before pulling the front door closed behind her.

‘Personally, I don’t blame her for rushing out of here. Mum was getting incredibly awkward with her questions. She seems to have Chloe’s entire future planned out.’

‘Thanks for looking after her.’

‘That’s what families are for. That and embarrassing teenagers. Is everything okay? Where’s Dom?’

‘Can I tell you later? It’s been a long day and I’m pretty tired.’

Archie squeezed her arm. ‘Of course. Now get out of here before our mother figures out you’ve returned and tells you of her plan to marry Chloe off to a rocket scientist.’

‘I... a what?’

‘Veronica? Who’s at the door?’

‘Go,’ Archie urged her, before re-entering the house.

Nicolette walked briskly down the path and climbed into the car.

‘Do up your seatbelt.’

‘What’s wrong with Nero? He’s acting dopey.’

Nicolette ensured they were safely away from the house before answering. ‘There was a break-in at home. Nothing was taken, but Nero was hurt.’

‘Someone broke into our house,’ Chloe said.

‘Yes. Uncle Dominic is there now checking it out.’

When Chloe didn’t reply, she risked a glance over. In the dim glow of passing streetlights, she could see her daughter looked upset.

‘Talk to me, Chloe.’

Chloe continued to stare out the window.

'On a scale of one to ten where are we?'

Chloe took a deep breath before replying. 'Seven.'

'Okay, seven on the freak out meter is pretty good.'

'Is it safe to go home?'

'I think so. No one will break in while your bad-arse mum is there.'

'I'm serious.'

'So am I. Listen to me, if anyone tries to get in the dogs will alert us. If anyone actually gets in, the baseball bat next to my bed will make sure they get carried out.'

'Mum!'

She reached over and grabbed Chloe's hand. 'Listen to me, I didn't take up martial arts because I liked the outfits, okay. I did it because you are the most precious thing in the entire world and if someone or something threatened you, then I wanted to be able to inflict the most pain possible in the easiest way.'

'Where were you when I got detention?'

Nicolette squeezed the hand and let go. 'Teachers are not a threat.'

'You've never met Mrs Ferguson,' Chloe shot back.

'I have met Mrs Ferguson and she's lovely.'

Chloe making jokes was a good sign. Her daughter was pretty resilient and, providing Dominic had not invaded her bedroom, she'd be alright.

When they got home, Chloe paused long enough to make a fuss over Teddy and Fig before disappearing into her room and closing the door.

Nicolette noted that Teddy lay next to Dominic, on the couch.

'He's not allowed up there,' she said.

Teddy looked at her and yawned.

'Look, it took him twenty minutes to just come and sit next to me. You want him down, you move him.'

Instead, she put some food in a bowl for Nero, then flopped into the chair opposite her traitor dog and brother.

'Find anything?' she asked.

'Yes, you're out of plastic bags.'

'We don't use plastic bags. They're bad for the environment, according to my teenage eco warrior.'

'They might be bad for the environment, but they're great for storing evidence.'

Tiredness forgotten, she leaned forward in her chair. 'What did you find?'

He shifted Teddy's head from his leg and shuffled forward to narrow the gap between them. From his jacket pocket he pulled out a small white envelope. Opening the flap, he showed her inside.

Nicolette, was hoping for a business card or something similar with the intruder's name and address on it. She was disappointed to see a small scrap of cloth.

'Not exactly a smoking gun.'

A flicker of frustration crossed his face. 'I found it caught on a nail sticking out of the wall by your front door. Whoever broke in obviously caught themselves on it. It matches the piece Fig had in her mouth. Unless it was you or Chloe that caught themselves.'

She shook her head. 'We both know it's there, so we avoid it.'

He sighed in frustration. 'If you know it's there, why don't you fix it?'

'Then how would we obtain crucial evidence like this?'

'Nic, all it would take is a couple whacks with a hammer.'

'I'm more worried about keeping a roof over our heads than a nail in the wall.'

Dominic frowned at her.

'Figuratively,' she added.

'Anyway, there might be some evidence on it, there's a dark stain which could be blood. I can't get the lab to analyse it, not without an active case to assign it to, but based on the height of the nail, I'd say you're looking for someone with a deep scratch on their left leg, just above the knee.'

Nicolette sat back and closed her eyes.

'You know who was wearing dark coloured pants. And who left the dinner party early.'

He looked at her blankly, then comprehension dawned. 'Lewis? You think Lewis broke into your place? Why?'

Her eyes still closed, Nicolette tried and failed to come up with a logical motive.

'He blames me for ending up in prison.'

'You didn't even testify against him.'

'I don't know then. If not him who? Can you run it against the Magnusson case?'

He pursed his lips. 'There's no direct connection – sorry, I should say there's no apparent connection. I'm already under the spotlight on this one, without running a piece of evidence I can't prove came from the crime scene. I'll hold on to it until we need it.'

Nicolette shrugged. The truth was without anyone to compare it to there was nothing to be gained from analysing it.

'I'll run you back to Archie's,' she said, climbing slowly to her feet.

'No need, she's on her way here with your car. I'll drop her home.'

'How? I've got my keys.'

'In the rush to get back here you left your jacket at her house, with your car keys in a pocket. I guess your house key isn't on the same ring.'

She blinked a few times, then collapsed back into her chair. 'Oh right. It's been a busy day, sorry.'

'No need to apologise, it has been a long couple of days. Wellington still doesn't get a large number of homicides, and to have two in the same day, possibly connected, has some of the brass nervous.'

He stood up and rolled his shoulders.

'I'll wait outside.'

'You don't have to.'

'No, but you need to get some sleep and I need to wake up and standing outside in the cold will do that.'

He paused in the hall to yell goodnight to Chloe, who yelled back. Then he paused on the front doorstep.

'I wasn't sure you'd remember Bartholomew.'

'Are you kidding? Bartholomew is the only reason I wasn't thrown in prison.'

'They don't throw fourteen-year-olds in prison, Nic. Not for beating up a bully. Or for getting beaten up by a bully.'

'Come on,' she protested. 'I could easily have taken that kid.'

'That kid was three years older, taller, wider, stronger. He could have sent you to hospital.'

She shrugged. 'I guess we'll never know.'

Dominic grinned at her. 'Oh, we know. The only one in denial is you.'

'Watch it, I might come across as sweet and innocent, but I could still kick your arse.'

'I have no doubt, but don't delude yourself. You come across as many things, but sweet and innocent are not on the list.'

She shut the door on his laughter.

'Who's Bartholomew?'

She jumped and whirled around, quickly masking her face when she saw Chloe.

'Sorry, Mum, I didn't mean to scare you.'

'Oh honey, you've been scaring me since I found out how smart you are,' she replied lightly.

'So, who is he?'

'Bartholomew is... a story for another time.'

'Was he an ex-boyfriend?'

'Most definitely not. Have you brushed your teeth?'

Chloe rolled her eyes and disappeared into the bathroom.

She stayed by the front door until she heard a car pull up, a door slam, and the car leave again. Only then did she walk slowly down the hallway to the lounge, where the three dogs were curled up next to each other.

Nicolette had heard the hero say in movies that there were no such things as coincidences, usually when they were trying to explain away a plot hole. She didn't subscribe to that, of course there were coincidences, but there were also facts. She'd been living in this house for almost fourteen years and not once in that time had there been a break-in, or vandalism, or anything along those lines. Until now.

Coincidence or not, the timing was suspicious. And if there was one thing Nicolette was good with, it was suspiciousness.

She let the dogs out and stood on the deck while they did their business. Fig normally raced around the lawn finding new and exciting smells, but tonight she stuck close to Nicolette.

Back inside she checked the doors and windows, then went to bed.

Two hours of wrestling with her over-stimulated brain later, she got up.

Leaving the lights off she paused at Chloe's door where she heard the soft sound of deep sleep, before continuing down to the lounge. She wrapped a blanket around herself and sat on the couch, Teddy one side, Fig the other, and Nero at her feet.

'Release the hounds,' she murmured before finally drifting off to sleep.

SIXTEEN

The next morning while she waited for Chloe to get ready for school, Nicolette wrote down everything she knew (or thought she knew) about the Maddy-Kalliana case. Using a piece of paper snagged from the printer, she drew a diagram showing everyone she'd met and how they connected to each other. There were plenty of blank spaces left on the page, but it was a start.

Nero was still sleeping. He'd managed to limp outside first thing that morning, and even half-heartedly chased after the other two, so Nicolette was feeling better about his injury.

Staring moodily at the paper she found herself turning over the question that had been bothering her all night. Why would someone break into her house? Were they expecting her to be there? Or were they hoping she wouldn't be?

Chloe clattered into the kitchen and slid a white envelope along the table.

'What's this?'

'Open it,' Chloe said, looking uncharacteristically nervous.

Nicolette picked up the envelope and lifted the flap to peer inside.

'What's this?' she repeated.

'Grandma gave me some money for my birthday.'

'And you thought you'd flaunt your newfound wealth?'

'It's two hundred dollars.'

Nicolette frowned. Her mother had always been generous when it came to Chloe, too generous. 'I hope you said thank you.'

'I want you to have it.'

'It's not my birthday.'

'Mum! I know things are tight. Put it towards the bills.'

Nicolette thrust the envelope towards her daughter. 'Nope.'

'Mum!'

'Chloe! We'll manage, we always do. I am not going to take your birthday present money. Can you imagine the whole new range of disapproving looks your grandmother would develop?'

Chloe reluctantly took the envelope back. 'I'll buy you a pair of jeans then, yours are getting holes in them.'

'Isn't that fashionable?'

'Not for old people like you.'

'Hey, I was putting holes in my clothes long before you were born.'

'Gross.'

Nicolette stood up and gave her daughter a hug. She was so proud of the young woman she'd made, even if Chloe reminded her of herself a little too much sometimes.

'Seriously kiddo, we will be fine. Money is my problem.' She released Chloe and looked into her eyes. 'Your problem is that big zit forming in the middle of your forehead.'

'Mum!'

'I mean, are you growing a unicorn horn or what?'

'Alright, when I do get money, you aren't getting any of it. I'll wave at you as I'm driving past in my limousine.'

'That's my girl.'

Chloe stepped back, then hesitated.

'Spit it out.'

'Okay, firstly, gross. Secondly, I was just wondering...' Chloe scrunched up her nose, a telltale sign she was working out whether to ask the question on her mind.

'An unasked question is a waste of a thought.'

'Who said that?'

'I did.'

'It's way too deep to have come from your brain.'

'My brain is plenty deep. Now hurry up before I die of old age.'

'It's my birthday in two days. I just... Is it still okay for...'

'Dinner! Yes, absolutely we can still go out for dinner. Are your friends all sorted to come?'

Chloe's face split into a relieved smile. 'Yeah, they'll be there...and I was wondering if one more could come as well.'

'Sure, I can call the restaurant and add one to the booking. Who is it?'

'Kirsten,' Chloe replied. She looked at her mother anxiously. 'You said I should give her a second chance.'

'And I meant it. That's fine. Alright, are you ready? Because if I get any more proud of you I might tear up and I won't be able to drop you at the station.'

'I just need to grab my lunch. Thanks, Mum, you're the best.'

'Remember that the next time you say I'm the worst mother in the world.'

'I would never say that!'

'You said it last week when I wouldn't buy you a new phone,' she called after her departing daughter.

'Can't hear you,' Chloe called back.

'I'll buy you that phone you wanted,' Nicolette whispered.

Chloe popped back into the room. 'Really?'

'Oh, so you can hear me.'

'That's cruel. I take it back. You're a terrible mother who psychologically tortures her daughter.'

After dropping Chloe at the train station, Nicolette went to pick up her car. Paying the bill felt like handing over one of her kidneys. She was thankful for Alice Atkinson's money even if she'd felt guilty taking it.

It was good to be back in her own car though, once she'd readjusted the seat, tilted the air conditioning vents so the cold air hit her just below the chin, and retuned the radio. It had that clean car smell, which made her realise how bad it normally smelt.

She headed home and spent the forty minutes before Nero's vet appointment searching the house. She had no doubt Dominic would have done a thorough job the night before, but it wasn't his house, and in the daylight she might see something missed the night before.

Starting at the front door, she slowly and methodically examined the hallway. The dogs thought it was some sort of game and she was constantly having to move one, then another so she could search properly.

Half an hour later, she slumped onto a dining room chair. She hadn't identified anything missing. She checked her watch. Ten minutes until she had to leave. Reaching across the table for the car keys, she accidentally knocked them off the table. When she got up, her left knee cracked against the solid wooden table leg.

'Son of a...' She cut herself off and looked at Fig. 'No offence.'

Fig cocked her head and sneezed.

'Bless you,' Nicolette said.

She hobbled around the table and picked up the keys. It was destined to be a long frustrating day.

'I've heard of pets resembling their owners, but this is the first time I've seen an owner trying to be like their pet,' Simon said when Nicolette limped into the exam room.

She scowled as she picked up Nero and placed him on the table.

Simon silently examined the patient, then smiled.

'He seems comfortable putting his weight on his leg again. No long walks for a few days at least. I'll send you home with some pain meds you can give him if it looks like he's in discomfort, but I think he should make a full recovery.'

Nicolette let out a sigh of relief.

'How are you doing?' he asked.

She looked at him in surprise, then shrugged. 'I'm not your patient.'

'No, but a happy owner equals a happy animal. Animals pick up on stress levels in humans.'

'I know that,' she snapped.

He smiled. 'And that answers my question.'

'Sorry. I'm fine.'

'Fine applies to wine and art, not to people. Not unless you're using the sentence, *damn girl you look fine*.'

She laughed and his cheeks went red.

'I... I mean, er....'

She put him out of his misery, patting his shoulder. 'Forget it.'

'So, anyway... How's the investigation going? The cat?'

'Oh, her owner has been located and she's doing well.'

'Did you discover who poisoned her?'

'Not yet. Things got a bit complicated.'

'Well, I hope you find out. There aren't many people prepared to go the extra mile for animals. They need all the voices they can get.'

'That's what I think too.'

Simon smiled, then handed her a card. 'That has my personal cell on it. In case Nero gets worse. Call me any time.'

'Isn't that a little cliche? The whole *here's my number* thing?'

He shrugged and his smiled broadened. 'Maybe I wouldn't be averse to you calling me about non-dog related things. But that's up to you.'

She stared at the card for a moment then slipped it into her pocket, making a mental note to throw it out later. The last thing she needed was another complication in her life.

She made a follow up appointment in reception and was getting into her car just as her phone rang.

'Nicolette Briggs? Detective Senior Sergeant Phelps. I need to ask you a few follow up questions. Please be at Central at 11am.'

He clicked off before she could respond.

'Yes sir,' she said angrily to the phone.

She took Nero home, drove back into the city, found a park, and walked to the Central police station. She was five minutes late. Phelps was waiting impatiently by the front desk.

'This way.'

He walked through an internal door, only to reappear a few moments later when he realised Nicolette wasn't following.

'You didn't say please.'

'I'm the police, I don't need to say please.'

She stayed exactly where she was, with Phelps glaring at her and a growing number of onlookers watching.

Realising he was drawing attention, Phelps smiled. 'My apologies. Ms Briggs, would you *please* follow me?'

'Of course, Detective Senior Sergeant Phelps. It would be my pleasure.'

She knew it had been petty to stage the mini protest in such a public forum, but she didn't want him having too much of the upper hand right from the start.

He led her into an internal interview room, with a table and two chairs. The walls were dull grey, the furniture worn and basic. A single manila folder lay in the middle of the table.

'Ms Briggs, can you tell me your relationship with Skylar Goodman?' He asked as soon as she sat.

Nicolette managed to keep surprise off her face as she replied, 'I don't have a relationship with her. We met once. Briefly.'

'At the gym, where you advised her to call your brother. Why?'

Suddenly she knew why she was here. This had nothing to do with her at all.

'In the course of my investigation I discovered a link between Ms Goodman and a murder victim, so I advised her to call Detective Senior Sergeant Lister.'

'Let me just clarify, you found a link between Skylar Goodman and my murder victim, the one that you were one of the last people to see alive, and you gave her *your brother's* phone number instead of mine?' He leaned forward, his eyes slipping to the corner of the room and back again. 'Did he ask you to do that?'

She didn't need to twist in her chair to know there was a camera mounted on the wall behind her.

Leaning forward, Nicolette placed both hands flat on the table, and said, 'No. Detective Senior Sergeant Dominic Lister did not ask me to do that. In fact, he has always insisted I not get involved with official police investigations.'

A flicker of disappointment crossed Phelps' face. He changed tack. 'We have spoken with a witness who states that you and the deceased argued moments before he was fatally stabbed.'

'I told you that already.'

'And that you physically assaulted him.'

'Again, you knew that already.'

'Something that you have done on several other occasions in the past.'

She felt a flutter of anxiety, mixed with indignation. 'Is this a formal interview?'

He paused long enough for her to realise it was for dramatic effect.

'No, just a fact-finding mission. You understand how it looks, right? You, with a history of violence, assaulting a man minutes before he's fatally stabbed.'

A voice inside her head was screaming for her lawyer. A quieter, more sensible voice told the screamer to shut up.

'History of violence,' she said casually, 'makes me sound tougher than I actually am. I've never been charged with anything.'

'I know,' he replied.

Leave it alone, leave it alone, leave it alone, her internal advisor said.

'What annoys you more, Phelps? That I haven't been convicted, or that I actually do some good?'

He snorted. 'Good? You harass people over animals. What you do is a waste of time.'

Hands clenched, she rose to her feet. She wasn't sure what she was going to do, but the flicker of triumph on his face made her pause. She forced her hands open and took a deep breath.

'Sorry,' she said, rubbing her leg. 'Bit of leg cramp.'

She pulled her chair back to the table and sat down. 'You were asking about Skylar Goodman? I assume that means you now know the *deceased's* real name.'

'Of course we know his name. We are the police, Briggs. *We* investigate things, *not* you. And despite what you seem to believe, we are very good at our jobs.'

Nicolette nodded. 'Absolutely. *Some* police are exceptional at their jobs.'

'Right.' He glared and it took a lot of effort to keep her face neutral. 'And you're maintaining you never met Grant Reed before the park?'

'That's an interesting word, isn't it? *Maintaining*. Such a fancy way of saying you think I'm lying.'

'*Are* you lying?'

'I never met Grant Reed before that day in the park. I did speak with him though, through the doorbell cam.'

She relayed the short conversation, and Phelps made a note in the file.

'So you think he poisoned the cat, and then he stole your dog. Your motives are stacking up.'

'Honestly, all this flip-flopping is making my head hurt, Phelps. Are you trying to ruin my brother's career or get me to confess to murder? Make up your mind.'

His eyes flicked to the corner of the room again as he leaned back in his chair and raised his hands in front of him. 'I would never try to derail a colleague's career. And I can't make you confess to anything you didn't do. That would be unethical. Having said that, if there's anything you'd like to get off your chest, then I'd be happy to hear it.'

She clamped her mouth shut, despite the perfect retort forming in her head. She'd probably annoyed him enough. It was time to go fishing.

'Was there anything else I can help you with, Detective Phelps?'

'Skylar Goodman was perturbed to learn her acquaintance had been murdered. A fact you withheld from her. Why?'

'It wasn't my place to make public the name of a murder victim.'

He almost seemed disappointed at her response.

'And I doubt she was too *perturbed*, she said they barely knew each other.'

'Funny way to refer to a four-month relationship. Did she say anything else?'

Nicolette started to shake her head, faltered, then followed through with it.

'Are you sure?'

'I've told you everything she said.' She had just remembered a moment in the conversation, when Nicolette had shown Skylar the photo of Kalliana Magnusson.

'Start from the beginning.'

'No, I don't think so.'

'Ms Briggs—'

‘Detective Phelps, I came here at your request, I answered your questions, and now I have things to do that don’t involve repeating myself.’

She stood up and was halfway to the door before he spoke.

‘I didn’t dismiss you!’

‘And I didn’t need you to.’

She opened the door and marched into the corridor, startling two uniformed officers walking past. They gave her a strange look as she pushed open the internal door to the stairwell.

Nicolette fully expected Phelps to try and stop her. Any second she thought she’d be tackled to the ground, or tasered. It wasn’t until she was outside the building that she relaxed a little.

‘Excuse me, Ms Briggs?’

She whirled around, fists up.

The man was neatly dressed in a grey suit, white shirt and red patterned tie. He appeared to be in his early forties, with dark closely cropped hair. He had bags under his eyes and at least two days stubble on his chin.

‘My apologies. I was hoping that we might speak. My name is Thomas Magnusson.’

SEVENTEEN

'I apologise for ambushing you in the street,' Thomas said. 'Thank you for allowing me buy you a coffee.' He spoke with a hint of an accent that she couldn't place.

She stirred a spoonful of sugar into her cup, tapped the spoon on the side and placed it on the saucer before replying.

'How did you know where I was?'

'I didn't,' he replied with a hint of smile. 'I happened to be on my way into the police station when I saw you emerge. It appears that the fates wished us to meet.'

Nicolette took a sip as she studied him. In her experience, fate rarely had anything to do with anything.

'And why would they wish that?' she asked.

He dabbed his top lip with a napkin, which he then refolded and placed on the table next to his drink.

'I have recently suffered the loss of someone. I have heard from various sources that you are involved on the peripheral of the investigation. I wanted to meet with you to say thank you in person for everything you are doing to find justice.'

'I'm sorry about your... sister?'

She waited for him to indicate whether she was right, but he just continued to stare at her with his dark eyes and a blank expression.

‘I’m not involved. It’s a police investigation.’

‘Yes, as it should be. However the police are restricted by policy and procedure and...’

‘The law,’ Nicolette finished.

Thomas inclined his head slightly. ‘Again, as it should be. However, restrictions do not always allow for an optimal outcome.’

Nicolette took another sip of her drink and leaned back in her chair. Around them a low buzz of conversation filled the small café. They were at a table tucked in the back. She’d noted with interest that Thomas had headed straight to it, passing several other empty tables.

‘Thomas, I haven’t been to a night club since I was eighteen years old. Since then, the only time I’ve danced was at my daughter’s daycare graduation. So please could you stop using a lot of words to say nothing and get to the point. My feet are tired.’

Thomas blinked several times rapidly, then relaxed into his chair. ‘My apologies. Years of working in the business world has taught me to choose my words carefully.’

‘Which is admirable, but it’s been a long week and my tolerance level is at an all-time low. Why don’t you just tell me what you want me to do.’

‘What makes you think I want you to do anything?’

She didn’t reply.

Eventually he nodded.

‘It’s simple, all I want is for you to tell me what you know. The police are being tight-lipped about the details of their investigation, which is, to get straight to the point, bloody frustrating. I don’t know if you have ever had someone close to you ripped away in such a fashion, but it is most... unsettling. And when I am unsettled, I look for answers. Do you understand?’

She was almost feeling sorry for him until he asked her that, like she was a toddler being told not to touch something because it was hot.

'Like I said, I'm not involved in the police investigation.'

Thomas leaned forward in his seat. 'Anything you know would help me understand who might have done this terrible thing.'

There was a hint of something in his words and his eyes that made her hesitate. This was more than a desire for information. She kept one hand on her coffee cup, ready to use it as a weapon should things take a turn.

'Perhaps if I knew more about Kalliana.'

'Why?'

Nicolette pretended to relax back into her chair, but her leg muscles were tense and she was aware of a lull in conversation around them.

'I might have seen something I wouldn't know was important, but if I knew a little more about her it would help me to put things into perspective.'

Thomas nodded thoughtfully. 'I'd hoped the things I'd heard about you were true. I apologise if I sounded intense before, this is a stressful time.'

He smiled and she felt some of the tension loosen from her shoulders. Of course it was stressful. She was overreacting.

'I get that.'

He sipped his drink, then dabbed with his napkin before replying.

'Kalliana was not my sister, at least not in the strict sense of the word. We are... were... cousins. Our families were very close so we grew up together. She was a wonderful woman, so kind and generous. To be violently murdered, and in her own home.' He shook his head. 'It is unconscionable.'

'Violently murdered? Do you know how she died?'

Thomas frowned with frustration. 'Not the specifics, but I know it was not natural causes. Do you know how she died?'

'I don't, but like you said, it wasn't natural causes.'

She hesitated. This was the ideal chance to get some important information, but she wasn't sure he'd be forthcoming.

'Did Kalliana have a boyfriend? Or girlfriend?'

'No.' Thomas's face twisted briefly in disgust and she wondered which option he'd found repellent.

'What about friends? If you two were close, you must know some of her friends. Perhaps they have an idea about who might have done this. Or...'

'Yes, I had considered that one of her friends might be responsible. However, Kalliana was particular with who she let into her life. I cannot see any of her friends doing such a thing.'

Again, she picked up a slight tone in his voice, that suggested irritation.

'When did you last talk to Kalliana?'

Thomas's eyes scanned the café as he considered her question. 'The night before she died. We were supposed to have dinner, but she wasn't feeling well. I promised to call her the next morning, but I became busy with work, and when I did call it was a police officer who answered. He informed me of her death. Are you sure you don't know anything?'

His tone had changed again, accusing and disbelieving. She was having a hard time keeping up with his abrupt shifts in mood.

'Sorry,' she replied. 'I've been busy being questioned on another matter. In fact, I'm due at a meeting shortly with Grant Reed.'

She was watching him closely to gauge his reaction. It was only there for a second, but he definitely knew the name.

'Do you know him?'

'No, I do not believe so.'

'Oh, he'd said he was doing some work for the Magnusson Family Trust. I just assumed because of your name that you were involved with the trust.'

'My cousin dealt with the day to day running of the trust.' Thomas looked pointedly at his watch, then reached into his suit jacket pocket and withdrew a business card.

'I also have a meeting to attend to. I wonder if you might get in contact with me should you remember anything, or learn anything that could help bring my cousin's killer to justice.'

She took the card. Thomas Magnusson, Director, Magnusson Family Trust.

'What exactly *is* the Magnusson Family Trust?'

'It is as it sounds, a trust formed to look after our family's interests,' Thomas said, rising from his seat. 'It was a pleasure meeting you, Ms Briggs. This has been informative.'

She was glad he thought so, because her initial assessment was that she'd learnt next to nothing.

As she sipped her coffee, she replayed the meeting in her head.

First and most important, Thomas Magnusson was a good liar. If she hadn't spent the last two years dealing with an increasingly confident teenager, she might not have caught it, but he'd lied to her at least twice.

Second, he hadn't seemed the sort of man to hold a meeting without a clear outcome. Yet he hadn't appeared surprised or disappointed by her lack of knowledge. In fact, almost the opposite – there'd been a touch of relief. It led her to wonder, as she drained the last of her coffee, if she'd just been sitting opposite the murderer himself.

She pondered that possibility all the way back to her car.

As she pulled out of the car park, she made a mental pro and con list.

On the pro side, he knew both victims, and had lied about knowing one of them. There was something about his cousin that he disapproved of, he would have known about the cameras at the house, and had a key to get in.

On the cons side, he didn't have a clear motive for either murder. And why break into Nicolette's house if he was prepared to meet her face to face?

No, although she didn't particularly warm to him, Nicolette wasn't prepared to brand Thomas Magnusson a killer. Yet.

Her thoughts turned to Skylar Goodman. Something was bugging her about the way Phelps had described Skylar's reaction to learning about Grant Reed's death. She'd had no reason to downplay that relationship to Nicolette, and yet she'd said they'd only seen each other a couple of times. Why?

Nicolette decided to find out. She rang Skylar. The woman cautiously agreed to meet her on Oriental Parade by the swimming pool.

Skylar was waiting outside, carrying a light blue sports bag, and shivering slightly in the cool breeze. She was on the phone as Nicolette walked up, but hung up and flashed Nicolette an annoyed expression.

'I've got a bone to pick with you. You didn't tell me Grant was dead.'

'I'm sorry. Like I told DSS Phelps, It wasn't my place to inform anyone of a murder victim's identity. Especially when you said you barely knew him. I really am sorry.'

Skylar's expression softened and she sighed. 'I understand.'

'Why didn't you tell me you were together for four months. I had no idea how important he was to you.'

'Yes, well, I might have lied about that.'

'To Phelps or me?'

A man on an electric scooter whizzed past, yelling something that was immediately snatched away by the wind.

'Did he say what I thought he did?' asked Nicolette.

Skylar shrugged. 'You get used to it when you're a celebrity.'

She didn't seem unhappy, despite the crudeness of the message.

'You were just saying you were a liar...?' Nicolette prompted.

Skylar's cheeks reddened, but that could have been the wind.

'Look, I'm not proud of it, alright, but the fact is part of my brand is about being single. It would hurt my career if people found out I was seeing someone. And anyway, that relationship was mostly just physical. I mean he was a good guy, but it was just a bit of fun.'

'Okay, I get that.' Although she didn't. It had been a long while since that sort of fun had been part of her life. 'What can you tell me about Grant? I only talked to him briefly but he seemed smart.'

Skylar grinned. 'He was super smart. He could think himself out of any situation. That's what made him great at his job. Everyone liked him.'

'My dog sure did,' Nicolette muttered.

'Oh,' Skylar laughed. 'That was his sausage.'

Nicolette blinked. 'Excuse me?'

'Grant told me he often had to go onto properties with dogs, so he always carried some cooked sausage in a plastic bag that he used to bribe them.'

Nicolette was impressed and annoyed that her dog had been so easily enticed away with a bit of meat.

Skylar shivered again and pulled up the zipper on her tracksuit. 'The police didn't tell me much, but I saw on the news that he was stabbed. Is that true?'

'I'm afraid so.'

'Why?' For a moment her mask slipped and Nicolette saw her genuine grief. 'Why would someone want to kill Grant? Everyone loved him.'

In Nicolette's experience that was only ever the case *after* someone died.

'Why is a good question. Had he seemed different recently? Worried about anything?'

'The police asked me that too,' Skylar said with a frown. 'He seemed fine.' Her frown deepened.

'But?'

'But after I talked to that detective I remembered something. A couple of days ago we were in bed together... post... you know.' She smiled at the memory. 'He was always good at that side of things.'

Nicolette looked away and shifted impatiently. She was no prude but had no desire to stand in the street with a virtual stranger while she reminisced about her sex life.

'Anyway, he got a call on his phone, and he looked worried after he hung up.'

'Could you hear what was said?'

'No, I was busy checking my own phone. But I asked him and he said a new client was causing some problems.'

'He didn't say who the client was?'

Skylar shrugged. 'It sounded like jibberish to me. *Rooproop* or something? It was such a weird name I figured I heard it wrong.'

'Maybe you did.'

'Probably.' Skylar shrugged again. 'Either way, he seemed... twitchy. Sort of jumpy. It took a while for him to mellow out after. Was there anything else? Only, I have to hit the pool now if I want to get my laps in before my spa appointment.'

'No, that's all. Thanks Skylar. Oh, just one more thing. Do you know Thomas Magnusson?'

Skylar thought for a moment then shook her head. 'Is he an influencer?'

'Not that I'm aware of. Thanks.'

Skylar disappeared inside the pool complex and Nicolette walked slowly towards her car. She paused to let a car exit the car park beside the pool, glanced towards the harbour and froze. Between the car park and the water, she saw a man yanking at a leash. A small hairy black dog cowered at the end of it. The man lifted his boot.

'Hey!' Nicolette yelled.

The man looked around.

'Hey!' she yelled again, starting across the car park.

The man sneered. 'What? he shouted back.

Nicolette quickened her pace as the dog whined and the man jerked on the leash again.

The man was tall and thin, wearing a baseball cap and a dirty long black coat.

'Mind your own business,' he said. He took a step and dragged the dog after him. 'Come on, you stupid b—'

Nicolette grabbed the hand holding the leash and twisted it.

The man grunted and pulled his hand free without difficulty. He went to raise it as he loomed over her, but the leash was still around his wrist, tethering it to the dog on the ground. He raised the other hand, palm facing towards her.

She stepped to the side and punched him in the stomach.

The man doubled up, his arms on his thighs.

The dog barked fiercely and pulled at the leash.

'Stop!'

She whirled at the shout from behind her, fist raised and knees bent slightly, ready to step into a punch.

Two uniformed police officers were jogging towards her. She didn't know the man, but she thought she recognised the woman constable.

'Step away from that man.'

Nicolette quickly lowered her hands and took a couple of steps away from the man with the dog.

'We're responding to a call about a disturbance. Can you tell me what happened here?'

'Well, I was—'

'Ma'am, I was speaking to the victim.'

Nicolette stared at the officer in disbelief then looked at the man who was still bent over. She watched him slowly straighten up, rubbing his stomach and looking nervously at her.

'I was just out for a walk and this absolute nutter attacked me and tried to steal my dog.'

'Now wait a sec—'

'Why don't I take your statement over here,' the woman constable said. She walked Nicolette a few metres away.

'He's lying.'

'Ms Briggs, I don't know if you remember me? I'm Constable Glen. We met about six months ago.'

'Oh, of course. Sonia, right?'

'Right. So why don't you tell me what happened here.'

It didn't take long, and Constable Glen made a few notes.

'You admit attacking him?'

'I suppose so, but it was just a tap to the stomach, and he was about to hit me, so it was self-defence.'

Glen looked over to where the man stood, cap in his hands, while his dog sat calmly at his feet.

'From where we were standing, it looked like more than a tap. You knocked the wind out of him.'

'Then you must have seen him raise his hand to me. Besides, look at me. I'm half his size, do you really think I could...?' Nicolette trailed off.

'Let's see what he has to say,' Glen said.

Her partner had finished talking to the man and approached. 'The victim says he was out for a walk, his dog was barking at a seagull and suddenly she came out of nowhere and punched him in the stomach.'

Nicolette stayed silent while Glen relayed her version of events.

'This isn't the first time you've been accused of assaulting people, is it, Ms Briggs?'

She kept her mouth clamped shut, despite words of protest clambering to be released.

'Let's go for a ride down to central.'

'Does he want to press charges?' she asked.

'It doesn't matter if he does or not. We witnessed the assault.'

'Like you said, this was just a misunderstanding. I'm happy to apologise if that'll help.'

'Mr Smith doesn't want to talk to you. He's pretty shaken up. I'm going to finish taking his statement then we'll take a ride.'

As he walked away, Nicolette pulled out her phone.

'What are you doing?' Glen asked.

'Making a call. Don't worry, I'm not going to do a runner.'

She hated herself, having sworn never to use family connections when she got in trouble, but something felt off about this incident and she wasn't going to leave anything to chance.

Unfortunately, Dominic didn't answer the phone. She left a brief message which she hoped managed to avoid sounding too stressed and annoyed.

'Let's go,' the male constable said.

Nicolette looked at Mr Smith. The flicker of a smug expression on his face confirmed her suspicions.

She was grateful for the absence of handcuffs, but still felt self-conscious as she was escorted through the car park and out to the pavement. She tried to ignore the stares by talking to Constable Glen.

'You got here pretty quickly.'

'We were just up the hill in Mt Victoria when we got the call.'

'You must drive fast.'

'Why?' the man said.

She turned her head. 'The whole thing from the time I saw the man to the time you arrived was two minutes at the most. The disturbance, as you call it, hadn't even happened yet when you got the phone call. You don't think that's weird?'

'Like I said, we were just up the hill.'

He had a stoic look on his face, so she gave up on him and turned to Glen. 'You see how something is strange here, can't you? Look.'

She glanced over her shoulder and after a moment so did the constable. Mr Smith was kneeling, his dog licking his face.

'Two minutes ago, that dog was acting terrified. Now it's all, he's the best owner ever.'

'Because the dog was never scared. You made it up and now you're trying to justify your actions. Come on.'

He made the mistake of grabbing her arm. It took all her will power to avoid adding assaulting a police officer to the list of her potential charges.

'Hey, Hayden, it's cool, she's not going to run,' Glen said.

He released her to open the backdoor of the patrol car.

Her phone rang. She checked the screen and was relieved to see it was Dominic.

'Just a sec, I need to answer this.'

'Nic, I've got two minutes. What's up?'

'I think I'm being arrested.'

She heard him swear, then ask what happened. She gave him the facts, minus her suspicions, and he asked to speak with one of the constables.

Nicolette handed the phone to Glen, but her partner snatched it first.

'Who is this?!'

His face grew increasingly sour as he listened. He relayed the story given by Mr Smith, listened some more, then handed the phone back to Nicolette. She put the phone to her ear.

'Don't say anything other than *thank you officer*,' Dominic said.

'You're free to go, Ms Briggs. Be careful how you approach things in future.'

'Thank you, officer.'

His sour expression deepened, but she got a hint of a friendly smile from Constable Glen.

She waited until they'd climbed into their patrol car before putting the phone back to her ear.

'What did you tell them?'

'I reminded them that they had the discretion to proceed or release you with a caution.'

'Thank you, officer.'

'You owe me, Nic. I'm trying to solve a murder and you've got me mucking around getting my sister off assault charges.'

'I think the two are related.'

'What?' He didn't bother hiding his frustration.

'What better way to stop me poking around asking questions than getting me arrested?'

'Why?'

'I don't know, maybe I'm getting too close to finding out the truth.'

'Are you?'

'I don't know,' she repeated.

'I don't think so, Nic, this sounds to me like you going off hot-headed like normal, only this time you dragged me into it.'

'That's bec—'

'I don't have time for this right now. I'll talk to you later.'

She sighed and put her phone away. It wasn't the first time a family member had hung up on her, but she usually got along with Dominic. And he was right. She had dragged him into her mess when she should have just sorted it herself.

She thought about going to talk with Mr Smith but decided against it. If he had been put up to it, he was hardly going to admit it. And if he was just an innocent – albeit nasty – man, then she didn't want him calling the police back. Something told her that constable would jump at the chance to put her in the back of the patrol car.

Outside the pool complex was a small kiosk that sold ice creams. Even though it wasn't the warmest day, Nicolette believed it was never too cold for ice cream. And she needed something with sugar in it.

She settled on wild berry gelato, carrying the cone to one of the small tables dotting the pavement.

Licking the pink drips away, she went over the events in her head. Then again. And once more for luck. No matter which way she looked at it, she couldn't avoid drawing the conclusion that someone wanted her out of the way. But why? Dominic was right. They must assume that she knew something. Which was a problem because she didn't think she knew anything. She took a big bite of gelato and winced as cold blasted her brain. She stuck her thumb onto the roof of her mouth and waited for the brain freeze to disappear. When it did, her thoughts came into focus. Forget why. The more important question was, who? Who had set this up?

There was only one person who'd known where she was. And only one who could have called the police to tip them off once she saw Nicolette take the bait.

Skylar Goodman had just rocketed to the top of the suspect list.

On reflection, that was where she should have been anyway, Nicolette thought. Skylar lied about her relationship with Grant Reed, and it was highly likely she'd also lied about not knowing Kalliana Magnusson.

As she finished her ice cream, Mr Smith walked past, his dog happily trotting by his side. He saw her and smirked. When she got to her feet, he picked up the pace and hurried away.

Nicolette headed back to her car and drove to Archie's house.

'Three times in a week. I don't know whether to feel blessed that I get to bask in your presence or sad that it took a murder investigation to get you to see me.'

'Or you could quit the melodrama and just let me in.'

Archie gave her a quick hug, then headed down the hall, leaving Nicolette to close the door and follow.

'What do you need me to do for you today? Hack a government database? Redirect some satellites? That sort of thing?'

'You can do that?'

Archie laughed. 'Not even a little bit.'

Far from the glamorous outfit she'd worn at the family dinner, Archie was wearing paint-stained tracksuit pants, an old faded T-shirt, and cat slippers.

'Is that the same Crowded House T-shirt you got in 2007? I can't believe you still wear it.'

'I can't believe it's still wearable,' Archie replied with a grin. 'But it's comfortable and reminds me of my youth.'

'Yeah, you're so old now.'

'Thirty-five is the new twenty-five I'll have you know. Now what can I do for you?'

'Skylar Goodman.'

She quickly explained her suspicions.

Archie sat at the dining table and opened her laptop.

'I never understood the concept of influencers,' she said as she typed. 'I'm hardly going to buy a bikini or eat at a café just because some woman tells me to. Although, that is a gorgeous bikini,' she said, clicking on a photo in Skylar's Instagram account.

'You would look good in that.'

'Please. I never wore bikinis even when I was young enough to think I could.'

'What happened to thirty-five being the new twenty-five?'

'Doesn't apply to swimwear. I've seen most of this, but was hoping you could make a magic breakthrough.'

Archie quickly scrolled through the photos.

'Stop!' Nicolette said. 'Go back up.'

Archie slowly rolled the screen back up.

'Now that's interesting.'

'If this is an a-ha moment, you're going to have to explain it to me.'

Nicolette pointed at the photo. 'That's Skylar Goodman.' She pointed again, 'And that's Kalliana Magnusson.'

'And the guy with his arms around them?'

'That is Grant Reed. Skylar told me that she'd only known him a few months, and that she'd never met Kalliana before. How old is that photo?'

Archie clicked a couple of times. 'According to the metadata this photo was taken April last year.'

Nicolette swore. 'That's the second time she's lied to me about Grant.'

'Sounds suss to me.'

'Very suss. Although no one says suss anymore.'

'Everybody says suss.'

'Sorry, Archie, according to my well-informed daughter, suss has gone the way of choice and awesome.'

'What? Awesome is out as well?'

'Chloe was quite clear on that when she told me how embarrassing I am.'

'Kids.'

'Are there any other pictures of these three together?'

It took five minutes to go through the many photos on Skylar's Instagram. They were almost at the end (or the beginning) of her posts when Nicolette pointed at the screen again.

'That could be a younger Kalliana Magnusson,' Archie said.

The picture didn't have the same professional quality as the later posts. The lighting was dim and both women were half turned away from the camera. The caption read “Besties out to change the world”.

‘When was this taken?’

Archie checked, then said, ‘It was posted in 2022, but that doesn’t mean it’s when it was taken.’

Nicolette sat back in her chair and pondered what that meant. ‘Besties out to change the world. Can you tell where they are?’

‘Of course I can, because I’m fabulous.’

‘Yes you are, but I’m being serious, can you?’

Archie sighed dramatically. ‘I’ll just pull the metadata, do a reverse image search, then calibrate the coordinates to know geo-locations.’

‘I understood about a third of that.’

‘Good, because it didn’t really make sense. However if you look at the wall behind them, it says Hyatt Regency, Sydney.’

Nicolette looked to where she was pointing and give herself a mental kick.

‘Alright, but my lack of observational skills doesn’t make you a genius.’

Archie laughed and they went back to studying the photo.

The two women were looking at something out of frame. There were empty seats either side of them and a glimpse of a row of seats in front and behind.

‘Is that a badge around Skylar’s neck?’

Archie did something with her mouse and the photo zoomed in, becoming more blurry as it did.

‘Before you ask, I can’t sharpen the image. This isn’t a movie. That’s as good as it gets.’

‘Fat lot of good you are. Can’t hack a satellite, can’t sharpen an image, what can you do?’

‘I can make fettuccine carbonara with mushrooms, and I can kick you out of my house.’

Nicolette put her arm around Archie and squeezed lightly. 'I do appreciate you, Veronica.'

'Don't call me that, I'll think you're dying or something.'

'I thought you wanted me to call you by your name.'

'I didn't think you'd actually do it. Anyway, look here, Kalliana has a similar badge around her neck. Maybe they were at a concert or a convention.'

Nicolette frowned. 'This is getting confusing. Grant told me he'd never met Kalliana, which was evidently a lie. Skylar told me she'd only met her once for a few minutes, which is also a lie. Why would everyone lie about knowing everyone else?'

Archie shrugged. 'Jealousy? Maybe the two women had a falling out over Grant.'

Nicolette had to admit it was plausible.

'That makes it even more likely Skylar's our killer, since the other two are dead.'

Archie spent a few minutes searching. 'The photo was posted on April 11th. Assuming there were more than ten conferences happening in Sydney on that day. If we rule out the unlikely ones, like the Symposium on International Space Exploration, that leaves three likely ones.'

'That one,' Nicolette pointed to the screen.

'Empowering Women into the 22nd Century. How can you be sure?'

'Skylar is an influencer. I agree it's an unlikely leap from that to space exploration. Anyway, the tag on the Instagram post said they were changing the world.'

'Makes sense. Give me a second to work some magic. In the meantime, can you make some tea.'

'What?'

'Hot drink, usually served with milk and sugar? Surely, you've heard of it. Make some while you explain to me why this photo from years ago is important.'

Nicolette collected her thoughts as she made the tea.

'I remember having a conversation with Dominic when he first became a detective. He said most homicides were committed by people known to the victim. There's something off about Skylar. When we first met, I dismissed it as her being a bit vapid. But there's something going on under the surface. She killed Kalliana, I'm sure of it. I thought Grant was collateral damage, just in the wrong place at the wrong time, but she might have intended that he would die all along. Except...' she frowned.

'Go on,' Archie urged as Nicolette placed a mug of tea in front of her.

'If Kalliana was killed by poison in her oil diffuser, as I suspect, then that had to be carefully planned. And discreetly. But Grant was stabbed in the open, in a park with any number of potential witnesses. It was risky and spontaneous. Do you think the crimes could have been committed by two different people? What?'

Archie was looking at her in amusement.

'Do you remember when we first came to live with you?'

'How can I forget? I was an only child who suddenly had to share her room with an annoying older sister.'

'I wasn't annoying.'

'You took half my closet space. Trust me, you were annoying.'

'Yeah, well it was no picnic for me either. One second Dad was a struggling widower trying to raise a moody teenager, the next he comes home and tells me that he's fallen in love and we have to move from Tauranga to Wellington so they could get married. I went from only child to having an annoying younger sister. I came home one day to find you'd packed all my stuff and put it out on the lawn with a sign saying it was all free. I had to fight a fifteen-year-old to get my iPod back.'

'Oh yeah,' Nicolette grinned. 'I'd forgotten about that.'

'Anyway, my point is, even then you were great at solving puzzles. I once made a bet with Mum that you were going to join the police when you left school.'

'I hope you didn't lose too much money.'

Archie grinned. 'Again, my point is, you're smart. You'll figure this out.'

'I wish I had your confidence in my abilities.'

Archie turned back to the laptop and tapped away for another minute before turning the screen to face Nicolette.

'What?'

'Just read.'

It was a copy of a newspaper article from four years ago, lauding Nicolette for reuniting owners with their dog that had been stolen for use in dog fighting.

'What's this?' she asked again.

'Scroll down.'

She did, finding article after article on her past cases.

'I haven't seen some of these,' Nicolette said.

'I thought it would be nice to have a copy of everything in one place. I know you would never do it yourself and, well, I'm proud of you.'

Nicolette felt a flutter in her chest and she swallowed several times before replying.

'I'm proud of you too.'

Archie waved her hand dismissively. 'As you should be, I'm fabulous. But my point is, you are very good at what you do. This proves it. So, stop doubting yourself. It doesn't suit you.'

'You're a little mean, you know that?'

'It's called being supportive. Now here's something else interesting. I've found an attendees list for the conference – don't ask me how – and neither Kalliana or Skylar are on the list. There is, however, a Katrina Matthewson and Sarah Gladstone.'

'Coincidence? Of course not,' Nicolette muttered. 'We know they were there, and the lanyards suggest they were registered. What can we find out about Katrina and Sarah?'

'They don't have any social media presence that I can find, not a current one anyway, but I'll do more digging.'

'Any news articles?'

'I'll check. It might take a while, I have a zoom meeting in a few minutes.'

'Text me when you get something.'

Nicolette headed for home. It was time to take the dogs for a walk. As she drove, she thought about her family. Her mother aside, her family had either directly or indirectly helped her out from the moment Chloe had been born, with the exception of Lewis. And she'd taken it for granted or hadn't even realised it was happening.

When she got home, the dogs were happy to see her. She pushed aside her melancholy and took them into the paddock next door. Her neighbours kindly let her use it when their horses were in one of the other fields. It was a great space for the dogs to tear around, and they only occasionally came back having rolled in horse manure.

She stood at the gate, throwing balls in different directions and having them returned at varying speeds and with varying degrees of slobber.

'You know who might know about the Skylar/Kalliana/Grant triangle?' she asked Teddy, flinging his ball as hard as she could. 'Thomas Magnusson,' she explained to Fig.

Nero barked and she jogged to pick up his ball. 'You know, the way this is supposed to work is you bring the ball to me and then I throw it.'

With his tongue out it looked like he was laughing at her. He barked happily as she gently tossed it and he hobbled after it, still favouring his injured leg but definitely more comfortable than the day before.

When she was tired of watching them, it still took five minutes of increasingly stern talking to get all three of them to sit by the gate so she could lead them home.

The distance between her yard and the paddock was only thirty metres, so she didn't bother putting the dogs onto leashes. They naturally hugged the fence line, stopping to sniff every post, and traffic was typically quiet along this stretch of road. Halfway home, Fig started digging at something in the dirt by the fence.

Teddy and Nero were almost at the gate and Nicolette had walked ahead a few paces before she realised Fig wasn't following. She turned and called, but Fig kept exploring with her nose. With a sigh, Nicolette started back.

Suddenly there was a roaring sound and she spun in time to glimpse a car heading straight for her. She tried to jump to the side but it was too late.

EIGHTEEN

Nicolette felt a sharp blow on her side. Then she was tumbling and smashing into something hard. For a moment the world went black, then it slowly rebooted. First her hearing came back and she became aware of barking. A lot of barking. Then parts of her began to hurt.

When she opened her eyes, an anxious Fig was standing over her.

'I'm okay,' she croaked, before wondering if that was in fact true.

She tested a few moving parts. Her arms and legs moved without much pain. She turned her neck to the left, no issue there. Then to the right. An intense pain shot down her side and she clamped her eyes shut and swore through a grimace.

Fig sniffed her and licked her face. Somewhere through the pain and the slobber, she was aware that the other two dogs were still barking. She looked around. The car was gone.

'Quit it,' she said to the dogs shakily.

They ignored her, which she found more annoying than the fact that someone had tried to run her over.

'Quit it!' she repeated more firmly. This time they listened, and reluctantly approached her.

‘I’m okay,’ she said again to Fig, but she didn’t need the dog’s sceptical expression to know she didn’t sound convincing.

‘Look, I’ll show you.’

She sat up quickly, figuring it was like pulling a Band Aid – quicker was better.

It was nothing like a Band Aid. Her head throbbed and her vision swarmed. And the sharp pain in her side sent her stomach rolling. She leaned to the side and threw up. The dogs came closer to sniff at the vomit.

‘Alright, I lied. I’m not okay.’

Fig whined and nudged Nicolette with her nose. Then she backed up, barked, and took off down the road.

‘Fair enough,’ said Nicolette.

She considered trying to stand, then dismissed it as a ridiculous idea and slumped back against the fence post. That must have been what she’d hit. It looked dented.

Her face felt wet and her fingers came away slicked with blood.

‘Chloe is going to be really upset with me. I better get this cleaned up before she gets home.’

She looked along the short distance to her house. It might as well be five hundred metres.

‘Maybe I should call the SPCA and tell them I’ve been broken and abandoned in a ditch.’ She laughed long and loud at that and only stopped when she heard the tinge of hysteria.

Nicolette reached into her pocket to get her phone. It wasn’t there. She wasted a few minutes looking on the ground around her, before remembering she’d left it charging on the kitchen counter.

‘Guess I’ll have to walk after all. Unless you two want to make a stretcher and pull me like sled dogs? No? And after all I’ve done for you.’

Nero crept closer and lay down while Teddy decided waiting was boring and wandered away to sniff something.

Nicolette gritted her teeth, took a deep breath (which she instantly regretted as the pain in her side returned), and rolled onto her knees. She grabbed the fence wire and waited for the world to stop jumping about. Ragged breathing nearby sent a flash of fear through her. She looked around expecting to see someone looming. Then she realised it was her.

'Never get hit by a car, Nero. It messes with your head.'

Another effort to stand left her panting and dizzy, but on her feet.

'You won't tell Chloe about all the swearing, will you?'

Nero barked.

'Good boy.'

Movement out of the corner of her eye made her turn her head slowly. Fig was running towards her. She skidded to a halt and dropped the object she had been holding in her mouth.

Nicolette blinked, tears threatening to spill as she looked down. She wiped them away, looking at her dog in amazement. She stooped and reality kicked back in.

'I don't want to be ungrateful, Fig, but any chance you could hand it up to me? I have a feeling if I get down, I'm not getting up again.'

Fig looked at the ground, then back at Nicolette. She shuffled anxiously.

'Good point,' Nicolette said.

Getting back down took less effort than standing, but still hurt. Only when she was safely propped against the fence post did she pick up her phone. She wiped the dog drool off with her T-shirt, then praised Fig again, taking a moment to scratch her behind the ears and ruffle her fur.

'You're the best.'

Teddy barked.

'And you too, and you, Nero. You're all very clever dogs.'

She paused for a moment, looking at the phone screen. Who to call? Her ribs said ambulance, her head said police, her gut said neither. Dominic would want her to file an official police report, which she might do at some point, but not right now. And Archie didn't like the sight of blood.

As she reviewed her short list of friends, she realised that her life had become increasingly about Chloe and work, not always in that order. Her old friends from college were long gone, she never got to go to university and, with a baby in tow, she hadn't managed many social engagements over the past fourteen years.

'I can't just sit here all day.' Although she was quite comfortable and the thought of getting up again wasn't a pleasant one.

She closed her eyes to think.

'Nicolette?'

Her eyes snapped open and she squeaked when she saw a figure standing over her.

He quickly took a step back. As he came into focus, she saw it was Simon Boland.

'What are you doing here?' she asked.

'I was driving past and I saw the dogs. I thought you might be having a rest, but when I called out you didn't answer.'

'Oh,' Nicolette was getting a sore neck looking up at him, 'I didn't hear you.'

'Are you alright?'

'Actually, I was hit by a car.'

'What! I'll call an ambulance.'

'No, I just need to get back home.'

He stopped, finger poised over his phone.

She braced herself for protests or follow up questions.

'Alright, let's get you up.' He reached out a hand and she took it, trying not to flinch as he pulled her gently to her feet.

'Where's home?'

She pointed, not trusting her voice until the throbbing pain subsided.

At first Simon held her arm, but she found after a couple of steps that she could manage, so she shook loose. The dogs raced ahead and were waiting for them by the front door.

Nicolette faltered when she saw the door was ajar, then she remembered that Fig had gone in to retrieve her phone. Her jumbled brain forgot to ask the obvious question, how had Fig opened the door?

Simon let her go in first, then insisted that she sit at the dining table while he examined her.

'I'm not a cat,' she complained as he checked her head, then asked where it hurt.

'No, you're much better. You can answer my questions rather than bite me. Does it hurt when I do this?'

He pressed his fingers into her ribs, and she slammed her hand onto the table and half leapt out of the chair. The dogs growled in unison. Teddy bared his teeth and took a step towards Simon.

'Yes, damn it, so don't do that. Or I *will* bite you.'

'Sorry, and sorry to you too,' he said to the dogs. 'I promise not to hurt her again. Now, can you take a deep breath and let it out slowly? On a scale of one to ten, how much agony was that?'

'Four. Okay six, maybe an eight.'

'My professional diagnosis is that you probably broke a rib. You need an x-ray.'

Nicolette shifted in her chair and nodded. 'No maybe about it. How's my head?'

'You probably have a concussion. I'll need to clean the wound properly, but the bleeding has stopped so I think you'll be fine. Paper towels?'

She pointed at the kitchen counter and watched him tear several off, soak them under the tap and carry them over to her. 'This is likely to hurt. Do you want to tell me what happened?'

'A hit and run.'

He continued cleaning her wound. He'd been right, it did hurt.

'You don't look surprised,' Nicolette said.

'Half my work is from hit and runs,' replied Simon.

'The thing is I don't think it was an accident.'

'It must have been an accident. Otherwise...'

'Someone tried to kill me.'

'You don't need to sound so cheerful about it.' Simon sat in the chair opposite and absentmindedly patted Nero. The other two dogs were keeping their distance, undecided whether Simon was friend or foe.

'I'm not cheerful, I'm bloody furious, but it's also interesting.'

'Interesting!' Simon shook his head. 'You've got a strange idea of interesting.'

'When you get to know me, you'll find I have a strange idea of lots of things.'

'What makes you think it wasn't an accident?'

'That was a straight piece of road, and I got hit about halfway down. Visibility is as good as it gets. And there's something else as well. I didn't hear the car, not until the last second. They gunned the engine.'

'You think if they'd been speeding the whole time, you would have heard it sooner?'

'Yes,' she said, pleased he'd picked it up so quickly.

'Then you have to call the police. That's attempted murder.'

'Vehicular manslaughter.'

'I don't understand you,' he complained.

'Good. Anyway, I'm pretty sure I left a decent sized dent in the car, so all I have to do is find the car and I'll have the culprit.' She looked at him suspiciously. 'Why were you driving past?'

'My sister lives further out in the valley. I had some time off this afternoon, so I thought I'd pop out to see her.' He studied Nicolette's face before adding, 'Would you like to examine the side of my car?' He sounded half sincere and half amused, but also a bit annoyed. 'I couldn't have known you lived around here.'

She did want to examine his car, but since he'd helped her it seemed unlikely that he'd also just tried to kill her. Unless he came back to finish her off.

Whether he sensed her uncertainty, or was oblivious to it, Simon just sat there patting Nero.

'No, that's okay,' Nicolette said. 'Thank you for helping me.'

He shrugged. 'What else was I going to do? My mother taught me to help women I find on the side of the road.'

She blinked and tilted her head slightly. 'You know that sounds a little creepy, right?'

'Does it? I always thought it was just a nice way of saying *help others*.'

Nicolette sighed. 'Sorry. Almost being killed tends to put me in a mood.'

'That makes it sound like it's happened before.'

She didn't reply. Things had been fraught on previous cases, sometimes leading to violence. But this was the first time someone had actually tried to kill her. Now that her brain was working again, her conversation with Archie came back to her. Deciding to run her down was impulsive and problematic, not careful and calculated like the poisoning of Kalliana Magnusson.

'Are you sure I can't persuade you to call the police?'

'I'll call my brother,' she replied. 'He's a detective.'

'Today.'

'I said I would,' she replied with a scowl.

Simon smiled. 'Sorry. I'm used to talking to patients that can't talk back.'

She reluctantly smiled.

'I'll see myself out. Let me know if you need anything. Like I said, my sister lives over this way so I come by quite often.'

'Thank you, but I'll be fine.'

He walked into the hallway and she heard the front door close.

Nicolette felt annoyed but couldn't pin down a reason. There were so many things she could be annoyed about, it was hard to narrow it down to just one. She picked up her phone, then put it down again. She needed to call someone. Whose reaction would be worst when they saw her cuts and bruises?

'Definitely Chloe,' she said to the dogs.

Their ears perked up at her name and Teddy trotted into the hallway to check the front door.

'You know, I pay for the dog food,' she called after him.

Her joints had started to stiffen up but she made it to the bathroom. Looking in the mirror, she decided it was a bit of a miracle that Simon hadn't immediately called an ambulance. Or an undertaker. Her skin was pale and fresh blood was oozing from the cut above her eyebrow, although it looked like Simon had done a good job cleaning the wound. Nicolette wet a face cloth and pressed it onto the cut, allowing herself the wince she had hidden from Simon.

There was something untrustworthy about Simon Boland. He'd said he didn't know where she lived but hadn't she given her address when she'd taken Nero to the clinic? Simon could easily have found it in their database.

She scowled at herself in the mirror. The throbbing in her side had subsided and she no longer felt like emptying her stomach when she touched it. That was a good sign. Cloth held to her face, she was leaving the bathroom just as the front door opened.

'Hi, Mum,' Chloe called from the hallway.

'You're home early,' Nicolette called back.

Chloe came into view and stopped in her tracks. 'What happened to you?'

Nicolette laughed. 'I took the dogs for a walk and tripped over on the way back. Smacked my head against a fence post.'

Chloe stared at her, then shrugged. 'Not smart.'

She didn't wait for an answer, just disappeared into her room and closed the door.

For once Nicolette was grateful for her teenager's lack of interest.

Easing herself down onto a chair, she pulled her phone towards her and mentally made a list of things to do. First, try and figure out where Skylar Goodman was when someone tried to turn her into roadkill. Second, find out whether Simon Boland had a sister, if she lived in the valley, and how close they were. (Early in her career, she'd made an assumption about a pair of siblings only to find out that they hadn't spoken in years. Never again.) She didn't know what his interest in her was, but the last man she'd been attracted to had left her with a baby.

She blinked. What a ridiculous thought. She wasn't attracted to him. Was she?

As she started making calls, she decided she wasn't lying to herself.

Not technically.

NINETEEN

When Nicolette woke up the next morning, she felt like she'd been hit by a car. She smiled at this thought. It was just as well, since her mouth was about the only part of her that hadn't stiffened up overnight.

'Mum! I need a ride to the station,' Chloe yelled from her room.

'What happened to the bus?'

'I missed it.'

'That wasn't very smart, was it?' Nicolette shouted in irritation.

'That's why I need to go to school. To get smarter.'

All this yelling was giving Nicolette a headache.

'Open my door,' she called out.

The bedroom door was pushed open and Chloe stood there in uniform, bag in hand.

'You're not even up. I'm going to be late.'

'Alright, alright, give me five minutes.'

'You've got three.'

Chloe disappeared from view before Nicolette could say something witty and sarcastic. She threw on sweatpants and yesterday's T-shirt much more slowly than normal, and with more wincing and swearing. Bending down to tie her shoes proved impossible so she settled for slip on sandals. She risked a look in the mirror above the chest of drawers. The cut looked angry and was crusted with blood, but at least she wasn't as pale as the day before. Most of her bruises were thankfully hidden by her clothes so she didn't look too much like a walking corpse.

Chloe was waiting by the front door with car keys in hand.

'Come on. The train isn't going to wait for me and it takes ten minutes to get to the station.'

Nicolette plucked the keys out of Chloe's hand. 'We'll make it in eight.'

That would have been optimistic on a normal day, and impossible when they got caught behind a learner driver. Seeing the L sign in the back window was the only reason Nicolette didn't honk her horn.

They arrived at the station in time to see the train pulling away.

'You'll have to drive me.'

'Honey, the list of things I *have* to do is short, and driving you to school because you missed the bus is not on there.'

Chloe opened her mouth to argue, then glanced at Nicolette's forehead.

'I'm sorry, Mum, could you please drive me to school this one time? I promise not to be late ever again.'

She smiled sweetly and Nicolette pursed her lips.

'I'll give it an eight out of ten. Almost believable, but you made a promise you can't possibly keep and the smile was a step too far.'

'Noted,' Chloe replied with a sad expression.

Nicolette sighed. 'You're lucky that I consider your education important.'

Chloe grinned and sat back in her seat, singing along to the radio as Nicolette pulled the car into traffic.

As they arrived outside the school, Chloe looked at her.

'Mum, you're okay, aren't you?'

'Of course I am. Why?'

'You've been holding the steering wheel like you were trying to strangle it.'

Nicolette forced her fingers to relax. 'Listen, Nancy Drew, we don't need another detective in the family.'

'Who's Nancy Drew?'

'What are they teaching you at that place? Get out of my car and don't come home until you're learnt about important literature.'

'You mean old people stuff.'

Chloe jumped out of the car and slammed the door, adding to Nicolette's headache.

Having left the house without the life-giving sustenance of morning coffee, she drove around the corner and parked, before heading into a café. Every part of her hurt as she stiffly tottered inside and placed her order. The last time she'd been this sore was when she'd fallen off a horse that got spooked by a rabbit. As she'd hit the ground, the horse and rabbit had fled in opposite directions.

While she waited for her coffee she studied her phone. Last night's investigation hadn't managed to pinpoint anything useful about Skylar Goodman's whereabouts the previous afternoon, but thanks to the power of the internet she had confirmed that Simon had a sister. Although whether he still talked to her or if she lived close by were still to be determined.

She carried her coffee out to the car. As she turned the engine on, her phone beeped with a message requesting her presence at the Silvermoon Retirement Village.

Short on anything to do in the interim, Nicolette messaged back that she was on her way. By the time she pulled into the carpark, the coffee was cool enough to sip without scalding her.

She was in the elevator when it occurred to her that showing up with a coffee in hand might be socially unacceptable. Especially when visiting your sort-of employer. Coming out of the elevator, she looked around the small landing for a place to stash the cup. The only possibility was the large pot plant in one corner, but before she could bend down, the front door swung open.

'Come on in,' Vanessa said.

'How did you...?'

Vanessa grinned. 'Alice has a security camera out here. She saw you arrive, and guessed you were trying to hide your coffee cup.'

'Smart woman,' Nicolette muttered.

Vanessa laughed. 'You have no idea.'

Alice was in the same spot on the couch, at the right end, side-on to the door. Nicolette sat opposite and was quietly pleased she managed to lower herself without letting out an old lady noise. She felt that would have been inappropriate in current company. But just in case she hadn't been as clever as she'd thought at hiding her discomfort, she decided to take charge of the conversation.

'I was under the impression that our business was complete.'

'Yet you came anyway,' Alice said.

Nicolette shrugged. 'It seemed polite.'

Alice grunted in disbelief. 'I told you at our first meeting, I understand people, and I get a strong sense you don't like leaving puzzles unsolved. Am I wrong? Are you not still investigating?'

Nicolette's silence seemed to be the only answer Alice required.

'As I told you last time you were here, the murder happened right next door to where I live. That makes me nervous.'

'Really?' Nicolette replied. 'From what I've read, this is the murder capital of retirement villages.'

Vanessa laughed when she saw Alice's sour expression.

'That's different. Now have you made any further progress?'

'Some.' She laid out everything that had happened since her previous visit. It took fifteen minutes by the time Alice interrupted several times to ask questions.

'I suppose you've thought of the obvious,' Alice said.

'That it's two different murderers? Yes, I have.'

'But you don't think it is,' said Vanessa.

Nicolette wanted to get up and pace, but stayed firmly where she was, since she'd omitted the hit and run from her summary.

'If they weren't so connected, I'd be inclined to think different people killed Kalliana and Grant. It's a hell of a coincidence if that's the case.'

'Coincidences do happen,' said Alice, 'but I think you're right. It's unlikely. What are your plans?'

'I'm not sure. I got an email this morning about another job, a paying one, so I might need to leave this one to the police.'

Alice snorted. 'I believe that as much as I believe you're sitting rigid in your seat because it's comfortable.'

Nicolette looked down at her clenched hands and forced them to open.

'You don't have to tell me, but it's obvious you're in discomfort.'

'Not to me it wasn't,' Vanessa said.

'I meant obvious to the observant, dear.'

Nicolette hesitated. 'I really did get an email about another job. I do have bills and chasing killers doesn't pay them. Homicide isn't my specialty.'

Alice leaned forward and fixed Nicolette with a stare. 'I have some experience with trying to juggle parenting with dangerous pursuits.'

'Oh?'

'Well, at my age I've had experience in most things. Usually twice.'

'And what age is that?'

'Oh, who remembers. Ninety-eight, nine, something like that. My memory isn't what it used to be.'

'I get the feeling that your memory loss is convenient rather than age related.'

'I like her. I like you,' Vanessa said to Nicolette. 'She can see right through you, Alice.'

'Don't be ridiculous,' Alice snapped.

Far from being chastised, Vanessa seemed to take the rebuke as a victory.

'We were talking about your plans, Nicolette. Do you think you are close to solving the murder and finding out the identity of who poisoned Maddy?'

'I don't know.'

'Alright, here's an easier question. Can you just walk away?'

'Sure. It'd be a slow walk, but definitely away.'

No one said anything.

Nicolette sighed. 'Alright, maybe I don't like leaving things unresolved.'

Alice nodded. 'And more importantly, it'll be difficult to walk away when someone obviously thinks you know something and is trying to kill you for it.'

'How did you...?'

'If you'd fallen off a bike you wouldn't be so reluctant to talk about it.'

'Who are you?'

'I told you, just an old woman who's seen a thing or two in her time. Vanessa, the envelope.'

Vanessa handed Nicolette a plain white envelope.

'That's payment for the next four days. I would feel better knowing for sure that these murders are not connected to Silvermoon in any way. But if you want to decline, I'll understand. You have a daughter to think of.'

Nicolette knew what Chloe would say if she told her about the hit and run. And most of it would not be repeatable in current company, no matter how worldly the older woman considered herself. In raising her daughter to be strong, independent and inquisitive, she'd also accidentally taught her to push back when pushed, and not to back down from a confrontation, but instead to look for different ways to resolve it. Walking away was not one of them.

She took the envelope. 'How's Maddy?'

'She brought me a headless bird this morning so I'm guessing she's feeling better.'

'Can I check on her before I go?'

Alice waved a hand. 'She's not here, but I'm sure if you wander the village, you'll find her being pampered by someone.'

Nicolette got to her feet, an involuntary groan slipping out before she could clamp her mouth closed. She walked over to the window and stared at the roofs of the houses below.

'How nosy are the residents?'

Alice joined her at the window. 'Moderately nosy, why?'

'So if someone for example was to use the fence to access the backyards of the property below, someone might be inclined to call the police? Hypothetically speaking.'

'Well, hypothetically speaking, depending on when this fence climbing was to take place, someone might be able to make sure that everyone is occupied elsewhere.'

'Well, just plucking a number off the top of my head, around 9pm tonight?'

'Done. Although at that time most of the residents are either in bed or about to be, so it's not a hardship.'

'What are you two talking about?' asked Vanessa.

'Nothing,' Nicolette replied. 'Goodbye Alice.'

Vanessa walked her to the elevator.

'I'm going to need that envelope back.'

'What? Why?'

'It's empty. Alice can be a little theatrical. She wanted to see you physically make the decision to continue. I'll transfer the money into your account after you're gone.'

As the elevator doors opened on the ground floor, Nicolette saw a woman carrying a large plastic box through the front door and disappear down a hallway. She looked vaguely familiar, but Nicolette couldn't remember where from. As she tried to work it out another woman came into the foyer wheeling a small trolley behind her. She headed in the same direction.

'It's a craft market.'

Nicolette looked over to the front desk to see the smiling receptionist pointing towards the hallway.

'They're setting up in the dining hall. It's a new thing that management thought would be good for the residents. You know, candles, jewellery, smelly stuff, that sort of thing.'

Nicolette nodded her thanks and started across the foyer. Halfway there she changed direction and headed towards the dining room instead.

It was the words *smelly stuff* that jogged the memory loose.

The dining room was large and brightly lit. All the chairs had been pushed to the walls and people were busily setting out their wares on the white table-clothed tables.

Nicolette spotted someone she recognised on the far side of the room, carefully lifting newspaper-wrapped objects from a plastic box and placing them on the table.

Nicolette approached. 'Hello, Angela.'

Angela Downing looked up, startled. She peered at Nicolette, then recognition dawned. 'You're the investigator, with Mum's cat.'

'Yes, Nicolette Briggs.'

'Right, er, what are you doing here?'

She continued to pull things from the box but didn't unwrap any of them.

'Just visiting someone. I didn't know you were the crafty type.'

Angela laughed. 'I'm not. These aren't mine. I'm just helping out for the day. Honestly, I'm just hoping I don't mess up and sell something for the wrong price.' She leaned in and lowered her voice conspiratorially. 'She's a bit of a nightmare when you make mistakes.'

'How's your mother?'

'She's fine. I think she might finally be settling into her new home.'

'Was she struggling?'

'Oh, not really,' Angela hurried on. 'I mean, she lived in the other house for so many years it's only natural it would take a while for her to get used to living somewhere else. Anyway, I really must finish setting up before we open to the residents.'

She turned her back, leaving Nicolette little choice but to stand there looking like an idiot or walk away.

One of the other tables drew Nicolette's attention. Several small animal figurines were laid out and one piece in the second row had caught her attention.

'May I?' she gestured to the piece.

The woman behind the table nodded and Nicolette picked it up to examine it more closely. It was a figurine of a dog, lying down with its head on its paws. The colour and shape reminded her of Teddy.

'Did you make this?'

'Yes. If you like it, twenty dollars.'

Nicolette placed it back down and dug out her wallet, only to find she had no cash.

'Here's my card,' the woman said. 'You can pay for it later. I'll put it aside for you.'

'Thanks. Do you have anything similar to these?' She showed a photo of Fig and Nero.

'Not yet, but I do commission pieces. Email me.'

Nicolette promised she would, then wandered around the room for a few more minutes. She glanced at Angela's table before leaving, noting that she hadn't made much progress in unpacking her goods. She seemed to be fussing over something but had her back to Nicolette so it was impossible to see what. Nicolette left thinking Angela better hurry if the residents were arriving soon.

Taking the steps down to the driveway, she made a note of the spot along the fence line for later, using a bench as a marker. Then she walked leisurely back to her car.

She followed the road down the hill and parked a few doors along from the old Downing house. There was no longer a police guard, but the door still had tape over it.

Nicolette went to the house next door and knocked.

The elderly neighbour answered, the same suspicious look on his face. Like before, a cell phone was gripped tightly in his hand.

'What do you want? I'm on the phone to my daughter.'

He waved the phone at her and she leaned back slightly to avoid being hit on the side of the head.

'Sorry to disturb you. Do you remember me? I was here the other day asking about a cat.'

'I don't have a cat, never liked them. I prefer dogs, but my daughter is allergic. She's a firefighter, you know.'

'I didn't know that. Good on her. I could never do it.'

The old man looked pleased. 'Yes, well, she's special.' He looked at his hand in surprise. 'Oh yes, I was about to call her.'

'I won't hold you up. I was asking about a cat. You told me she lived next door?'

'Oh, that wretched beast. The worst day ever when Gladys brought that thing home. She's been using my vege garden as a toilet.'

'Gladys?' Nicolette asked innocently.

'What? No, the cat of course. It's not good for the beets. I was glad when she moved, but the damn cat didn't go with her.'

'I was just wondering if you'd seen either of these two people around at all.' Nicolette quickly showed him her phone screen before he could delve into more detail about cat poop and vegetables.

He peered closely, leaning in until the phone was inches from his face.

'I saw the blonde next door a couple of times. The other one was poking around outside with a ladder. I think he was up to no good. I was going to tell my daughter, she's a police officer you know.'

'You must be so proud that both your daughters have careers that help people.'

'Eh? What are you talking about? I only have the one daughter. She's going to be here any minute. You should go.'

'Just one more thing. Can you remember the last time you saw the woman next door?'

'A few days ago. I was opening my curtains and saw her getting in her car. Took off like her tail was on fire.'

'Can you remember what day that was?'

He shrugged. 'The day the woman who lived there after Gladys got up early.'

Nicolette stifled her frustration and thanked the man, who once again proclaimed his daughter was on the phone and he needed to get back to her. Not exactly a reliable witness.

Walking back down the path she spotted Abbie leaving her house, with Emma in a front pack, and holding a bag in each hand. She paused at her front gate and Nicolette hurried along to unlatch it for her.

'Thanks,' Abbie said with a tired smile. 'One thing they never told me was how much baggage babies come with.'

'I know what you mean. I swear it felt like I was leaving home for six months every time I went out with my daughter. Don't tell me you're walking somewhere with all this.'

'Only to the bus stop. My husband took the car to work, and I need to get this one to a Baby and Music session in the city. And...'

'You needed some adult company to keep you sane?' Nicolette guessed.

'Does that make me a bad mother?'

'It makes you a mother. I was nineteen when I had Chloe and for a while I thought I'd never have a conversation again that didn't involve baby talk or talking about the baby. Come on, I'll walk you to the bus stop. I'd offer you a lift, but my car doesn't have a baby seat.'

'Mine does. It's in the back of the car that Gary forgot to tell me he was taking until he walked out the door.'

As they walked past the old Downing house, Abbie looked at it and frowned.

'I've been thinking about something. I don't know if it's important.'

'Let's assume it is,' replied Nicolette.

Abbie shot her a wry smile. 'It's hard to get things in perspective these days. I used to be so detail-orientated. It would drive my workmates crazy. Now I'm pretty sure I'm still wearing yesterday's underwear, and I spent ten minutes this morning looking for the car keys before I remembered my husband had them.'

'I promise you it'll get better. What did you remember?'

'The night before the...' she glanced down at Emma, then mouthed the word *murder* to Nicolette, 'I was up with this one. I think it was just after midnight, and I heard a loud bang. I thought someone had hit our car, so I looked out the front curtain.'

Emma let out a soft cry and began wriggling. Abbie shushed her and waited until she'd settled before continuing.

'I saw a man standing by his car, staring at the Downing house. He yelled something but I couldn't make out what. Then he got into the car and drove away, far too fast for our narrow road.'

'Had you seen him before?'

'I can't be sure.'

'Was it this man?' Nicolette showed her the photo of Grant, Kalliana, and Skylar.

'I don't think so. I mean, it was pretty dark, but he was standing under a streetlight.'

Nicolette thought for a moment. Then she described Thomas Magnusson.

'That sounds more like him, but like I said, it was dark so I couldn't be absolutely certain. I could tell he was angry though. He kicked the fence. And he was waving his hands around, he was clearly upset.'

'Had you seen him around the neighbourhood before that night? Or after it?'

'I don't think so.' She sighed. 'Things were so much nicer when the Downings lived there. Gladys is such a nice lady. She brought me a week's worth of food when Emma was born. She was so upset at having to move.'

'Oh? I understood she wanted to sell the house because it reminded her of her husband.'

They turned the corner at the end of the block and Nicolette saw the bus stop twenty metres away.

'Word around the neighbourhood is her husband took out a mortgage without telling her and she couldn't afford the repayments after he died. The last thing she wanted to do was leave that house. Oh, there's the bus.'

They hustled the last few feet to the bus stop, arriving at the same time as the bus. Nicolette handed over the bags and made sure Abbie was onboard safely, then walked back to her car. She felt like she was finally getting some of the missing pieces to the puzzle and decided to call Dominic.

'Let me guess, you've been arrested again.'

'Not today, but it's still early.'

'What do you want, Nic?'

'How hard are you looking at Thomas Magnusson?'

'You know I can't—'

'Did you know he was seen the night before the murder, outside the house, angry.'

There was silence, then he said, 'How did you find that out?'

'Sleepless mother. And did you know he came to see me wanting to know what I knew about the murder?'

'No, but that doesn't surprise me. He's been pestering me for information and getting nothing. Makes sense he would look for someone else to supply it. I hope you didn't actually tell him anything.'

'Of course not. So how hard are you looking at Thomas?'

'Nic!'

'Okay, okay, you don't need to say anything. How about you grunt once for very hard and twice for he's been dismissed from consideration.'

'I'm not one of your dogs.'

'No, they're better trained,' she muttered.

'Goodbye, Nicolette.'

'Wait, I'm sorry, Dom. The last twenty-four hours have been a little stressful. Did you know about the connection between Grant Reed, Kalliana Magnusson, and Skylar Goodman?'

'What connection?'

She told him about the photo she'd found online.

There was a long pause, then Dominic said, 'Mum was right, you would make a good detective.'

'I am a good detective.'

'I meant a proper one.'

She hung up on him and threw her phone onto the passenger seat, where it bounced, hit the door, and slid into the gap between the door and the seat.

It shouldn't still get under her skin that some of her family considered what she did as a cute little hobby, a phase she was going through before getting a real job. But it did. What she did was important. And despite what they thought, it wasn't just finding lost cats or missing dogs. More often than not her cases required the same amount of investigative skills as any other detective's case.

Nicolette sighed.

Stupid family getting under her stupid skin.

A faint ringing came from somewhere in the car and she dove across the seat and shoved her hand into the gap to try and snag her phone. She managed to pinch it between two fingers and pull it free, answering without looking at the screen.

'Ms Briggs? Thomas Magnusson. Have I caught you at a bad time?'

Just suffering an existential crisis, she thought. 'Not at all. What can I do for you?'

'I wanted to apologise for waylaying you outside the police station and was wondering if you'd heard anything further.'

'I've found out a few things. For example, that you were at the house the night before Kalliana died, and there was some sort of argument.'

There was a short pause before he replied, 'more like a robust discussion.'

'Most robust discussions don't involve yelling outside a house at midnight.'

Thomas chuckled. 'Alright, you got me. Kalliana and I had dinner to discuss some business, then had a disagreement, but I didn't kill her. It wouldn't be terribly smart of me to commit murder, then stand outside the house shouting about it.'

'What was the disagreement about?'

'Does it matter now she's dead?'

'Possibly not, or it might point to a motive.'

He laughed again. 'I knew approaching you was going to come back to bite me. Alright, as I told the police, I didn't approve of some of Kalliana's relationship choices. She thought I was interfering, which in hindsight I was, and we quarrelled. It wasn't the first time... and I didn't believe it would be the last. Although sadly that was the case.'

Nicolette thought he sounded more annoyed than regretful.

'Either way, it was simply a case of family quarrelling. Surely you fight with yours.'

Nicolette didn't reply.

'I didn't kill my cousin.'

'What sort of car do you drive?' she asked.

'Oh, it's an Outlander. And before you ask, yes my car was outside the house that night, because as you so rightly pointed out, so was I.'

She tried to make sense of the split-second jumble of images from the hit and run, but even if she had gotten a clear look, cars were not her thing. She wasn't exactly sure what an Outlander looked like.

'What were you fighting about?'

Thomas sighed. 'Like I said, we didn't see eye to eye on her relationship choices.'

She waited for him to elaborate and when it looked like he wasn't going to she said, 'Did it involve Grant Reed or Skylar Johnson?'

It took so long for him to answer she pulled her phone away to check the screen that he was still there.

'One was a distraction and the other a danger,' he finally said.

'Danger?'

'To Kalliana's mental health, not her life,' clarified Thomas. 'I don't know either of them well, but some of the stories my cousin told led to me forming a less than favourable opinion of both of them.'

'Yet you employed Grant Reed to install cameras in the house in Wadestown.'

'That was Kalliana's idea. Although personally I think it was his idea, especially the cameras inside. Wadestown is not exactly known for its high crime rate. I believe Grant Reed persuaded her to have them installed.'

'For the money?' asked Nicolette.

'Possibly, although I suspect a more nefarious reason.'

She didn't think anyone used the word nefarious anymore, but he'd managed to easily slip it into the conversation.

'You think he wanted to watch her,' she said.

'All I know is that I did not authorise the installation of any indoor cameras.'

A sharp tune came down the phone line.

'Excuse me, that's my other phone. Please keep me apprised.'

He hung up before she could respond.

As she put her phone onto the passenger seat, she realised she hadn't asked an obvious question. Who'd asked Grant Reed to take the cameras down? It wasn't Kalliana Magnusson, because she was already dead. Unless Grant had lied. One theory was he'd killed Kalliana himself, then taken the cameras to remove any trace of him at the house. But then who killed Grant?

TWENTY

Nicolette drummed the steering wheel in frustration. All the questions were going round and round and ending up in the same spot. She decided to go back to the park where Grant was murdered. Maybe something there would jog her memory, or better yet, maybe the killer dropped a business card which the police miraculously missed.

As she stood near the spot where Grant Reed had died, neither appeared likely. At least the lack of police or cordon tape meant she was free to poke around. It hadn't rained since the murder and, although the body was long gone, a dark stain on the grass remained. Nicolette shuddered and tried not to look at it.

She hadn't seen anyone else lurking around the field that day, so the murderer had to have been hidden in the shrubbery. Carefully pushing between two chest-high bushes, she came to a tiny space surrounded by shrubbery. The ground was hard and dry. There was no sign of anyone having been in there. Turning, she gently lifted a branch, exposing a clear view across the field to the playground and the bench where she and Grant had sat. It was also just a couple of steps to where his body had fallen to the ground.

Had the killer stepped briefly into the open to commit murder? Or had Grant got too close to the bush and it had been as simple as pushing a knife through the branches and into Grant's chest?

Nicolette forced her way out of the bushes. It wasn't quick or quiet, her T-shirt snagged on a branch and the shaking leaves sounded like rain falling. There's no way she would have heard it from the other side of the park, but Grant would surely have noticed someone coming out. Why would he just have stood there while someone came at him with a knife? Unless he knew the person.

She pushed back into cover and went deeper. The bushes lasted a few metres before opening onto a footpath where the road twisted away in both directions. Across the road, a row of houses sat back from the curb. The killer could have parked here, murdered Grant, then driven off. But how did they know Grant would come over to this side of the field?

She checked her watch. It must be almost time to...

She checked her watch again, the simple turn of the wrist sparking a memory. Grant had checked his watch twice. Had he arranged to meet someone at a particular time? Was that why he'd gone for the run? Even at the time, she'd thought it strange that he'd decided the best time for a jog was in the middle of their conversation.

She needed to see his phone. It would be in the police evidence locker. Phelps would rather rip off all his toenails than let her look at it and Dom was on thin ice there already so there was no way he would do her a favour.

Nicolette pushed back into the bushes and came out the other side just in time to startle a little boy. He fell over and promptly burst into tears.

'I'm so sorry,' Nicolette said.

'Jasper, you're alright,' his mother hustled over and plucked him off the ground, where he quickly decided life wasn't too bad after all.

'I didn't mean to scare him.'

The woman shrugged. 'If it wasn't you, it would have been a butterfly, or the grass moving in the wrong direction. He's going through a big scared-of-everything phase.'

'My dogs do that.'

The woman frowned, then her eyes narrowed widened in recognition. 'You're the woman who was talking to the man before he was murdered.'

'Murdered,' Jasper repeated.

'That was you sitting over there?' asked Nicolette. 'Thanks for telling the police I wasn't anywhere near him when that happened.'

The woman shrugged again. 'I also told them you'd hit him.'

'*Assaulted* was the term the police used.'

'*Gave him what he deserved* was what I said. Did he really take your dog?'

'Yes, but Teddy is alright. Were you here when he arrived?'

'Sure was. We'd already been on the swings for two songs. Jasper gets a three-song limit on the swings, otherwise he'd be there all day.'

'Swings,' Jasper repeated and reached two hands out in the direction of the playground.

'In a minute, honey.'

'Let's walk and talk. I remember what my daughter was like when she saw a playground. It's like catnip for kids.'

'Catnip for kids,' the woman repeated. 'So accurate.'

She placed Jasper on the ground and he immediately ran towards the playground, occasionally falling over when his legs couldn't match the speed his brain wanted them to go.

'You were two songs in,' prompted Nicolette.

'Yes, anyway I saw the man approach, well, mainly the dog to be honest. Jasper wants to hug every dog he meets and doesn't always wait to ask permission. He doesn't seem to be scared of dogs yet. I was planning to go over and ask after we'd finished on the swings, but Jasper got distracted by the slide.'

'Did you see him make any calls?'

'Yes, I think he did make a call. Either that or he was crazy.'

Nicolette blinked. 'Sorry?'

'He was talking into his watch. I assumed it was one of those smart watches that can take and send messages and calls. I had one once. Until Jasper decided to use it as a paint brush.'

Nicolette felt a hint of triumph. She was on the right track. He hadn't been on the other side of the field by accident. He definitely knew his killer.

Her phone rang and she excused herself to take the call. 'Hey, Archie.'

'Tell me I'm brilliant.'

'You're brilliant.'

'Aw shucks, you don't need to say that.'

'Brilliant but needy.'

'Okay, that's fair. I did some digging into the convention in Australia the two women were at. There were a bunch of news articles about hotel guests being robbed around the same time as the convention.'

'Okay,' Nicolette replied uncertainly.

'You're unimpressed, but that's just the warmup. You remember that other photo we found? The two girls with the guy that stole Teddy?'

'Sure.'

'I managed to track down where it was taken.'

'Where? How?'

'Did you not just hear how brilliant I am? I managed to figure out where that was taken as well. Melbourne, six months after the other picture. I checked on conventions happening at the same time and I found one where a number of thefts reported at the hotel.'

'They were thieves,' Nicolette said.

'Or the unluckiest people around.'

'So, thieves.'

'Given that the conferences were run by different people and held in different cities, then that does seem most likely.'

'You're brilliant.'

'I know.' Archie hung up, having captured praise and the last word.

Nicolette thanked the woman who was singing 'Twinkle Twinkle Little Star' and pushing her son on the swings, then headed to her car. By the time she got there the headache that had been threatening was playing the drums inside her head. She rummaged through the glovebox for her emergency supply of painkillers, finally finding the box underneath an overdue reminder for a car service. It was empty.

'Chloe!'

With a sigh of despair, she leaned her forehead on the steering wheel and closed her eyes.

Only to open them a few seconds later.

She'd been doing this entire investigation with one hand tied behind her back. And that was all going to change at 9pm that night.

TWENTY ONE

There were too many lights on for her liking but by hugging the fence line Nicolette was able to get from the main gate to the rose garden with relative confidence that she hadn't been spotted. The weather at least had cooperated by being cloudy. She wore dark clothes, carried a bag, and was currently cruising on pharmacy pain relief.

Reaching the right spot on the fence, she paused to look around. Alice had been right. The Silvermoon Retirement Village was quiet, except... She caught movement out of the corner of her eye. Dropping to the ground, she watched a man striding towards the exercise building. He was too far away and too focussed on his destination to spot her but, just in case, she waited until he was inside and counted to thirty before springing to her feet.

Normally she would have leapt up and pulled herself over, but thanks to her injuries that wasn't possible. Instead she had brought a short step-ladder that she had purchased years earlier for outings such as these. Even with the assist she still grimaced at the impact on her knee when she hit the ground on the other side. Rubbing her leg, she surveyed the Downing backyard. All was quiet here just as expected. The houses either side were dark as well.

Swiftly crossing the lawn, she picked the back door lock and slipped inside. Picking a lock was never as easy as it looked in the movies, but she practiced at home every week.

The kitchen was cold and dark. Reaching into her pocket, she pulled out a small torch and switched it on, keeping it low. The thin beam of light was unlikely to be seen from outside, but she moved quickly anyway. Her search revealed nothing other than a lot of takeaway boxes in the refrigerator. Nicolette scanned the walls by the ceiling and spotted a small security camera. She frowned. Instead of facing into the kitchen, the camera was pointed towards the hallway. But at that angle it couldn't possibly capture everything, only the first two doors in the hallway.

The first door was the bathroom. There was no indication that a few days ago a dead body had lain here. There was also no sign of an oil diffuser, although Nicolette spotted a ring on the wooden bench top. She also spotted a small Bluetooth speaker on the windowsill. That was probably where the music Abby had heard from the front door came from. As she surveyed the room a shiver went down her spine and she became aware of how quiet the house was. She gave the bathroom one more look, then moved further into the house.

The second door opened into a room with no external windows. It was only about two metres square and was completely empty. The walls were painted pale blue and the ceiling was white and Nicolette remembered Gladys Downing saying the new owner had wanted to measure up this one room. Her frown deepened.

Closing the door behind her she switched on the overhead light, confident it wouldn't be seen from outside.

'Why this room?' she murmured.

She was about to head out again when something caught her eye. She paused. At first she thought it was a trick of the light. She ran her flashlight over it. Examining one wall then the next, she swept the light from the floor up as high as her stiff muscles would allow. She was almost definitely sure. The paint on one wall was a slightly different shade to the others. The question was, assuming she wasn't imagining it, why?

She ran a hand over the surface and pushed gently. Nothing happened. She rapped it with her knuckles, then knocked on the other walls. There was a definite sound difference. The differently painted wall sounded hollow.

She spent ten minutes testing every inch of the wall, but the secret door that she was positive existed refused to reveal itself.

'You're losing it Briggs,' she muttered.

Despite her brain telling her she was wrong, her gut told her there was something more to this. Grant had asked to measure this particular room. The camera in the kitchen was pointed towards this door. It couldn't be a coincidence.

So she started again, examining the wall furthest from the door, and found it almost immediately. There was a hole in the baseboard, small enough for her to have missed it the first time. She lay down to get a better view and shone her torch directly onto it. Something glinted in the light. Getting to her feet she went into the kitchen to find something she could poke into the hole. All the cutlery was too big, but she found a short, spiked object with a large flat head. She recognised it as a baking skewer although, since she didn't bake, she'd never actually used one.

The skewer slid easily into the hole in the wall. When she felt resistance, she pushed firmly. There was a click and one side of the wall popped out an inch. Still on her knees she gripped the edge and pulled. It swung open on a hinge to reveal a narrow cavity. Narrow but not empty. Floor to ceiling shelves were crammed with plastic boxes. Nicolette opened one at random and gasped. It was filled with diamond earrings. The next one held an emerald necklace, and a third contained Australian one-hundred-dollar bank notes. She flicked through and stopped counting at eleven hundred with most of the pile still to go.

Carefully she replaced everything and closed the wall back up. Several things were beginning to slide into place. But they raised more questions. The biggest one was how Dominic was going to react to her breaking into a crime scene.

Not well was the answer.

'Now you could get angry at me.'

'I am—'

'Or,' she hurried on, 'you can accept that all those highly trained police officers missed a wall full of stolen merchandise in the room next to where a woman was murdered.'

There was silence as he struggled to find a good argument. 'You shouldn't have been in there anyway. I'm on my way. Are you going to wait there for me?'

'I can't, I've got something else to do. Besides, I was never here. You, being the clever detective that you are, acted on a hunch, and found this hidden compartment. You might want to reach out to the Sydney police next. They should be able to match some of the items against those stolen during a conference at the start of ... oh I don't know... 2020.'

He didn't reply.

'You have also discovered a motive for the murder,' Nicolette added.

'Damn it, Nic, the only thing I hate more than you breaking the law is when you're right about it. What do you mean about Sydney?'

She briefed him on everything she'd found out.

He swore again. 'Why didn't we know this?'

'Because you had no reason to speak to the previous owner of the house.'

'But we still should have checked.'

His tone disturbed her. Much as she liked one upping her brother, she didn't like seeing him doubting himself.

'Look, we both know you're the second-best detective in the family,' she said, hoping the well-worn joke would lift his spirits. 'And this puts Skylar Goodman in the frame as lead suspect.'

Dominic sighed. 'I'd tell you not to touch anything else, but you've already left enough trace evidence around the place to raise some difficult questions. Please don't screw things up further.'

'Bye, Dom.' She hung up and slipped her phone away.

Leaving the small room, she stopped to wipe her fingerprints from the door handle, then walked quickly to the back door. Just as she was about to open it, she looked down and stopped. She'd seen plenty of cat doors over the years, and this one had been installed a while ago. It had a dial to turn to either lock or unlock the door from the inside. What had caught her attention was that the cat door was locked. Maybe the lock was broken.

Squatting, she pushed on the cat door from the outside. It didn't budge.

'How did Maddy get in?' she said to herself.

She called Dom back who sounded more annoyed than ever when she told him her discovery.

'I'm trying to solve a murder case and you're worried about how a damn cat got into the house. Get out now, Nic, or I'll arrest you myself.'

'You wouldn't!'

'Wouldn't I?'

'Mum would never forgive you.'

'She'd understand,' he shot back. 'She's surprised it hasn't happened already.'

'Yeah well, I could say the same about her.'

'What are you talking about?'

'I don't know!'

'Nic, you got lucky, but luck eventually runs out. Get out of the house now.'

He hung up and it took all her restraint not to slam the door behind her. She was halfway across the lawn before she realised she was holding her breath.

She stopped, blinking away a rogue tear or two. How dare he imply her investigative skills were lucky. She wanted to hit something, more specifically someone, but any object would do. She grabbed her phone and pulled up her mother's number, then clenched her fist and changed to her home number. When the answer phone clicked in Nicolette opened her mouth, ready to let out years of frustration. Then she hung up. She couldn't risk the neighbours hearing her. And Chloe was at home. She didn't need to listen to her mother's frustration.

She knew she was a disappointment to her mother. She also knew that several other members of her family thought she was wasting her life playing detective instead of getting a real job. She wasn't sure even she fully understood what drove her to try and protect those that couldn't protect themselves. Or maybe she did. Maybe she didn't want to raise Chloe in a world where bad people got away with things. Her anger gave away to a rueful smile. She was a walking cliché. She would die of embarrassment if she said that to her mother.

The truth was she felt like she was doing good. And Chloe wasn't deprived of anything. And that was enough. But with a disapproving family it was tiring constantly having to remind herself of that. She'd always thought Dominic was different. She thought he (almost) got her. It was disappointing to find out he was as bad as the rest.

Well, the best way to show them would be to solve the case before her brother did. And now she had another piece of the puzzle. If the cat door was locked, how did Maddy get into the house and become poisoned?

Nicolette felt like she already had the answer, but it remained frustratingly out of sight in the corner of her mind.

She checked her watch and saw that she'd been standing in the open for five minutes. Taking a deep breath, she forced herself to move. Not towards the back fence, but the one separating the old Downing house from the neighbour.

She was over the fence and across the lawn in a few seconds, repeating the action twice more, before dropping to the ground at her destination. A startled barking split the silence.

'Hush, baby,' she said quietly.

The dog growled and backed away nervously.

'It's okay, baby, good boy.'

She glanced at the house, but there was no sign of life within. Reaching into her bag she withdrew a small plastic bag filled with bits of sausage. She held a piece out to the dog who crept forward and gently took it from her hand.

'Aren't you a clever boy.'

The dog's tail gave a tentative wag as he took a second piece of sausage. She continued to feed him the rest of the bag's contents as she scratched behind his ear with one hand, then withdrew a harness from her bag. Slowly and carefully she fitted the dog with the harness, making sure it was fixed tightly without hurting him.

'Ready to go on an adventure?'

That earned Nicolette a lick on the hand.

'Okay, this is going to be strange, but I promise you'll be safe, and fed, and loved.'

She grabbed the harness and tensed her leg muscles.

'Here we go, baby.'

With a grunt, she picked the dog up and swung him onto her back, slipping her arms through the straps as she went. He was surprisingly light, but Nicolette knew the next part was going to hurt.

'Ready, baby?'

She felt the dog shudder, and whispered encouragement as she walked over to the back fence and looked up. It was taller than she remembered. For a second, she thought about taking the dog out the front and onto the street. But she couldn't risk being seen. She refused to get her brother into trouble, no matter how annoyed she was with him. Catching her stealing a dog was just the thing Phelps would use to undermine Dominic's career.

The fence might have been high, but she had an advantage. Going to the corner of the property she carefully climbed the side fence, pressing both hands onto the wood of the back fence to help her balance. Aware of how exposed she was, and the wriggling dog on her back, Nicolette reached up and managed to hook her fingers onto the top of the fence. Cursing her height, she went up on her tip toes... and slipped. A shooting pain down her side reminded her of her injuries.

For the longest moment she teetered.

The dog yelped and she felt herself slip further. Just as she was about jump down, she managed to right herself.

'It's okay, baby.' Although it wasn't clear if she was talking to the dog or herself.

To her right came a sudden flare of light. The back light in the house two doors down had switched on.

Bending her legs slightly she tensed, then jumped as high as she could, catching the top of the fence with her hands, and scrabbling with her feet, she dragged herself up. She paused on the top, panting. A movement caught her eye and she watched a black and white cat cross the back lawn and jump a fence with ease that made Nicolette curse.

Probably going home, Nicolette thought. The elusive thought from earlier came back, teasingly staying just out of reach.

Dropping to the ground on the Silvermoon side, she shrugged off the harness and released the dog. He seemed relatively relaxed about the adventure, more so when Nicolette delved into her bag and retrieved a second bag of sausage which the dog devoured. Nicolette remained on her knees, every ragged breath sending fresh waves of pain through her ribs. If she was going to do this sort of thing again she needed to invest in some new equipment. Something she could use on both sides on the fence. Or at the very least not get hit by any more cars.

Releasing the dog from the harness, she clipped a leash to the collar and lead him out the Silvermoon gates and onto the main road.

Retrieving her phone, she called an acquaintance from the SPCA, claiming she'd found a dog wandering the streets.

'Wandering, eh? Okay, bring him in.'

Andrew often joked that she was the luckiest person in the world with the number of animals Nicolette had just happened to come across wandering the street. But he was a softie who knew not to ask too many questions. He'd get the dog checked out by a vet, and if there was a cause for concern they would persuade the owner to give him up for adoption. And if not, Nicolette would just have to find him wandering the street again.

Nicolette was loading the dog into her car, which she'd parked several streets away, when the elusive thought finally presented itself.

'No,' she said to the empty car.

She needed more information and there was one person who could provide it.

TWENTY-TWO

'This is nice, you didn't need to pay though.'

Nicolette smiled at Gladys Downing as the older woman took a big bite of chocolate cake.

'My daughter doesn't let me eat chocolate cake anymore,' Gladys said, wiping her mouth on a napkin. 'She says it's for my own good, but I think she likes sucking the enjoyment out of the world.'

'Sounds like my mother,' replied Nicolette.

They grinned at each other and Nicolette waited for Gladys to finish a second bite of cake before pressing on.

'I was hoping you could provide me with some insight into Maddy – sorry Kanga's – habits.'

'Yes, so you said on the phone, dear, but I don't understand why. She's alright now, isn't she? Whatever happened was just a terrible accident.'

'You're right, she is fine, but I haven't found out who poisoned her, accident or not, and I'd like to avoid it happening to any other animals. If you could just clear a few things up while you finish that delicious looking cake? Seriously, is that the richest thing you've ever tasted? I wish I'd gotten a piece now.'

Gladys put her hand over the cake. 'This was the last bit.'

She looked so fierce that Nicolette had to smother a smile. 'It's okay,' she said. 'I need to watch what I'm eating anyway. It's my daughter's birthday dinner tonight and I'm bound to eat too many things I shouldn't.'

A look of relief came over Gladys' face and Nicolette wondered just how strict Angela Downing was with her mother.

'It was first noticed that Kanga was unwell last Friday. When was the last time you saw her before that?'

'Oh, I'm not sure. She's always flitting in and out. Let me think. It must have been the night before. She wasn't home when I got up on Friday morning but I definitely remember feeding her some treats before going to bed.'

'Did she often wander off without breakfast?'

'Angela must have given her breakfast that day. I remember because there was an empty can of cat food on the bench that wasn't there the night before, and I was annoyed at Angela for feeding Kanga the whole can. She is a food hog you see. She'll eat everything put down in front of her, even when she shouldn't. She had a problem with her weight for a while and the vet was clear that she needed to lose it or she would die young.'

'Did Angela often feed her?'

Gladys frowned. 'No. She's never liked Kanga. I just thought she was doing something nice for me. I'd slept in that day, you see. I was a bit under the weather.'

'Oh dear,' Nicolette said. 'It must be nice to have someone in the house to look after you.'

'It is,' Gladys said unconvincingly.

'I don't have the best relationship with my mother, but I know if she needed me, I'd be there for her.'

'Reluctantly,' Gladys finished for her.

Nicolette nodded slowly. 'Maybe a little, but I'd still be there.'

'Angela is a good girl. But she was ever so angry with me when I sold the house.'

'Do you know why?'

'It was her childhood home,' Gladys said, as if that explained her daughter's reaction.

Personally Nicolette had no real sentimental attachment to her childhood home, but she could understand how others saw things differently.

'But it was your home for longer. It must have been hard to give up,' she said.

Gladys wiped her mouth and shrugged sadly. 'It wasn't like I had a choice. My husband was a wonderful man, with a terrible sense of money. And I couldn't afford to pay a mortgage, not on a government pension. Now I have enough to live comfortably once my apartment is ready at the retirement village.'

'Silvermoon?'

Gladys laughed. 'That place is out of my price range. But I'm happy with where I'm going.' She glanced around with a guilty expression then leaned in. 'I love my daughter, but she's not the easiest person to live with. Honestly I thought her hobby would make her relax more, but she's still so tightly wound. Muttering about buying the house back. I told her, it's gone, time to move on, but she just glares at me. I suppose I shouldn't have said that. You won't tell her will you?'

'I promise I won't. Thank you for taking the time to talk to me.'

'Of course, I'd do anything for cake. Oh dear, that makes me sound terrible, doesn't it?'

'Not at all, between you and me, I'd do anything for cake as well.'

Nicolette stood up and was about to say goodbye when she remembered one more question she wanted to ask. 'I saw Angela at the Silvermoon Retirement Village doing some sort of craft market. Is that her hobby?'

Gladys snorted. 'She was always a sensible girl growing up, but now it's all oils and health kicks.'

Nicolette felt a flutter of triumph. 'You mean essential oils?' When the other woman nodded, she pressed on. 'Does she make her own?'

'Yes, locked away in the bathroom for hours at a time cooking up things. If you ask me they all smell the same. I mean, what does a *tropical sunset* even smell like?'

'No idea, I share my bathroom with a fourteen-year-old so it smells of face cleanser and apple shampoo.'

'I miss those days.'

Nicolette walked away struggling to quell the triumphant feeling bubbling up inside of her. However, every step she took towards her car brought fresh questions. Like, would buying someone's childhood home be enough to make you a target for murder? And if so, then what was the motive for killing Grant?

She went to call Dominic, but stopped before the call could connect. It was still just suspicions and theories. She had nothing concrete to pin Angela Downing to the murder of Kalliana Magnusson.

Her phone trilled with the ring tone she'd assigned to Chloe.

'Mum, what are you doing? We have to leave soon for dinner.'

Nicolette glanced at her watch before taking a deep breath. 'Chloe, dinner is in five hours.'

'Yes, but my hair appointment is in forty minutes.'

Nicolette winced. She'd completely forgotten Chloe wanted to get her hair styled for the big day,

'And you haven't even wished me happy birthday or given me a present.'

'That's not true,' protested Nicolette. 'I wished you happy birthday this morning.'

'Was it before ten? You know I don't function before ten on a Saturday.'

'Your inability to hear it doesn't negate that I said it.'

'Are you going to be home to take me to the hairdresser?'

'I'm already on the way,' Nicolette lied.

'I can't hear you driving.'

'I'm going to lose you, I'm driving through a tunnel.'

'You're lying.'

'See– u– oon.'

She hung up and jumped into the car, mentally calculating how long it would take to get home, and then get back to Johnsonville to the hairdresser. If she didn't hit traffic, she'd just make it.

They pulled up outside the hairdresser's ten minutes late for the appointment. The temperature in the car rose several degrees after Chloe got out and slammed the door. Like any teenager, she seemed to forget where the funds for the haircut and dinner that night were coming from, and assumed Nicolette would pay for everything regardless of the iciness between them.

By the time Nicolette had found a park and walked into the shop, Chloe was in the seat chatting away excitedly about her dinner plans. Nicolette waved to Holly. She'd been cutting their hair since Chloe could sit in the seat by herself.

Nicolette was about to send Dominic a message telling him of her suspicions around Angela Downing, but then remembered she currently wasn't talking to her brother. And there was no way she was going to talk to Detective Senior Sergeant Pain in the Butt. He wouldn't listen anyway, let alone take action.

As she watched the hairdresser work magic on Chloe's hair, Nicolette's mood slipped lower. Her body hurt, her head hurt, she had no proof. There was a reason she didn't do humans.

'Mum!'

She roused herself from the pity party to see Chloe and the hairdresser watching her.

'What do you think?'

Nicolette smiled. 'I think you look beautiful.'

Chloe rolled her eyes but seemed pleased at the compliment.

'For an ungrateful urchin,' Nicolette added.

'What's an urchin?'

'A mischievous ragged youngster,' said Holly.

'That sounds about right. I'm treated no better than the dogs she brings home. Do you know, she locks me in the bedroom every night with newspaper for a toilet.'

Holly grinned at her. 'Newspaper? Lucky, my parents used to lock me in the shed with nothing to eat but bugs.'

'Really?'

Holly laughed and patted her on the shoulder. 'It's about as true as what you said about your Mum.'

Chloe nodded, then gave Nicolette a sly smile. 'Do you have time to do my mum's hair? It's looking a bit flat and tangled.'

'You know those tracksuit pants of mine that you hate?'

'The red ones with the rips in the knees?'

'Yeah, I'm thinking I might wear those tonight.'

'You wouldn't.'

'It'll distract people from my flat, tangled hair,' Nicolette said innocently.

Chloe glared at her then slumped in her chair. 'Fine, you win. Your hair looks good.'

'But not so good you aren't due for a cut,' Holly quickly added.

Nicolette reluctantly made an appointment as she paid for Chloe's haircut, then trailed her daughter through the mall, only being acknowledged when it came to paying for things. By the time they'd finished Chloe had forgiven her enough to chat excitedly all the way back home.

Nicolette listened to roughly half of it. The other half of the time she was formulating and discarding various ideas for the next steps in her investigation.

She pushed it all aside when she pulled into the driveway and saw a car parked there. Visitors were scarce enough that she knew all the regular cars. This one looked familiar but she couldn't place it.

'Wait here,' she said as she got out of the car.

'What? Why?'

Ignoring Chloe, she cautiously approached the car. There was no one in it. Walking around the outside she checked for damage but there was nothing resembling a Nicolette-sized dent.

'Mum, what's going on?'

Nicolette jumped and rounded on her daughter standing right behind her.

'I told you to stay in the car.'

'Yeah, and you left it unlocked, so not so safe.'

'You could have locked it yourself.'

'Then how could I ask you what's going on from all the way over there?'

'Nothing's going on.'

'Yeah, like I believe that.'

'Just stay behind me.'

Nicolette crept to the side of the house. It was too quiet. By now, there should have been three excited dogs racing up and down the fence line. She cocked her head and listened intently.

There was a low murmuring from the back of the house.

'Get your phone out,' she whispered to Chloe.

'Why? So I can take a photo of you getting murdered?'

'So you can call for help. And after this we're going to talk about the videos you're watching online.'

Nicolette carefully climbed the fence and inched along the side of the house. The murmuring got louder but she couldn't make out what was being said.

All sense of stealth went out the window when she heard a whimper. She barged around the corner, fists raised, eyes flashing, ready to deal to the person hurting her dogs.

And stopped dead.

Sitting on the lawn surrounded by dogs in various states of bliss, sat Simon Boland. He paused from rubbing Teddy's stomach and smiled at Nicolette.

'Hi, sorry to drop in unannounced, I wanted to check on the patient.'

Nicolette felt a pang of irritation watching the dogs she'd rescued from horrible situations cavorting around a man they barely knew.

'Shall I call the police now?' Chloe asked.

'Oh, shut up,' Nicolette replied.

Simon stood up and attempted to brush dog hair off his pants. 'I should have called first, but I was driving past and stopped on a whim. When I saw the dogs at the fence, I thought a quick check up wouldn't hurt. I didn't mean to overstep.'

'It's fine.'

'Ah,' Simon said. 'Never have two words so much meant the opposite. Nero's leg is healing fine, and I'm late so I'll be going.'

Chloe nudged her mother in the ribs.

'What?' Nicolette whispered to her.

'Don't be rude to the hot vet.'

'He's not hot.'

'He is so hot.'

'I'm not having this conversation with you right now. Or ever.'

'Well, I think I...'

In horror Nicolette realised their whispered conversation hadn't been as whispered as she'd thought. Simon's cheeks were red as he stepped past. He paused for a moment to look her in the eyes.

'Just for the record, I don't think I'm hot either.'

He moved off before she could stammer an apology.

'You should come to my birthday dinner tonight,' Chloe called after him.

'What?'

'Nothing, she's young and uneducated.'

'Oh.'

'I'm sending her to Boarding school tomorrow, far, far away.'

'It's my birthday, and you said I could invite anyone I wanted.'

Nicolette pushed her daughter behind her. 'Far, far way.'

Simon laughed then easily vaulted the fence. Nicolette waited until she heard the car engine start before turning around.

'What was that?'

'One of us should have a date tonight,' Chloe replied with a shrug. 'And you won't let me bring one, so it'll have to be you.'

Nicolette glared at her daughter. 'For a start, when *I* decide I'm going on a date, chaperoning a bunch of teenagers won't be part of the plan. As for you.' She turned her glare on the dogs. 'Where's the loyalty?'

'Mum, you're scaring Fig.'

Fig's head and tail had dropped and she whined softly.

Nicolette dropped her to knees and opened her arms. Teddy and Nero immediately swamped her and after a moment Fig slunk in for a pat.

'Sorry, baby,' she murmured as she scratched behind Fig's ears. 'Sometimes I overreact.'

Fig licked her cheek to show she was forgiven and Nicolette felt her stomach unclench.

'Sorry, Mum,' Chloe said, sitting on the grass beside her. 'I just want you to be happy.'

'What makes you think I'm not happy?'

Chloe rocked back slightly as Nero leaned on her. She scratched his rump and he flopped onto her lap. 'I've seen you worrying about money, and I know it costs a lot to send me to college, and I...'

'You think a man will take my mind off all of that?'

Chloe grinned. 'It sounds stupid now you say it.'

'Listen to me, Chloe Mackenzie Briggs. You and these three maniacs are all I need to be happy. And you're going to go to that school and get a good education and then get a high powered job that pays squillions of dollars so I can retire and live off you for the rest of my life.'

'Deal.' She grinned again. 'It'll be like my version of taking in strays.' She pushed Nero away and jumped to her feet. 'I'm going to try on outfits for tonight.'

'I wasn't kidding about Boarding school,' Nicolette called after her.

'Yes you were,' Chloe yelled back.

Nicolette stayed on the lawn for a while longer, enjoying the sun and the company. The dogs cuddled up next to her and she let her mind wander. Slowly her brain started drifting through fragments from the last few days. Things that people said or saw, things she'd seen herself, things that didn't make sense.

Somewhere along the way, her mind drifted too far, and she fell asleep.

TWENTY THREE

Chloe's birthday dinner went well. The biggest surprise for Nicolette was how Chloe and her friends welcomed Kirsten, the girl who according to her knowledgeable daughter, no one liked. It had been a little awkward at the beginning, but after a while Kirsten had joined in on the conversation and by the end of dinner it was like they had all been friends forever. When Nicolette asked her about it on the way home, Chloe had shrugged, and said, 'She's not that bad.' Which was teenager for Kirsten was on her way to becoming part of the inner circle.

Sunday morning Nicolette went for a long walk with the dogs. When she got back Chloe was still in bed, so Nicolette sent Teddy in. Seconds later there was a yelp followed by a demand for Teddy to stop breathing on her. A minute later, Chloe staggered into the kitchen.

'How is it that you went to bed before me, and yet you still look like you haven't slept in days?'

'Luck?' Chloe replied as she slid onto a stool and slumped her head onto her hands.

'You're in charge of the dogs today, I have to go out.'

'Where are you going? Can I come?'

Nicolette eyed her daughter. 'I'm not going near any clothes shops.'

'Never mind then. Where are you going?'

'Just a couple of errands to do with the case.'

Chloe raised her head with a look of concern. 'Be careful.'

'Always, kiddo.'

'Kiddo?'

'Trying it out. So that's a no?'

'No.'

'Fair enough.'

Nicolette climbed into the car and read the message on her phone once. *I have some information. Meet me tomorrow at 12pm outside Te Papa. Thomas Magnusson.*

She wondered again why he didn't just take his information to the police. Since she hadn't ruled him out as a suspect, was it was a smart move meeting with him? But he'd suggested a public place, so she thought she'd be safe.

She turned the key. There was a clicking sound but the car didn't start.

'Come on, I just got you fixed.'

She tried again with the same result. She got out and looked under the bonnet, without having any clue what she was looking at. Nothing screamed to her "I'm broken". She slammed it shut and got back behind the wheel.

'Come on you piece of....'

The engine coughed into life. She didn't waste any time, slipping it into reverse and pulling out of the driveway before the engine could change its mind.

She spent the drive into the city alternating between worrying about the case and worrying about how she was going to afford a new car, because this one was definitely on its last tyres.

She hadn't solved either problem by the time she parked.

Thomas Magnusson sat on a bench seat enjoying the sun in designer sunglasses and clothes that were probably worth more than her car. He smiled as she approached.

'Thank you for coming. I have arranged for a private meeting room upstairs where we can talk.'

Nicolette couldn't detect anything sinister in his words, but that didn't mean they weren't there.

'I've found that nowhere is more private than a stroll on the waterfront,' she replied. 'People are usually too caught up in their own thing to listen to anyone else. Shall we?'

Not waiting for him to agree, she set off around the side of the building.

After a short distance he caught up with her.

'You are determined. You remind me of my cousin. She too had the right mix of stubbornness and self-belief. Very well, a walk in the sun it is.'

'Can I ask you a question? Where is your accent from?'

'Accent?' he replied with a startled expression. Suddenly he chuckled and when he spoke again his voice had a distinct New Zealand twang. 'Originally I'm from Whitianga, but that doesn't open as many doors as an unknown European accent does.'

'I'm guessing your name is the same?'

Thomas smiled. 'Thomas is my real name, but Magnusson is a bit fancier than the real thing.'

'Which is?'

'Not important,' he said with a grin.

'Fair enough, I presume that Magnusson came into existence about three years ago?'

'Spot on, detective. See? I knew there was a reason I came to you rather than the police.'

She'd been giving that some thought and took a swing with her main theory. 'Are you sure it wasn't because you didn't want to admit to being part of a gang of thieves that rips off hotel guests across Australasia?'

He winced. 'I wouldn't call four people a gang. How much do you know?'

'I don't know anything for sure, but I can guess a few things.'

She turned right and they dodged around a small child on a push bike way too big for him. He careered towards the edge of the boardwalk and Nicolette was poised to intervene when the kid's father scooped him up. She'd been accurate on her description though. Sunday lunchtime brought out everyone, and as people could walk from Frank Kitts Park to Oriental Parade without leaving the edge of the water, there were throngs of people all over the place.

'One, you've been operating for a few years. Two, you filtered the proceeds from the thefts through the Magnusson Family Trust to clean it. Three, Kalliana, Skylar, and Grant ran the operations, and you were... what, supervisor? Don't like getting your hands dirty?'

His mouth tightened but he didn't reply, instead gesturing for her to continue.

'You bought the house from Gladys Downing intending to use it as a base of operations. Until...' she paused and glanced across at him, '... something went wrong.'

'Yes, my cousin was murdered.'

Nicolette saw a passing group give them startled expressions.

'Yes, I'm sorry for your loss. You said in your text that you had some information.'

Thomas looked around then took her elbow and steered her to a bench seat facing the marina.

'Skylar Goodman has booked a flight to Australia tomorrow.'

He sat back to see what effect his words would have.

'You think she's fleeing the country because she's guilty?'

'She's the only one left alive. It makes sense that she'd want to get away.'

'Why now? If she'd killed Kalliana, why not flee straight away? Why wait to be questioned by the police or risk have her part in the thefts revealed?'

'I would have thought that obvious,' replied Thomas. 'Money. Her share was still sitting in that house. If she left without it, she'd have to start with nothing. She called me frantic about it, but I don't have the equity to give her what she wanted.'

'Not until you've sold everything in the hidden compartment in the room in the house.'

His eyes widened and he swore. 'So they found that.'

'Actually...' Nicolette paused, considering telling him that it was she that found it. 'Yes, they did,' she finished.

'Damn.' He stared across the water for a while, then shrugged. 'Ah well, we'll just have to start again. Taking it is most of the fun anyway.' He grinned.

'You'll need to get a new group.'

The smile dropped away and he sighed. 'I'll miss Kalliana, she's family. Grant was a pain, but he knew his stuff. Good tech guys are surprisingly hard to find. At least ones willing to make a little bit on the side.'

'And Skylar?'

'Skylar is... complicated. We used to.... you know, and I still have feelings for her, but I think she might have killed the others, so I'm less enamoured than I was.'

'Why, though? Why would she kill the others?'

'I can't say for sure. I know she had been talking to Grant about cutting Kalliana out. Kalliana found out and confronted her. It got quite heated.'

'I'm surprised the police haven't talked to you about the room of stolen jewellery.'

'I did miss a call from the detective this morning. That was probably what he wanted to talk about. My name is on the sale and purchase agreement on behalf of the Trust, but of course I never lived there so I had no idea what had been hidden away.'

Nicolette thought for a moment. 'And *you* can't tell them Skylar is fleeing the country because that would mean admitting that you know her, which places you one step closer to the thefts.'

'I knew you were smart as soon as I met you. They already know you've met Skylar so you could easily tell the detective she's planning on leaving.'

'What makes you think I'm not going to tell them about this conversation as well?'

He reached over and took her hands. She tensed, but all he did was turn them face up, then placed his own hands on top of them.

'I am in your hands.'

He looked so earnest that she wavered. Then she took her hands away.

'I'm sure that look must work on a lot of women.'

'Most of them,' he replied with a laugh.

Nicolette stood up. 'Look, I can't prove this conversation ever took place, so there's no benefit in repeating it, but I'll pass on the info about Skylar. Thank you, Thomas.'

He also stood and looked at her, the world behind her reflected in his sunglasses.

'I'd appreciate that. If there's ever anything I can do for you, let me know.'

'I am curious about something. If you think Skylar really killed Kalliana why don't you do something about it?'

Thomas' expression turned hard. 'Nothing would give me more pleasure, but I don't trust myself to stop from going too far.'

Despite the warm day Nicolette shivered at the menace in his voice. As he walked away she sat back down.

Everything he'd said about Skylar made sense, maybe a little too much sense. He had just given her several reasons to think Skylar Goodman was the murderer. All she had to do was phone Dominic, then Skylar would be arrested. Case closed.

There were just two problems.

One, it blew her theory that Angela Downing was involved in Kalliana's death. Two, Thomas was lying. She didn't know about what exactly, but he hadn't told her the whole truth, and once she suspected that, everything he'd told her after that was shaky.

So she *would* go to the cops, but not quite yet.

Pulling out her phone she made two calls, both went to answerphone. She left messages then headed back to her car.

Thankfully it started first time and thoughts of having to get a new car were banished to the background as she ran through her plan (though the word plan assigned it a level of organisation it didn't deserve).

Fifteen minutes later, she pulled up outside the old Downing house. As she got out of the car, she saw the curtains pull back at the house next door and the old man stare at her. She waved and he instantly turned to look down the street in the other direction. She kept looking at him and when he glanced back, he gave a tiny wave and let the curtain fall into place.

Good. She couldn't do anything about him seeing her arrive, but she didn't want an audience when she broke into the house.

Luckily the lock on the front door was similar to the back and picking it was easier the second time. Within a minute she was inside. A quick check showed that the hidden space had been emptied. The camera in the kitchen had also been taken down. Not knowing how much time she had, Nicolette quickly unpacked the box she'd brought with her, set everything up, then settled down to wait.

Her phone was silent. She thought about calling again but was worried that would undermine her casualness. She'd tried to sound breezy on the calls, an unnatural concept for her, and she didn't think she'd be able to do it again without causing some sort of internal damage.

There was a soft noise at the front door and a moment later she heard it open. It closed again before the visitor spoke.

'Hello?'

Nicolette stepped into view.

At the other end of the hallway, Skylar Goodman gave a little jump. 'You scared me.'

'Sorry,' said Nicolette in an unapologetic tone.

Skylar took a couple of steps down the hall, then stopped beside the closed door to the internal room.

'You said you had something for me?' she asked.

'I do. Thomas told me everything. I figured if you were leaving the country, you'd want some capital to take with you.'

Skylar opened the door and looked into the room. 'Everything's gone. What can you give me?'

Nicolette shrugged. 'I might have hidden a few things before showing the stash to the cops.'

Nicolette mentally winced. She sounded like a bad mob movie.

Skylar didn't seem to notice. 'What sort of things?'

'Watches, and a necklace.'

Skylar idly took a step towards her. 'And you're going to give them to me, just like that? I thought you were a detective. Don't you have to follow the law?'

'Usually, but right now the law and I aren't talking.'

'Huh?'

'Never mind. The point is, I'll let you have them.'

'In exchange for what?'

Nicolette pretended not to notice Skylar inching closer.

'The truth. To satisfy my curiosity. Why did you try and run me down?'

Skylar looked genuinely confused by the question.

'Okay, that wasn't you,' Nicolette continued. 'But you did try and have me arrested that day by Freyberg pool.'

Skylar shrugged. 'I couldn't do anything about the cops asking questions. But you kept showing up and I couldn't figure out what your angle was, so I decided to get rid of you.'

'Thanks,' Nicolette replied dryly.

'It didn't work anyway, so no harm, right?'

'Except it made me more suspicious of you.'

Nicolette shuffled her feet, managing to regain a little distance, which Skylar immediately closed again.

'Whatever. I didn't kill Kalliana, I loved her.'

'Yes, I believe both of those things. But you did kill Grant Reed.'

Skylar snorted. 'Rubbish, I didn't kill anyone.'

'You thought he killed Kalliana, and like you said, you loved her.'

'No wonder you didn't go to the cops. You're disturbed.'

'Grant called you that morning to tell you about Kalliana's death. And I'm betting you were the one who helped him take my dog. What did you do? Tell him you'd wait in the bushes, then lured him over with a message and stabbed him. Why?'

Instead of answering, Skylar stepped forward. Now she was in the doorway leading to the kitchen. Nicolette moved to her left, putting the edge of the breakfast bar between them.

'Are you going to give me the jewellery or do I have to hear more of your fairy tales?'

'It always bothered me that the two murders were so different. Poisoning and stabbing, because they're quite different methods, aren't they? One is less violent than the other.'

'Both kill people.'

'Yes, but there's killing people and there's murdering people.'

'What's the difference? Dead is dead.'

'I can see you're a real black and white sort of girl.'

'I actually prefer pastels.'

Nicolette laughed and a wry smile crossed Skylar's face as she moved around the breakfast bar.

'But the biggest difference between the two is that one is hands off, the killer doesn't need to be there, while the other is close up and personal.'

'I knew Grant for years and he had a temper. He said more stupid things than most men. Hell, he even threatened to kill me a couple of times, but I never did anything about it. I knew he was all talk. He was harmless. And if I believed that, why would I think he killed Kalliana?'

Nicolette didn't reply. Skylar's argument made sense but she was sure she was right.

'Well, this is an interesting development.'

They both turned to see Gladys Downing standing in the kitchen doorway.

'Who the hell are you?' asked Skylar.

'I'm Gladys Downing and this is my house, so I should be asking you that question.'

Skylar looked at Nicolette in confusion.

'This *was* her house. Until Thomas bought it.'

'No. This *is* my house.'

Nicolette realised she'd made a big mistake.

Hopefully not a fatal one.

TWENTY FOUR

'Is your daughter here too? I left a message for her.'

'No,' Gladys replied with a shake of her head. 'You left a message on my daughter's phone, which I listened to, and deleted.'

'What's going on?' Skylar demanded.

Nicolette thought quickly. She'd arranged to meet both Skylar and Angela here at different times, never imagining that they might show up together. Now she was in a kitchen with two potential murderers and, thanks to going left rather than right, she was blocked from the back door.

She decided to keep them talking while she figured out an exit plan.

'What's going on is this. Gladys lived in this house for decades. She had her daughter here, her husband died here, and she fully expected to die here as well. Only, her husband made some bad investments and she couldn't pay the mortgage and had to sell.'

'He was a wonderful man,' Gladys said. 'Except with money. He took away my home.'

'And since you couldn't get back at him, you decided to take your anger out on the person who bought the house.'

Skylar stared at Gladys in horror. 'You killed Kalliana?'

'Was that her name? Such a tragedy, but she shouldn't have been living in my house,' Gladys said with a smile.

'You're bonkers.'

'Now, dear, don't make me wash your mouth out with soap. Besides, from what I just overheard, you got your hands dirty too.'

Skylar stared incredulously at the older lady, then at Nicolette, and back again.

Gladys's expression turned thoughtful. 'Seems we could benefit from some cooperation. We both have a problem. Someone knows our secrets and could blab them to the police.'

'You're suggesting we kill her?'

'It's not ideal, I realise, but you've already done it once, so you know you're capable,' Gladys pointed out.

To Nicolette's dismay, Skylar nodded slowly.

'My car is parked in front. We should take her somewhere else so her death isn't linked to my house. She's very annoying, I'm sure there's a long list of people who want her dead.'

Nicolette opened her mouth to object, then decided silence was more conducive to a longer life.

'Yeah,' murmured Skylar. 'She asks a lot of questions and just won't go away. She's like a clingy ex-boyfriend I had once.'

'Did you kill him too?' Nicolette immediately regretted saying it but calling her clingy was just a step too far. 'You may have killed Grant, but that was out of anger. Did he say something that made you believe he'd killed Kalliana?

Skylar looked troubled. 'I drove him and your dog to the park. Just as he was getting out of the car, he said that now she was gone we could split everything in half. The way he said it, with a stupid grin on his face. I was sure he'd done it. The more I thought about it the more I was convinced. So I sent him a message to come over to where I was waiting and when he did I stabbed him.'

'With a knife you just happened to have in your purse.'

Skylar looked at her coldly. 'Wellington is a dangerous place.'

'It was a spur of the moment thing. I'm sure the police will take that into account. It's completely different killing someone without emotion.'

Gladys shook her finger at Nicolette. 'You know, that's what I thought to, but it turns out it's surprisingly easy. The hardest part was practicing on Kanga. She didn't like being locked in the toilet but it was the smallest room in Angela's house and I had to make sure it would work.'

'Who's Kanga?' asked Skylar.

'Her cat. Gladys poisoned her then dumped her around here to make it look like it happened in this house. But the cat door is locked so she couldn't have gotten in on her own. It never made sense that it was an accident.'

'Oh?'

'People don't leave oil diffusers going when they're not home. She would have had to be exposed at the same time as Kalliana, who if you remember, was killed. And the cat wasn't.'

Skylar's faced change as she connected the dots and she turned angrily towards Gladys. 'You killed Kalliana!'

'Yes, dear, we went over this.'

Skylar shook her head and sat on the kitchen stool next to the breakfast bar. 'This is nuts,' she muttered.

Gladys stepped up to the breakfast bar, completing the triangle. 'Yes dear, but there is a simple solution. You get her to give you what you came for, then you help me take care of her and we both get what we want. No one has to know.'

Nicolette saw Skylar thinking about the offer, and quickly said. 'Which one of you tried to run me down?'

Gladys rolled her eyes and she raised her hand. 'Guilty. I began panicking a little, which is completely not like me. I do not panic, but you were sniffing around and, even the slowest of detectives might strike it lucky. The idea just popped into my head. I followed you home and waited.' She shook her head sadly. 'Unfortunately, I was wearing the wrong glasses and misjudged where you were. You glanced off the side of the car instead of being hit straight on. Even so, I hit you quite hard. How are you feeling, dear?'

'And Angela has a hybrid car, that's why I didn't hear you coming, not until you sped up. I can't believe you tried to kill me, I bought you cake.'

'*Trying,* dear, *trying* to kill you. If our friend here would commit, we could get on with it.' Gladys looked around. 'I don't like what they've done with the place. It's going to take a lot of work to get it back the way it should be.'

Nicolette eyed the exits and weighed her options. She was pretty sure she could get past Gladys without difficulty, but Skylar was the unknown.

She shifted her eyes around the room looking for anything she could use as a weapon. Kalliana had either never used her kitchen or she was the tidiest person in the world. The only thing sitting out was a box of tea bags. Nicolette could throw them, but that would be more annoying than anything else, and although tea leaves could be irritating if they got into eyes, she didn't think her attackers would stay put while she ripped the bags open.

She glanced at her watch, an action caught by Skylar.

'Got some place to be?' she sneered.

'No, expecting someone,' replied Nicolette.

'Another murderer?'

'No, the police. You didn't think I would set all this up without calling them first. They should be bursting through the front door any second.'

Gladys and Skylar turned to towards the front door and Nicolette sprang. She rushed past Gladys and was halfway down the hall before she heard them react. With the sound of footsteps echoing on the wooden floor behind her, Nicolette reached the front door and reached for the handle. It wouldn't open. She tugged again but it remained stubbornly closed.

Gladys advanced down the hall towards her.

'I locked it as I came in.'

Nicolette glanced at the doors on either side of her. 'Good to know.'

She darted into a bedroom and slammed the door closed after her. Quickly turning the key, she sighed with relief when she heard the click of the lock.

Something slammed into the door and she jumped back.

Pulling her phone out, she jabbed a finger at the screen to bring up her contacts. Dialling Dominic, she waited an agonisingly long time before the call connected and it rang.

'Nic, I—'

'Old Downing house, now.'

'Okay.'

He hung up and she fumbled her phone back into her pocket. She dropped it. As she bent to pick it up, there was another crash at the door and her hand jerked, sending the phone sliding under the bed.

'You said you'd already called the police,' Gladys called out.

'Yeah, little tip, people lie when confronted by killers.'

From under the bed, her phone rang. She dropped to her knees to grab it, when she heard a scraping sound. Shooting a look at the door she was horrified to see it swing open.

'Another tip, dear. When someone has lived in a house for years, they get to know all the quirks of the building, like for example that the bedroom door can be opened from the outside even if it's locked. You just need the right key.' She held her hand up to show off a small silver key. 'And luckily for me they didn't change where the spares are kept.'

Before Nicolette replied, Skylar pushed into the room and took a swing with her fist.

Nicolette ducked, feeling the whoosh of air as it missed by millimetres. She launched herself up, and shouldered Skylar in the chest, sending her flying into the doorframe.

Gladys cried out and went tumbling to the ground. Nicolette's first reaction was to check on her, but the old woman rolled onto her back and let loose with an impressively comprehensive range of swear words.

Nicolette rushed out into the hall, heading for the back door, but Gladys grabbed her ankle and she went sprawling onto the wood floor, banging her head against the wall on the way down. Scrambling to her feet, she fled down the hall, into the kitchen and across to the back door. It was locked but the key was in it. She fumbled, her fingers suddenly the size of jumbo sausages. Finally it clicked and she flung it open and jumped down the steps onto the back lawn. She ran to the side of the house and sprinted to the front yard. Just as she rounded the corner someone bowled her and she went tumbling across the grass into the fence. She looked up in time to see Skylar lifting her foot to stomp on her head. Grabbing the foot in both hands, she shoved upwards. Skylar's arms windmilled as she fell backwards.

'Hey! What's going on here!'

Nicolette sat up and saw a police officer standing on the other side of the fence.

'She's a murderer,' Nicolette said.

'No, she is,' Skylar yelled.

'My brother is Detective Senior Sergeant Dominic Lister. She stabbed a man in the park near here a few days ago.'

The officer looked at her with narrowed eyes. 'How is Dom?'

Nicolette climbed slowly to her feet. 'He hates being called Dom.'

'Yes he does.'

'That's why I do it. He should be here any minute.'

Out of the corner of her eye she saw Skylar move towards the front gate. Seconds later she was lying on the ground, being zip tied, with a knee in her back.

'You're hurting me,' she complained.

'You shouldn't have run. Up you get.'

Once standing, Skylar shot a look at Nicolette that made her glad the woman was restrained.

'There's another one, inside the house,' Nicolette said.

The officer nodded. 'Well unless she's able to scale the back fence then she's only got one way out.'

'You know the property well then?'

'Sure,' the officer replied. 'My dad lives next door.'

Nicolette looked across to see the old man standing in his front doorway. She gave him a wave and he waved back.

'I have to admit, I didn't believe him when he said his daughter was a police officer. The second time I talked to him he said you were a firefighter.'

'Oh, that's my sister,' the officer laughed.

Just then a car screeched to a halt and Dominic jumped out.

'You alright?' he asked.

'Couldn't be better.'

'Do you realise you've got blood all over your face?'

'What?' She reached up and touched her cheek and her fingers came away red. 'I thought that was sweat. Must have happened when I hit the fence.'

Dominic's face relaxed a little and he turned to the constable and introduced himself.

'I know who you are, sir. She said she was your sister.'

'Yes,' Dominic replied. 'She likes to say that when it can get her out of trouble.'

'Gladys Downing is inside the house. She murdered Kalliana Magnusson. Skylar murdered Grant Reed.'

'Stay here. The others should be here shortly.'

He started towards the entrance and Nicolette called after him, 'Be careful, she's a bit crazy.'

He waved over his shoulder and went inside.

While they waited, Nicolette tried to clean her face using a tissue from her pocket.

'You're making it worse,' the officer cheerfully told her. 'Dad! Can you bring out some paper towels?'

The towels arrived at the same time as the Dominic emerged from the house, leading Gladys Downing by the arm.

'Mrs Downing claims that she was lured here by you and attacked without provocation. And that this young lady was passing by and came to her rescue when she heard cries for help.'

Gladys Downing looked around her with a confused expression as Skylar nodded vigorously.

'That's exactly what happened. She was crazy, I managed to get her outside, but I was so worried that she was going to hurt that poor old lady.'

'Nic?'

Nicolette pulled out her phone and opened an app. Pressing a few buttons she turned the screen so the others could see it.

'The camera in the kitchen had been taken, but luckily I brought my own. Everything is on video.'

Dominic gave her a faint smile.

Gladys' expression hardened. 'If only I'd worn my glasses.'

TWENTY FIVE

'I can't believe she was so desperate to get back into the house, she killed for it.'

Nicolette nodded at Vanessa. 'She thought that no one would want a house where a murder was committed and she'd be able to buy it back for next to nothing.'

They were sitting in Alice's apartment, the afternoon sun streaming through the window, prickling Nicolette's skin. Alice and Vanessa sat opposite her, and she was surprised that Alice hadn't been more surprised when she'd related the events of the previous weekend.

'In my experience, old people can be just as unpredictable as young people,' Alice said. 'Usually for different reasons.'

'How so?' asked Vanessa.

'Young people are impulsive because they haven't learnt how to control their emotions. Old people have been feeling those emotions for a lot longer. Gladys Downing felt safe in her house, and that was taken away from her, so she acted. What about Skylar Goodman?'

'She was the young, impulsive flip side of that. She loved Kalliana and when she thought Grant had killed her, she acted without thinking.'

'And you knew that but still invited her to the house?'

Nicolette shrugged. 'I didn't *know* it, not for sure. My idea was to try and get her to confess to something on camera that I could take to the police. In hindsight not the best plan, something my brother and sister and mother have all pointed out more than once.'

'Not Chloe?' asked Alice.

'I haven't told her what happened. No need for her to worry.'

'Who broke into your house and hurt your dog?'

Nicolette frowned. 'That's the one thing that neither of them admitted to. I thought it might have been Thomas Magnusson, but I checked and he was out of town the night it happened.

'Just a regular burglar perhaps?'

'Maybe.' She wasn't going to divulge that she still suspected her step-brother of doing it. She hadn't managed to follow up on that theory yet though.

Alice nodded thoughtfully. 'Angela Downing came to see me yesterday. She doesn't want the cat at her house so the Silvermoon Retirement Village has officially adopted her.'

Nicolette looked over to the empty spot on the carpet by the window.

'I believe she is currently being spoiled by Les and Freda. I fear for her life expectancy with all the extra meals she will be getting. And what's next for you, dear?'

Nicolette would have liked to take a week or two off to fully recover, but her conscience and bank account wouldn't let her.

'I start a new job tomorrow. Someone's prize Leonberger has gone missing and she thinks her ex-husband has taken her.'

'Well, if you ever want to try something different, I could use someone with your attributes,' replied Alice.

Nicolette held up her hand.

'Sorry, I don't do humans.'

THE END

Author's Note:

I personally love it when characters from other shows or books make cameo appearances in other work. Alice and her companion Vanessa are from the Silvermoon Retirement Village series of cozy mysteries where, as you might suspect, Alice solves murders that do include humans.

About the Author

Rodney Strong is a New Zealand author, primarily of cosy mysteries. He has been writing all his life and decided in 2016 to pursue a full-time career in creating worlds. His most popular character is a 98-year-old retired con artist, but he loves all of his characters, even if some of them don't do as they're told.

He has published a total of 17 books and delights in freaking people out by telling them that he essentially kills people for a living but that it was alright because he'd made the people up in the first place.

He lives in Porirua with his family, including two kittens who are still of the age they believe all toes are fair game.

More info about Rodney at www.rodneystrongauthor.com

Printed in Dunstable, United Kingdom

74692828R00147